Faking Lucky

Romance: A Touch of Steam + A Twist of Humor

Q. D. Purdu

ISBN: 0692780971
ISBN 13: 9780692780978
Library of Congress Control Number: 2016915162
Q.D.Purdu, Manor, TX

1

So I'm home alone on Saturday night in my comfy T-shirt, relaxed on my denim sofa, eating fudge and brazil nuts, and channel surfing. *Jewelry channel*—maybe a flashy gem would jazz up my life. Gag—tonight it's cameos. *Sex in the City*—I bet they all faked it, even Samantha. *Marriage Exposure*—where do they find people who will go on TV and argue about their sex lives?

Wait.

I don't believe my eyes. It looks like Burt on *Marriage Exposure*. I raise the volume and edge closer to the screen. It is him, the same reddish-brown hair and sharp features. He's even worn his favorite green-striped polo shirt. I haven't seen him since we broke up a year ago, and he has on that same shirt. The short-haired woman sitting next to him has her hands covering her face. She wails something like, "You never loved me! You never loved me!"

It can't be. Burt's in an L-word relationship? Married? I edge closer to the screen, hardly breathing.

Burt pulls at the back of his neck with one hand, the way he always does when he's stressed, and looks down toward his feet. "I wouldn't have married you if I didn't love you." Unbelievable. He's married to her.

She uncovers her red, puffy face and leans close to him. "You never loved me." Spit flies out with her words. "You've always loved..." She gives a big, gasping sob and then slowly, distinctly blurts out my name. "Desdemona. With...with...her beautiful dark eyes. Her perfect body. Her incredible piano playing." More spit with the *p's*. "Her long, thick raven hair." She raises both hands to her head and pulls at her brownish spikes.

No. I must have misheard.

But she repeats my name, dragging out each syllable as if it causes her physical pain. "Des...de...mon...a."

Could Burt have dated another Desdemona?

Something mushes between my toes. Fudge under my foot oozes out onto my creamy-white lamb's-wool throw, which is now on the floor. I must have stood up when she wailed my name. Brazil nuts are all over the floor.

Burt takes her by the shoulders. "Jenny, no." He always was considerate of everyone's feelings. "I could never love Desdemona. She...she's a freak. She fakes orgasms."

A crazy giggle snakes its way up from my chest. *Is this really happening? How could he have known? Guys can't really tell, can they?* The giggle morphs into a nauseated groan. *Am I dreaming? Drugged? In a parallel universe? Has Burt just announced my unspeakable flaw to the world?*

And so what if I don't get the big O every single time? Well, I guess I hardly ever get it... OK, I got it three times, and it would have been four if my vibrator had not quit working. But I'm not even twenty-seven yet—far from the sexual peak of forty.

At some point during the last minute, my phone starts buzzing. My autopilot eyes glance at it. Friends text me about Burt being on TV. So there is something worse than being a nonorgasmic faker. It's being a nonorgasmic faker and having the whole world know it.

A loud, animalistic howl shocks the breath out of me. *What is that?* I freeze and listen for a split second before I realize the roar comes from me.

I muffle my howls, hoping I haven't alarmed my landlady, who lives in the attached duplex. With foot in fudge and phone facedown, I'm transfixed.

Burt embraces his sobbing wife and mutters endearments. The MC hoofs it into the audience, whose members clamor to speak into the mic.

A long-haired, leather-vested guy gets the first shot. "Hey, Burt." He's got an oily, smooth voice—could be a talk-show host himself. "Ah, maybe you just ain't man enough for Mona."

Mona. I hate when people call me Mona. But this could be good. Maybe the world will forget my real name. Yes! Mona.

Next a clean-cut, older guy steps up and glares at the leather vest. "Des. De. Mon. A. Not Mona." *Crap.* "You should be respectful enough to pronounce her complete name."

The audience interrupts with hoots that could be boos or cheers or random insanity. The MC swings the mic toward an elderly lady, but the clean-cut guy jerks him back. "I'm not finished. The first gentleman"— he rolls his eyes toward the leather vest—"was correct about one thing."

The impatient grandma reaches for the mic, and the MC blocks her hand and tries to hurry the clean-cut guy, who looks like he's gearing up for a long lecture. "If Desdemona is not satisfied, it's clearly a sign of the male's lack of technique. Research shows…"

Grandma's hand darts between the two men and snatches the mic. She runs down an aisle with the MC in pursuit. "Burt!" Her voice is surprisingly loud and shrill. "Did you ask Desdemona what's a matter?" She screams out questions as the MC chases, grabbing futilely for the mic. "Did you ask her why?" This elderly woman sprints like a teenager. "How do you know she faked? Did you go down?" The audience is out of control now.

In a shuffle of arms, a tall, skinny guy commandeers the mic. "Hey, Desdemona." It's as if he's looking straight at me—in the room with me— seeing me. "Come to me." Hairs skitter across the back of my neck. "I'll get you there, baby."

Somehow the MC has produced a second mic that overrides the other one and muffles the noise of the audience. "Thanks for being with us for another shocking episode of *Marriage Exposure*. Tune in tomorrow for an unbelievable brother-in-law who sneaks into bed with his own brother's wife"—he pauses, moves close to the camera, and raises both eyebrows several times—"without her knowing it. You're not going to want to miss this."

The camera pans over the audience that is now chanting, "Desdemona, Desdemona, Desdemona..."

A diet-pill commercial is halfway over before I shake off the shock enough to silence the TV. Eleanor, my cat, bats a Brazil nut across the floor. My phone rings. *Ugh. It's Mom.* I grab the phone and the ruined lamb's wool, scoop up the nuts, and hop toward the kitchen to stick my foot in the sink. I would ignore my mother, but if I don't answer, she'll call my landlady to come over and make sure I'm not bound and gagged, unconscious, or murdered.

How will I deal with my mother's shock about Burt's revelation?

"Mija, where are you?"

"Home."

"Alone?" She'd like me to be married and have several kids by now. *Alone* is never a word she welcomes.

"Yes."

"On Saturday night—home alone? With all there is to do in Austin?"

"Yes."

She lets a long silence hang. I would normally fill it with disclaimers about being too tired to go out or the last-minute cancellation of my gig tonight. Instead of chatting her up, I wait her out and run water over my foot. Eleanor, maybe sensing my misery, rubs against my other leg. Nothing I could say will divert Mother from Burt's blast. I take deep breaths, steadying myself for the onslaught.

She finally seems to realize she's not getting an explanation about my solitary Saturday night. "How do I say this?" She sighs loudly. "It's one thing to know people privately, but to see them as a nationally known personality...it's...it's..."

"Mom, just say it." Tears well in my eyes. The reality of an insane TV show barging into my life stabs in places I didn't know I could hurt.

"OK, OK. Well, it happened while I was with my book-club group at the bookstore." It's really just a book corner in the general store on Main Street.

"You're at the store?" This makes no sense. It's too late for the store to be open.

"No, I'm not there now. We were there from six to eight tonight for our weekly meeting, and then we went to ladies' night at the margarita bar and had two-for-ones. I just now got home. You know that new bar that opened where the bakery used to be?"

There are only a dozen stores in my hometown of Garcia. How could I forget? "Yeah."

"The antique store is also adding a coffee shop—oh, I'm rambling. Want me to just get to the point?"

I force out a whisper and blot my tear-slicked face with a paper towel. "Yes."

She takes a deep breath again. No question that she's unnerved by the conversation we're about to have. My stomach knots. It will be worse to hear my mother talking about Burt and fake orgasms than it was to hear strangers on national TV. I lower my wet but clean foot from the sink so I stand solidly. I pick up Eleanor, who allows one of her rare cuddles. She must know I need it.

"Hunter Johns."

I gasp. His name triggers the same *pow* in my chest that happens every time I think of him, or see a stranger tilt his head that certain way, or hear a laugh that mimics Hunter's deep ring, or dream of kissing him only to wake and remember it will never happen again. *Pow.*

"Desdemona, are you there? Did you hear me?"

I should answer Mom—say something. It's been over nine years since Hunter and I were seniors in high school and he left the campus in handcuffs. Nine years since we swore our love to each other. Nine years since I ruined our chances of ever being together. But still the regret and loss slice razor sharp.

"Desdemona?"

"What about Hunter?" My voice scrapes.

"Oh, good, I thought we'd been cut off. Well, we were about to discuss our new novel when all these people flooded in. Not locals, but people from San Antonio, Austin, Houston. It was just amazing. Our quiet little Saturday-night book talk was turning into—"

"What about Hunter?" I can't fathom where this is going. I'm so caught off guard that for a full two seconds I forget *Marriage Exposure.*

"I'm getting to him. So Alma went up to the manager and asked, 'What's going on?' And he said a national best-selling mystery writer was here for a book signing. Have you read Des Amone's books?"

"Yes. Sure I have."

"Did you read the one that was made into a movie?"

"Mom. Where is this going? What does it have to do with Hunter?"

"Des Amone is Hunter's pen name. And Hunter came to Garcia to do a hometown launch of his new book tour. It's all over the Internet, but none of us noticed. You know we mainly stick to romances."

"Des Amone..." I repeat her words to make sense of them, "is Hunter's pen name."

"Isn't that a hoot? And ya'll were in school together." Mom is oblivious to the relationship I had with Hunter. She lives in her own little world that revolves around her tiny, barely-break-even flower shop with her upstairs living quarters—my home until I moved to Austin. "So we each bought his book, and when he signed mine, he asked about you. Can you believe it—a famous, rich author still remembering a classmate from all those years ago? Isn't it funny how his pen name kind of sounds like *Desdemona*?"

She doesn't wait for me to answer. "So for our next meeting, we're all reading Hunter's book. You know, it's just so much fun to read a book with a group—"

"What did he say about me? What did you tell him?"

"He just asked how you are, and I told him you were playing all over Austin and giving lessons. I showed him that picture of you in your long red dress, playing that red baby grand. I think it was taken in some bar on Sixth Street. He said, 'Still beautiful as ever.'" I shut my eyes and make myself breathe. "We could have talked and talked, but there was a line behind me, so I moved on. I told him to look you up when he goes to Austin on his book tour. And I gave him your number."

The *pow* that hit me when she said his name evolves into a melody that fills my chest while she drones on. The melody, not one that I could ever put to music no matter how hard I try, is always there—inside—below the surface. But at times like this it expands, presses, and hurts in the middle of my chest.

— —

Until nine years ago, Hunter's and my lives had always bordered each other. Garcia has only one high school, which at that time had fewer than eight hundred students. Hunter stood apart—confident, smart, athletic. For years my eyes were drawn to him whenever we had a class together—his height and his thick mahogany hair, always in a short buzz cut like all the athletes, were like banners catching my attention. Even the bones in his face seemed more substantive than anyone else's. His strong nose, his forehead with its masculine bulge above his eyebrows, the vertical line that creased each cheek, making his face strong even when relaxed. Our art teacher in ninth grade had said, "Hunter, with your bones, you'll look the same when you're an old man as you do now."

Throughout high school, whether I was in class or the hallway or a common area, my ears sought out his deep voice and warm laugh. Every day, no matter what else was going on, a part of me was always listening for Hunter.

In our junior year, we had homeroom together. During the first semester, he sat in the middle of the room, usually surrounded by three cheerleaders, who acted as if it were their official role to keep him entertained. I sat in the back, pretended to study, and wished I could be pretty, blond, blue-eyed Georgina, the one sitting behind Hunter. *Get over it. He's a nice guy—nice to everyone. His occasional smile at me is just that—a simple smile*, I said to myself. I was totally out of the in-crowd, and piano practice took all my time. So I never knew for sure who he was dating.

One morning in homeroom, his three groupies were giggling about some whispered joke, and Hunter turned around to face Georgina, who was tapping his shoulder. I watched her hand relax onto his bicep and imagined it was my hand—imagined I was stroking those prominent muscles. When I let my gaze slide up his arm to his face, I was shocked that his eyes were waiting to meet mine. An involuntary gasp escaped from me, and somehow my soft sound pierced the giggling, and all three girls followed his gaze and turned to stare at me.

I shook my head, and frowned down at whatever textbook was lying open in front of me. I pretended to be perplexed at some academic mystery. Then I gazed slightly to the right of Hunter, hoping they would think I was deep in thought and not that I had been salivating for him.

After that embarrassment, I vowed to myself that I would keep my eyes off of Hunter, but the very next day, I was again drawn into watching Georgina and him. She slid into her desk and pulled a tightly folded sheet of notebook paper out of her jeans pocket. Hunter seemed to be ignoring her, focusing on an open book on his desk. She grabbed his shoulder and squeezed, but he just held up one finger as if to acknowledge her. He didn't turn to face her. She stood up, leaned her whole body over his shoulder, and passed the note to the cheerleader sitting in front of Hunter.

The cheerleader unfolded the note, scanned, and instantly turned and slapped the paper onto Hunter's desk. "Hardcore." She grinned wickedly at Hunter.

Hunter shook his head, covered the note with his hand, and slid it under his book. Clearly whatever he'd seen written on the paper was something he saw fit to cover up. By now a smattering of giggles all around Hunter caught the teacher's attention at the exact moment Hunter tried to hide the note.

Miss Gomez walked purposefully down his aisle, halted at his desk, and held out her hand. "Let's have it, young man." She was a first-year teacher, and she took her role as disciplinarian very seriously.

Hunter gave her the note.

The teacher's eyebrows shot up above her black-framed glasses. Her tan skin flushed a burgundy red. "Does this..." she asked, her voice shook, "this thing belong to you?"

Hunter nodded solemnly, with his eyes cast downward toward his desk. "Yes, ma'am."

She wadded the note, stomped back to her desk, and started writing furiously on her pink pad. Hunter, anticipating a discipline referral to the office, dropped his book into his bag and stood up, ready for the pink slip as soon as she ripped it off the pad.

Unbelievable. He was innocent. It was Georgina's note. He had nothing to do with it. I gaped at Georgina, waiting for her to own up, but she slumped into her chair and guiltily stared at Hunter as he walked out of the room.

I fumed all morning. And Georgina's weeping in the hallway, telling her friends about Hunter taking the blame for her, didn't soften my resolve. She needed to own up.

I'd always been so frozen by my crush on Hunter that I'd never actually walked up to him and initiated a conversation. But now. Now I was determined to help him. At lunch I waited near his locker, hoping to talk with him. The hallway was almost empty. It looked as if he wasn't coming. My heart sank lower as each second ticked by. Then he rounded the corner and started toward his locker.

I blurted out, "Hunter." My voice was too loud in the quiet hallway. "I..." I lowered my volume. "Could I talk to you?"

He grinned and picked up his pace. In a few long strides, he was next to me, looking down at me. Warmth radiated from his body. The scent of him made my heart rate speed up—made me want to inhale deeply. His neck, up close, was strong and muscled, and I could see his pulse beat on one side. He had black stubble on his chin. His lips, the bottom one thicker than the top one, were slightly parted, as if waiting for me to say or do something. For long moments we stared at each other. Was he remembering the time in our sophomore year when he rescued me and we almost had a date? My face became hot, and then I did what I always do when nervous. I babbled. "Georgina brought that note in. You had nothing to do with it. You even ignored her when she tried to get your attention. She practically bowled you over leaning across you to pass the note. You are innocent. And it wasn't fair for you to take the fall. I witnessed the whole—"

He put his hands on my upper arms and gently squeezed. "Are you worried about me?" He grinned, and his eyes lit up as he peered into mine.

"Well, I...it just isn't right. I don't think you should be blamed for something—"

He squeezed again. The touch of his hands on my bare arms arrested my thoughts and my words. It wouldn't have mattered what he said at that moment; I was speechless just from the touch of him.

"Don't worry. Nothing will happen to me. Coach will just make me run extra laps. It's no big deal."

I shook my head—mainly in an effort to clear my head. Then I said as much for myself as for him, "You must really, truly love her."

"Georgina?" He huffed out a laugh. "Everyone loves Georgina. But she's with Leo. They're solid." Leo had graduated the prior year—I had known they were an item while he was still in high school; I didn't know they were still dating. "He probably gave her the joke—saw him with it last weekend."

My head was reeling with this new information. "But, still, you shouldn't have to take—"

"Desdemona." My heart stopped when he said my name, especially when he squeezed my arms again and moved a little closer. "Georgina wants to be class president. If she took the wrap for the note, they'd probably DQ her. All that will happen to me is laps. And I do laps every day. It's nothing."

My need to babble had ceased. All I knew was that Hunter, gorgeous Hunter, wasn't with Georgina, and he was standing closer to me than necessary, and he was holding my arms way longer than he needed to, and his breath was warm on my face, and if I were to stand on tiptoes and lean four and one-half inches forward, I could put my lips on that pulse beat on the side of his neck.

And then one side of his lips tilted upward in a grin that tugged at a secret place deep inside my body. He whispered into my ear, "It will be worth every single lap just to know it matters to you."

And the next morning in homeroom, Hunter dragged a desk to the back of the room and sat behind me. No one questioned it. We were suddenly together. We didn't get to actually go out on dates that year—neither of us had a car, and Hunter had huge responsibilities helping his mom take care of his dad, who had suffered a brain injury in a construction accident. But all day, every day at school, we were together. And within weeks we started having stolen moments alone in the piano room.

The band director had given me keys to the high school's main entry door and the small piano room because I spent so much time there either practicing alone or accompanying a student instrumentalist. From my freshman year on, my piano teacher often hooked me up with paying gigs in the community, so with no piano at home, I needed lots of practice time at school. During our junior year, Hunter's mother took the job as school secretary, and often, hours after most people had left the campus, she and I would be the only ones in the building. Usually, few people ever came down to the small piano room, wedged between janitor's supply and book storage.

But sometimes Hunter would come in before he checked in with his mother after athletic practice. At first I would be surprised to look up from my music and find him listening to me play. But soon I tingled with hope every day—hope that he would come in and tell me about his day.

The first time we kissed was on the piano bench.

He had been standing in the doorway while I was practicing "Always on My Mind" for a fiftieth-wedding-anniversary party the next weekend. The small spinet piano was angled so that my side faced the doorway, and I could see him in my peripheral vision. After the last measure, I turned toward him. The word *huggable* flashed through my mind. That's how he looked with his shower-wet hair, gray sweats, and sleeveless T-shirt.

His head was tilted in his reflective way. "That's beautiful." Our eyes connected. "You'll play it this weekend, right?"

"Yeah—and some others—all their favorites."

He stepped closer. "Will it bother your playing if I sit beside you while you practice?"

"Of course not." I patted the bench.

Instead of facing the piano, he straddled the bench and faced me. His closeness set every cell in my body dancing. His warm exhale touched my neck. My body breathed in on its own as if hungry to capture his breath. My eyes dropped from his eyes to his lips—and lower. As if my hands had a will of their own, they moved to reach for him. I caught myself. Forced my eyes forward. Forced my hands to the keyboard.

But he leaned closer, his gaze on my face. I turned back toward him.

"Maybe..." His brown eyes burrowed into mine. He seemed to be casting for his next words. "Maybe someday you and I"—I inhaled the breath of his words—"will have a lifetime"—he moved so close that I felt his lips moving with his last words—"of favorite songs."

I wanted to say, "That's the sweetest, most romantic, most touching, beautiful thing anyone could say." I wanted to say, "You've just probed into my deepest, most wonderful fantasy." I wanted to say, "Hunter, I love you, love you, love you." But I froze. Somehow his eyes asked me if I was OK. I must have nodded, because the distance between our lips closed. The feeling of being connected to him—of not knowing where I ended and he started—blurred out everything else the same way that playing a beautiful, complex melody can absorb all conscious thought in rare moments. For a time, I lost track of where our hands were, of how his legs were embracing me along with his arms, of how our bodies were pressed together, of how his secret bulge was speaking to my thigh.

Footfalls, his mother's high-heeled shoes clanking up the empty hallway, pulled us apart.

Hunter stood up, and I played the opening measures of "Always on My Mind" as she opened the door.

2

There are seven texts from the past ten minutes. It's crazy. I barely know seven people. How could news travel so fast? All the texts say basically the same thing:

"Turn on Channel 6—quick."

"Burt on TV."

"Burt. Channel 6. Dirtbag—talking about you."

Most of the messages are from Kari, first telling me to watch—later telling me not to worry, no one will believe Burt. Sweet Kari. She's the only person on the planet who I might talk to about this, but I'm not ready.

I click my Facebook icon, hoping no one has posted on my page about it. Relief. There are no new posts, but that sliver of relief skids into a boulder of shock that stops my breath. Sixteen messages and more than twenty notifications—mostly friend requests from guys I don't know. With shaking hands, I drop the phone and turn on my computer—I've got to get myself out of Facebook. Fifteen minutes of fumbling through delete and deactivate options, and Desdemona Lorents is no longer on social media.

I should Google my name and *Marriage Exposure*. But instead, I key in Des Amone. Amazing that Hunter has been there boldly all these years, and I never recognized him. I've searched for his real name many times, and the only thing I was able to glean from the Internet was that he became a ranch manager and lives on a large ranch out in west Texas. I assumed he wasn't into social media, while all this time his Internet presence was huge. In all his photos as Des Amone, he's worn an Indiana Jones hat pulled low to one side, and he has a thick, dark beard. Now that I know he's Hunter, I'm amazed I didn't recognize him before. Seeing his picture as a mature man transports me right back to the piano room— into our first sexual moment.

— ⁓

By the beginning of our senior year, Hunter was slipping into the practice room almost every day before he checked in with his mother. One day he closed the door and propped a chair against the doorknob. I stopped playing and started to stand up.

He stepped toward me, his eyes locked with mine. "Would you keep playing?" His thick, husky voice sparked electric energy through me.

The air between us was charged like a living, magnetic field that sucked me toward him. I wanted to press myself against him, but I did as he asked—dropped back onto the bench and began to play.

This time he sat behind me with each leg wrapped around me and his body pressed against me. Luckily, "Always on My Mind" is an easy song, so I was able to continue as he lifted my hair and kissed my neck. He put one hand on my thigh and the other on the bare skin of my waist just under the edge of my blouse. He paused his hand that was moving upward toward my breast as if asking me if this was OK. Even though I was playing, I could have pressed my arm against his hand and prevented him from moving further up. But I didn't do that. Instead I leaned into him and kept my arm lifted from my side. Our heat had been building for years, and now finally we were going beyond just kissing. His hand moved upward until he was cupping my breast through my bra. His breathing—rapid and hot on my neck—shifted into a low moan, and his hard-on pressed against my rear.

My playing stopped. My breathing aligned with his. Every sense in my body tuned into his hand on my breast, his other hand on my thigh with only my thin, gauzy skirt separating us, and his erection against my butt triggering a heavenly melting between my legs. I realized I had stopped playing, so I made myself begin again. He chuckled softly in my ear as if happy about the effect he was having on me. Then, when I thought I could not possibly feel closer or more connected with him than I already was, he moved his hand off my bra cup and edged his fingers below the bra until he was caressing my bare breast. I twisted my face toward him—needing to have his lips on mine.

My music stopped again. Nothing—not a fire, not a bomb—nothing could make me play this time. His hand slid up my leg and slipped under my skirt, not stopping until he reached my panties. His breath caught, and his fingers explored, stroking against the thin material and gently pushing it aside. I turned, wrapping my legs around him—pressing against his hardness.

The chair propped against the door rattled. Somehow we pulled apart, and I started playing that old "Heart and Soul" song my dad taught me when I was six. It was a default melody for me. I could play it without thinking.

A custodian called from the hallway. "Something's wrong with the door."

Hunter moved the chair and rattled the knob. "Yeah, you're right. It's stuck." He swung it open and showed the custodian a large twig that I hadn't noticed before. "This was stuck under it." In his other hand, Hunter held my sheet music in front of his crotch. He must have been shielding his hard-on. He studied the music for a long, long time that day while the custodian swept.

After Hunter and I hooked up, the rest of the world faded away. School, my mother, my old sorrow about Dad, and my resentment about not having my own piano, everything faded into the background like a boring movie I was half-watching. The real world for me consisted of moments with Hunter—mostly in the piano room, but sometimes at events after school or on weekends. We both had our driver's licenses, but neither of us had a car, so the alone time that lots of our friends had wasn't an option for us.

Seeing him each day in class, in the cafeteria, in the hallway was on-going foreplay—knowing that after school we'd have our time. His touch had unleashed something wild in me.

One day when I was practicing and tingling with anticipation that Hunter would be with me soon, his mother surprised me by coming into the room. "I'm sorry to interrupt, but could I ask you to sit at my desk for a few minutes?" Her eyes were red, her face blotchy, and her normally smoothed-back, light-brown hair was slipping from its low ponytail.

A flash of fear jolted me. *Had something happened to Hunter out on the practice field?* I stood up quickly. "What is it?" I searched her face, feeling more alarmed by the second. "Is something wrong, Mrs. Johns?"

She gave a slight nod and then immediately shook her head. She looked past me as she spoke—not making eye contact. "I have to run to the nursing home, but I'm waiting for a call from the cheerleader uni-form company with an adjusted quote." I followed her down the hall to the office. When we got to her desk, she thrust a notepad at me. "I'd let the uniform company leave a message, but I have a few questions that I need to go over with them."

I glanced at the questions and nodded. "Makes sense."

"I'll just be gone a few minutes." Her eyes became teary, and her chin trembled, and for the first time, her eyes met mine. "The nursing home needs me to sign so they can restrain my husband." Hunter's dad, a former construction supervisor, had suffered extensive brain damage from a head injury when he fell off a scaffold two years earlier. Everyone in town knew about the building accident and the struggle that Hunter, his mom, and his younger sister, Clara, were still having. The whole town had participated in fund raisers. "The cheerleader sponsor needs the info tonight."

She took one slow step toward the door and then turned back to face me. "I never thought I'd have him restrained. Never. I told them to never do it." Her eyes welled up with tears. "That's why I have to sign a release now. They say he's...he's combative...going to hurt himself or someone else if they don't tie him down."

I stepped toward her and wrapped my arms around her. "I'm so sorry." I wished I could offer some comfort or advice, but there were no words in my world to help with what she was going through.

After that day, I helped Mrs. Johns several times—filling in if she had to leave, or helping her count cash from fund raisers, or just straightening up the front office. Sometimes she had to go to the nursing home, and sometimes she had to pick up Clara. The family had only one car, so she and Clara generally stayed around until Hunter finished practice. Then they would all go home together.

One day Mrs. Johns was called to the nursing home again for some problem with Mr. Johns. Soon as I was alone at her desk, a school-board member phoned, wanting information about the agenda for an upcoming meeting. I checked the in-basket and opened the file drawer, trying desperately to find what he wanted so that Mrs. Johns wouldn't get in trouble for not being there. I pulled open a drawer that was normally locked. I had seen Mrs. Johns pull out her keys when she needed to open it. There, underneath a small, childlike, plastic-bound journal was the agenda draft.

As I lifted the draft to find the information he was looking for, the journal, pink with pictures of happy faces on it, fell open.

"Sir," I said. "Which item were you wanting?"

He droned on about the agenda order, wanting to know what was first, second, third. While we talked I couldn't help that my eyes scanned the open page, handwritten dates, dollar amounts, and account names. Finally, he ended the call.

The dates in the journal started shortly after the beginning of the school year and continued through the current week. Most of the amounts were subtractions of between two hundred and seven hundred dollars. The total subtractions came to $26,300. A couple of dates indicated additions adding up to $420.

The account names—cheerleaders, band boosters, athletic club, agriculture club, football and volleyball gate receipts, concession income—covered just about every fund-raising group in the school.

What did this mean? Lots of cash came through the office. I had helped count money, wrap coins, and enter amounts into the online ledger many times. I had never seen this little journal before. My stomach sank as I realized she must be stealing money and using this book to keep track of it. And she must be trying to pay it back. But the miserable $420 was far short of the $26,300 owed.

I put the agenda back in the drawer and started to lay the journal on top when I noticed a folded sheet inside the back cover. I knew I shouldn't look at it, but at that moment my mind was racing with my fear about what this ledger meant. I think I looked at the folded sheet because I hoped it was an explanation showing that I was wrong—that Hunter's mother was not stealing from the cash receipts. I unfolded the paper—a statement from a health-insurance company listing the nursing-home bill and the amount that the insurance company was paying. In boldface it stated, "The insured is responsible for the following amount: $11,700."

The main door of the hallway opened, and Mrs. Johns's distinctive footfalls came toward the office. I put the little journal back in its place and closed the drawer. But as she entered the office, I opened the drawer again and stood to greet her. I didn't want to lie—make her think I hadn't seen anything. "The board president called and wanted to know the sequence of the agenda items." I pointed toward the drawer. "I found your draft in this drawer and read it to him."

"Thanks." She barely glanced at me. She looked down at her purse in her hands as if she'd never seen it before, and then her gaze slid back to the drawer.

We stood still for long seconds. I couldn't guess whether she was still thinking about her husband or worried that I'd seen her ledger. I reached into the drawer and lifted the little journal so that she could see it. "Mrs. Johns, I didn't mean—"

The office door swung open. Hunter came in. Instantly the atmosphere was charged with the energy I always felt when I was near him.

Surprise and happiness lifted the corners of his mouth when he saw me. "Hey." But a heartbeat later, his smile dropped, as he must have sensed our tension. He looked from his mother to me and then back to her again. "What's—"

His mother pulled her eyes away from the journal, stepped toward him, and folded her arms around him. She was about five-foot-four, like me, so he could look over her head at me as she wept into his chest and told him about his dad becoming more combative and being restrained.

Our gazes locked, and I wanted to take their pain away. I slowly lowered the journal and closed the drawer as my heart filled with love and my mind filled with questions. *Is it ever OK to steal money? Is it ever OK to lie and cover up a crime?*

3

fter a few hours of sleep Sunday morning, I force myself out
of my duplex. I wish I could stay home for the next five years
or until *Marriage Exposure* is forgotten, but I have a gig at the
Hilton—four hours of playing a grand piano near the bar in the main
lobby. Several conferences will be launched this afternoon. People
will be arriving, visiting in the bar and requesting songs. I wear an elegant, cream-colored, satin backless dress that compliments the pale,
velvety carpet on the raised circular platform staging a coffee-colored
Wurlitzer. I hope to go home with lots of tips and no recognition. *Yikes!*
The social director of the Hilton has placed a small plaque with my name
in calligraphy on a stand nearby. I slip the plaque into a huge plant.
Desdemona is too strange of a name—someone could link me to *Marriage
Exposure.*

I finish Chopin's Etude No. 2 and try to think of music that might
appeal to the group of middle-aged, athletic-looking men gathering in
the bar.

A familiar voice tickles my ear. "Hello, my beautiful lady."
Miguel San Felipe Rodriguez, a classical guitarist I've played duets
with, stands close behind me—so close his breath warms my neck and
shoulders. "Will you play a piece for me?" He moves to my side. We've

socialized together a lot, but only with other musicians. I've always made an excuse when he suggests something that involves only the two of us.

Did he see Burt on TV? "Hi, Miguel." Even though I cringe about *Marriage Exposure*, my training takes over—you never, never stop playing. Never. I grin and spring into the *Rocky* theme song. Miguel's totally kind, hot, and talented, and even though his flirting throws me off-balance, his boyish sense of humor always gives me a lift. Today, after the nightmare of yesterday, he shines even brighter.

He shakes his head and clamps his hands over his ears. "How can a beautiful woman corrupt this magnificent instrument with that racket?"

I laugh for the first time in at least twenty-four hours. "Tips, Miguel. A girl has to eat." Actually, as I think of it, I probably haven't laughed like this since the last time I saw Miguel a few days ago. And he's probably one of the few people in the civilized world who hasn't seen a clip of last night's show. Miguel never wastes time on TV or Internet. I hope.

We stop talking for a moment when one of the buffed men from the bar steps up onto the platform and drops a ten into the porcelain tip bowl. I nod my thanks and then ask Miguel, "Are you playing today?"

"No." He smiles like a playful boy. *Oh no. Has he seen a clip?*

"Are you here for one of the conferences?"

"No." *He's being cryptic. He has to have seen it.*

"OK, Miguel." My stomach knots. "Why are you here?" I gaze at him while I replay a simple refrain. My throat tightens, but I force out the question. "Did you see a clip of *Marriage Exposure?*"

An expression of genuine confusion emotes from his honest eyes. "I come because I know that the beautiful Desdemona is playing." He lightly traces his fingers across my bare back, almost as if he's strumming his guitar. *Maybe he didn't see a clip.* Relief flows through me. "And I am under her spell." He can get by with outrageous flirting. He's fortyish, but he's one of those men who will look better with each passing year. His straight black hair hangs below his collar and has a few strands of gray at the temples. He's fit as a runner, even though I'm sure he doesn't spend much time exercising. His world is his guitar.

An involuntary chuckle of relief ripples through me, and I shake my head at him.

"Tell me, beautiful Desdemona, do you really think I joke? Or do you choose to receive my heartfelt declarations as jest?"

When I glance at him, my laugh freezes.

He's serious. "May I come back for you when you finish? I will take you for a glass of wine? Dinner?" He makes his statements sound like questions. *Is he acting different? Or am I being paranoid?*

"Sure," I say. The bar fills with middle-aged couples dressed in western attire, so I switch to classic country. One couple starts to dance a slow two-step in the small area between the piano and the bar.

A low growl comes from Miguel. He plays only classical pieces—no bastardizing to meet a bar crowd's whims. Somehow he shows his disapproval with humor.

"You finish at six, yes?"

I nod.

"I shall return for you then. I promise."

He strolls toward the bar.

Two gorgeous young women, both in strapless minidresses and seated at a small table near the bar, check him out as he passes by. He pays no attention to them, takes a stool at the end of the bar, and turns toward me. He nods at me as though we've just shared a secret.

I feel myself flush—somehow his gaze from across the room feels more intimate than the whispers in my ear did moments ago. The bartender approaches him as if asking for his order. Miguel simply shakes his head and continues to watch me.

A woman in her midforties—I think she's with the buffed man who left the *Rocky* tip—steps up onto the platform. "Can you play that wonderful eighties hit—'To All the Girls I've Loved Before'?"

I nod and smile while finishing the two-step melody. "But it won't be the same without Julio or Willie."

She shrugs. "Maybe not, but I just love it."

I love it, too. And the song makes me think of Miguel, Julio Iglesias's Spanish accent and handsome good looks, and even the message of the song—no judgment, no heartbreak, no disappointment—just a tribute to women loved.

She leaves as I play the opening measures. My eyes, on their own accord, shift back toward the end of the bar. Miguel is gone. And suddenly I feel a deep disappointment. I miss his smile, his assurance. My eyes dart around, searching. And there he is to my right, leaning against a pillar in the large open space that flows into the lobby. Still watching me, still smiling as though we're sharing a secret. *He must have seen the show. OK. OK.* Everyone I know will have heard about what Burt said. I'll have to deal with it sooner or later. And Miguel will be a good person to start with. Shake it off. Play. Wine and dinner with him will be fun. It will be good to get to know him better. Paradoxically, now that he stands farther away, he feels even closer.

The hours flow by, and Miguel disappears for short periods, but he always reappears somewhere among the crowd—sometimes sitting, sometimes standing, but always focused on me.

As promised, at 6:00 p.m. sharp he comes onto the piano platform and offers me his arm. "Shall we dine in the hotel restaurant? Or may I take you to Indrianna's?"

"Here," I squeak too quickly. Indrianna's is an intimate, obscenely expensive place out on Lake Travis, a thirty-minute drive away. I want to spend time with him, but in public. I clear my throat and calm my voice. "I love the restaurant here."

We stroll into the dining area. Red wine, incredible steak, soft music, Miguel's accent—perfect ending to a Sunday with no mention of the TV show.

Every time we've been together in the past, the conversation has revolved around music and gigs. But tonight he talks about his family, how his grandmother taught him to play violin when he was three and piano when he was five. In spite of frequent interruptions by our cute, blond, ponytailed, eager-to-please waitress, Miguel shares himself in ways I wouldn't have imagined. He grew up with a golden Lab that slept on the foot of his bed. He knows how to juggle, and he has a younger sister who is blind in one eye.

While he orders dessert, I excuse myself to go to the ladies' room. My face in the beveled mirror surprises me—relaxed, content. The melody from "To All the Girls I've Loved Before" spins in my head. I stand straighter. I want to be a woman loved. A normal, happy woman loved. Not a *Marriage Exposure* freak. I don't want to be defined by Burt and some insane TV show. When I return to our table, the ponytail still stands next to Miguel.

Her demeanor stiffens when she spots me. She was leaning into him, smiling into his face. Now she's upright again, with pad in hand, pencil poised. "Two Chilean crème de menthe liquors with vanilla ice cream." She starts backing away. "I'll get those right out."

I slide into my seat. "You have an admirer."

"Yes." He nods with an almost sad expression. "But not the one I would like to have."

Before I can think of a comeback to this, he leans forward and covers my hand with his. "Will you come to my home tonight?"

"Ah." I shake my head, trying to come up with a soft way to say no.

Cute ponytail, rushing back to our table, saves me. "Sir, I'm so sorry, but we're out of the Chilean liquor. We do have a Californian."

"Hmmm." Miguel stands up. "Let me talk with the bartender. I think he has another that will serve well." He turns toward me. "Will you excuse me, Desdemona?"

Cute ponytail's jaw drops as Miguel leaves the restaurant area, heading back toward the main bar. "Desdemona? *The* Desdemona?"

I'm a moderately well-known entertainer within the Austin music scene, but the tone of her "*the* Desdemona" doesn't align with my status as a pianist.

Her gaping, her question, the whole nightmare of last night pounce onto my panic button, which triggers my babbling. "It's not what you think." Her mouth opens even wider. "Burt doesn't know what he's talking about. They just make stuff up for those shows. And even if it were true, guys can't really tell. Everyone knows that." Her eyes are round balls—the whites show all around her blue irises. "You can't believe anything you see on a reality TV show." I leap to my feet. It's the only way

I can shut myself up. But as I dash back toward the ladies' room, I say, "You have the wrong person. That girl's name is Mona."

I rush into a stall, lock it, and collapse against the door, slowly sliding toward the floor. *How could this be happening? How could a random waitress recognize my name from the show?* Tears stream down my face. My cream satin dress will probably pick up smudges from the floor if I don't stop my downward slide. I make myself stand up, and I blot my eyes with toilet tissue. I've been in tougher spots than this on stage. *Just play through it. Deep breaths, keep performing. March on.*

After repairing my face the best I can with water and a hand towel, I return to the table where Miguel waits with tiny glasses of green liquor and crystal bowls of ice cream. He stands up as soon as he spots me and reaches an arm toward me. "Desdemona, are you unwell?" His brow is creased with worry. He squeezes my hand.

"No, I'm fine." I return his squeeze. "You don't watch *Marriage Exposure*, do you?"

His befuddled expression answers even before he speaks. "You asked me this earlier. Is this a new music show?"

I laugh with relief. "No. It's the most stupid reality show on the planet. Never, never watch it. It's a total waste of time."

"But why do you ask me this?"

I sip the liquor. "Nothing. Please forget it. This crème de menthe is amazing. Thank you for going to all the trouble you did to get it for us."

He beams. "I'm so glad you like it. Nothing is too much trouble for you, my Desdemona. Nothing." He pauses then and speaks slowly, carefully, as if he's worried that he'll ask the wrong thing. "Shall we go to Armando's for some music after we finish?" He clearly picked up on my negative response to his earlier invitation to go to his home. "Philippe and his band perform tonight."

"No." My voice is decisive, crisp. He peers at me, puzzled and concerned, as if he's afraid I'm going to say that I don't want to go anywhere else with him.

He nods slowly. "Is there another place you wish to go?"

"Yes."

The silence between us is heavy. I reach across the table and place my hand on his. "I'd like very much to visit your home tonight."

He brings my hand to his lips and presses a soft kiss into my palm. "You honor me."

In minutes we're on the sidewalk, and I assume we're walking to wherever he's parked. But he pauses at an iron gate, presses in a code, and leads me down a stone path bordered by tall rosebushes and lit with candle-shaped lamps. The path winds along the side of a tall building that seems to be a combination of offices and apartments. I've figured out that we're not headed for a parking garage. "Is this where you live?"

"Yes, welcome to *mi casa*." He pauses at another coded entry. This one, a doorway, leads into a small lobby with elevators. The elevator he selects has a glass exterior wall. We whiz upward, and the already beautiful Austin skyline shifts from a horizontal city scene to a breathtaking view of Town Lake, the Capitol Building, and the surrounding skyscrapers.

Another bottle of wine and another hour of talk in Miguel's apartment overlooking the magical night scene creates a new distance from yesterday and *Marriage Exposure*. And Miguel's romantic guitar music makes me almost forget my nine-year ache for Hunter.

Miguel sets his guitar back on its stand and refills my glass. Then he slides his guitarist's calloused fingers along my cheek. His eyes go to my lips. *Is he going to kiss me?* He leans in closer, brushing his lips over mine. *My steak was loaded with garlic. My breath must be awful. Why didn't I finger brush my teeth when I went to the bathroom? Hopefully, his steak was as garlicky as mine. Isn't it true that if you both eat the same thing, you won't notice it on each other's breath?*

The lip brushing slowly becomes a deep kiss. It's long and almost symphonic in the leisurely way his tongue explores my mouth as though he's following his own secret melody. He breaks the kiss and peers into my eyes. "Why is it that you never consented to come to my home before? I ask you so many times, and always you say no. Until this night."

He must be reading my mind, because I ask myself the same question. I answer with complete honesty. "I don't know." Maybe I've been a little scared of being alone with someone as polished and talented as Miguel. Maybe the shocks of last night have jarred me into trying a new path.

He lifts my feet, one at a time, and slides off my cream-colored pumps. I'm suddenly aware of how little I'm wearing. He shifts my feet onto his solid onyx coffee table. The smooth, clingy dress with a built-in bra that was great for a performance feels too insubstantial when alone with a man. The dress, now with my legs propped up, falls open at the slit so that my thigh is exposed almost to my panty line.

He takes a deep breath. "You are exquisite."

Why am I so frozen with self-consciousness? Why don't I just go with the flow? Why not have sex with Miguel? Maybe if I plow through my inhibitions, I'll become a frequent flier of the big O. Maybe my failure is a result of the fact that the two lovers I've had—I'm not counting Hunter since we didn't go all the way—Burt and Victor, just weren't skilled. Maybe it's not my fault at all. Hunter and I had rushed make-out sessions in our stolen, alone moments. After Hunter went to juvie, I waited five years, thinking somehow we'd find our way back to each other. Victor, my first, was a short fling on spring break. And Burt was a safe habit to alleviate aloneness. Maybe I just need the right man.

Miguel moves his fingers slowly up my calves. Classical guitarists have uniquely shaped calluses on the tips of their fingers, providing an amazing sensation when rubbed against skin. He keeps one hand on my knee, and with his free hand he reaches toward the side table. The music of mixed strings fills the room. There must be hidden speakers everywhere. The lights magically dim.

My surprise breaks my muteness—and the mood. "How did you do that?"

He smiles and tilts his head toward a smoothly receding control panel on the side table.

"How can you afford all this?" I ask. "All the musicians I know live on a shoestring."

"Shoestring?" He raises his eyebrows in confusion.

Even though his English is great, some idioms are lost. "I mean most musicians don't make much money."

"Ah. *Mi familia* in Caracas." He massages both my legs just above the knees. "And Venezuela reveres classical musicians—sponsors them."

"Wow." His hands move up higher on my thighs. It's clear where this is going. I need to make a decision, either leap up and get out now or resolve to have sex with him. "My rented duplex and my old spinet are the sum total of my wealth." I talk too fast, and his hands squeeze my thighs. He leans down and puts a soft kiss on my knee. "And I was lucky to score low rent—I had to agree to adopt the cat from the previous owner, and my landlady's hard of hearing, so she says my playing doesn't bother her." He kisses around to the back of my knee. "She plays her television too loud and has it next to our common wall, but she only watches it in the afternoons—Dr. Oz and Dr. Phil every day." One hand slowly moves up my inner thigh. "But even with my bargain rate, rent and food pretty much consume my income, but I'm an expert on Dr. Oz and Dr. Phil." *Why am I telling him this stuff?* He kisses my neck and one hand is almost to my panty line. "You know Austin is a music mecca with performers on every street, but lots of musicians are willing to play for free, so substantial income is scarce."

He stops my monologue with a deep kiss, and both his hands creep further up my thigh until he strokes me along the leg bands of my panties. He runs his thumbs underneath the edge and breaks our kiss. "I would like to take you to my country."

"My passport is out-of-date, I think." It's now or never. I can still leave. *Do I want to have sex with Miguel?* "But I've been planning to renew it." I visualize his hands on his guitar a few minutes earlier. *Maybe an older man with this amazing touch can be my solution.*

"Desdemona—" His fingers slip further into the rarely-trespassed-under-panty zone. "I would like to awaken the sleeping woman in you." I gasp. And it's not because of his fingers. It's his words. "I would like to find your music." He had to have seen the show. Right? But earlier he said he didn't, and it's true that he has been asking me out for years. Maybe this is just the universe sending me forward.

I should do it. Why not? He's nice. I've known him a long time. He tugs my panties, lifts my buttocks, and slowly slips the flimsy silk down—taking his time. He watches his own hands as he moves the panties down to my feet.

What will he do next? Take off my dress? Take off his own clothes? Where does he keep condoms? What if he doesn't want to use a condom? Should I ask now? My armpits get moist. Do I have body odor? I showered at noon, played for four hours, walked with Miguel to the restaurant—then six blocks to his loft. How many hours is that? How long have I been here? Is my deodorant still working?

He lifts my feet one by one as he removes the panties. He leans back beside me on the sofa. "You are so beautiful—exquisite." One hand is on my thigh. The other hand strokes my shoulder. He leans closer to my face.

OK, relax. Worrying will not solve the body odor or bad breath. Relax.

I swear Miguel reads my mind. "Relax, beautiful Desdemona." He kisses my neck. First on the front. Then he kisses his way to the back and uses one hand and his mouth to unfasten the closure at the back of my neck. *OK. The whole front of my dress will fall down at any moment.*

Should I sort of hold it up or just let it fall? Should I be undressing him? I'm about to be naked, and he's fully clothed. I bet he still has his shoes on. I take a quick glance. Yep. Perfectly polished black loafers.

His hand on my thigh edges closer to my center. OK. This is every girl's dream—a handsome man with talented hands intent on awakening the sleeping woman.

The thigh hand slides over and covers my mound, with one finger pressed flat against my clitoral area. The end of his finger edges into my vagina. *Am I getting wet? Hello, if I were wet, I wouldn't be wondering if I'm wet. Should I be wet? Will he notice if I'm not?* His kisses move back to the front of my neck. With his free hand, he edges the dress down. *Crap.* Like an idiot I clamp my arms against my dress to keep it up. *Relax.* I loosen my arms so the dress can fall.

He says something in Spanish while he pushes the dress below my breasts with his face. I wish my mother had taught me more Spanish. Even though it's her first language, she wanted me to be a natural English speaker like my Anglo dad. Miguel kisses my breasts for a long time—not the nipples—just the flesh all around. At the same time, he edges his finger deeper inside. *Still not wet...I think.*

I hadn't noticed before, but he has a clock reflected on his ceiling. I wonder where it is being projected from. It's 9:15 p.m., and his nose is five inches from my armpit. My deodorant is for sure gone by now. I should have used the toxic kind with the super antiperspirant in it. I'm pretty sure I used the organic kind this morning—smells great, feels great, but lasts only a few hours. I've read that of all the human sub-groups on the planet, the female Caucasian has the most unpleasant body odor. But maybe since I'm only half Caucasian, I'm not so bad. But wait, would Latinas have been grouped with Caucasians in that study?

He takes one nipple into his mouth and rolls his tongue around it with the same slow, smooth rhythm that he uses on my clitoris. It's nice. Really nice. *But what should I be doing? Oh no! I've done nothing but lounge here. I need to do something to him.*

I quickly unbutton his shirt and try to slide it down his arms, which of course doesn't work, because both his hands are engaged. He breaks from his rhythm, one arm at a time, to get the shirt off. Then he smoothly gets back to work. I reach for his zipper. *Shouldn't I take his shoes off first? Oh well, I can't reach them.* Maybe he won't even need them off. He'll just need his pants down. *Can't they just clump around his ankles?*

Now he has one finger in, one hand on one breast, and his mouth on the other.

I find his zipper. Down it goes. I push my hands beneath the waist-band of his underwear, and his erection springs out when I lift his underwear up and over. For a moment I stare. I'm fascinated with pe-nises—the amazing way they transform from a soft, resting cushy into a large, firm appendage; the way the silky skin glides over the hard muscle underneath; and the way a penis is so strong yet so weak. Strong in that when erect, it literally takes over a man's body, leading the man wher-ever it needs to go. And weak because an erect penis has no choice but to enter a woman or find some sort of release. And all this strength and weakness is intermingled with passion, and ideally, love. It has been over a year since Burt and I ended, and I've missed touching and exploring. Should I rub around on the tip or pump the shaft up and down? I decide to do both.

I've just about got a rhythm going when he raises his head to mine, kisses me long and slow, and then takes his finger out, bringing me to my feet at the same time. He steps out of his pants and shoes. He's muscular and sleek, and the most hairless man I've ever seen. A solid dark tan from head to toe. His erection stands at attention—a redder tan than the rest of him.

I step toward him and grab for his penis, but he stops me. "You must not be in a hurry. We have time." I halt my hands midreach. "Let me," he says as he clasps my elbows. I unconsciously clamp my elbows against my dress even though it has dropped to my waistline. I must look like some kind of robot girl stiffly trying to caress him with my elbows locked to my side.

I take a deep breath. *Relax.* And let the dress fall. *What do I do with my hands now?* He slowly circles me, looking up and down my body as if he's measuring—his hands at his side, his erection leading like a flag. His slow prance and inspection reminds me of the matador circling the bull. I can almost hear the bullring trumpets and the cheers of the crowd. He mutters more Spanish.

In a swift move, he scoops me into his arms and carries me toward what I figure must be his bedroom. Yes. It is indeed a bedroom. A large round bed covered in some kind of fur, a full wall of windows looking over the lake and city lights, another wall of displayed guitars—two of which I've never seen him play. Those two must be antiques—I think I saw one at an instrument auction somewhere.

He lowers me onto the fur covering of the bed, still muttering Spanish with an occasional "Desdemona" thrown in. *I should be saying something. But what? Miguel? You are gorgeous? That sounds good.*

"Miguel, you are gorgeous—a gorgeous man."

This gets me another long, long kiss. I wonder if it will be weird the next time we run into each other at a gig or concert. This kiss is really long. And his erection presses into my belly. *When will he put it in?* I still haven't figured out the condom thing yet—I didn't notice anything like a bedside table with a handy condom drawer. Maybe round beds don't have bedside tables.

Just when I think he might be shifting around to get himself in-side me, he moves his whole body off me and kisses my breasts again. This time he goes straight for the nipples and switches back and forth—left nipple, right nipple, left nipple, right nipple...I wonder if I should touch or kiss his nipples? Burt liked that, but spring-break Victor did not. And, of course, I was too inexperienced to even think of male-nipple preferences with Hunter. *Pow.* That choking, I-could-cry feeling surges through my chest. *Stop thinking about Hunter.* I've never read the best protocol to find out whether a guy likes nipple play. I almost giggle out loud when I imagine myself saying, "Excuse me, Miguel, could you in-form me of your nipple preferences?"

He puts his hands on both breasts and kisses my belly. Rolling each nipple between his textured thumb and forefinger, he works his way lower down my belly. *Uh oh.* I think he's going to go down on me. *Crap.* I'm totally not ready for a close-up down there. I should have done the French bath thing when I used his bathroom earlier. Now he's reached the top of my pubic hair. My shower was nine hours ago. If I had known about this, I could have gotten waxed. But then some men don't like that. Victor liked it. Burt did not. And, of course, I don't know which Hunter preferred. *Pow.*

I've got to stop him. "Miguel, I need you to—"

"Desdemona, I need you, too." He spreads me open with his fin-gers and positions his face so that he gazes directly into my displayed everything. His lips part as he exhales hard. His fingers, holding me open, slowly massage the sensitive flesh bordering my clitoris. He leans in closer, takes a deep breath, and then blows warm air gently onto me. He glances at my face for a moment and says something in Spanish. He looks back down where he still holds me open. His lips part again, and he starts a downward dive.

Suddenly Dr. Oz looms before my mind's eye—I mean ear. "Wait." I screech. Miguel jerks his head back and looks at me with a puzzled expression. "I heard a Dr. Oz show about this. You can get human pap-illomaviruses from this." His eyebrows shoot upward, and his mouth drops open. "He said to use a dam like Saran Wrap." His confounded expression tells me he's still not getting it. I give up. Too hard to explain. I know enough Spanish to say, "No oral, *por favor*."

He smiles, puts his hand back over my mound, and kisses me just above my pubic hair. He kisses me across my lower belly and continues massaging on the sides of my clitoris. Slowly, slowly he works his way up my belly and finally back to my breast, where he rolls the nipple in his mouth in sync with the rhythm his hand uses on my core.

All I can think to do is pat his head and shoulders. This beautiful man works so hard for me. He's the kindest, most considerate, most handsome, talented creature I know. It's beautiful.

OK, big O. If you're in there anywhere, it's time to show yourself. It won't get any better than this. I guess he senses that my music isn't where it needs to be yet. He eases a finger all the way inside. *Rats. Still too dry.* He is such a dear that I use my vaginal muscles to squeeze his finger with gratitude.

He growls deep in his chest and slows his mouth work on my nipple. He must think those squeezes were an orgasm. What the hell—it's not my fault he thinks that. I give a little moan just for good measure. He growls some more.

In the semidarkness, I can see that he's smiling at me as he reaches down on the side of the bed. I hear a drawer open. *Hmm, a built-in, hidden drawer. Clever.* With one hand still caressing my mound, he uses his free hand to bring a condom to his mouth. He rips the wrapper open with his teeth. OK, that was great foreplay; maybe this will be the time I come. Just before he slips the condom on, I reach for his penis. "No more, Desdemona. I can wait no longer."

The condom is on, but suddenly he turns his back to me and reaches down into that hidden drawer again. *What is he doing?* I sit up and try to peek over his shoulder so I can see.

But too quickly he turns back toward me. *Click.* There's a soft sound as something hits the hardwood floor beside the bed. Before I can check it out, he's face-to-face with me, lowering me back down to the bed, alternately kissing and whispering, "You are ready, my beautiful Desdemona. It is time." We fall back onto the bed. I do a quick visual of the condom, but it's too dark to tell if it's still in place. Just before he positions for his entry, I reach down and feel for the rubber roll at the base. *Yes, condom is in place, and he's sliding in—yes, sliding—I'm wet enough for sliding.* I expect he'll give a few quick pumps and be done. But he surprises me by being slow and rolling his body around so that his pubic bone finds all kinds of pressure points between my legs. If my music could be found, this would do it.

He whispers, "I want you to come again with me inside."
Uh oh.

He kisses me. His tongue caresses mine. He's managed to get one hand between us, and he rolls my nipple again. I wrap my legs around him and press my pelvis into him. For a moment I'm sure I feel a little flutter of life, a little hint of response. This could be it. How I would love to get the big O with someone inside me (my three, almost four happened with a clitoral vibrator and an empty vagina)! This could be it. He moves so slowly, so gently—circling his body so that he literally massages my mound while he kisses me and rolls my nipple. This could be it. It's beautiful. He's a precious, kind man. This could be it. I press my pelvis even harder into him and Kegel for all I'm worth.

His rhythm speeds up. His breathing accelerates. He says my name over and over. He collapses on top of me. He's not too heavy—it's actually very comfortable and cozy. But after a few minutes, he rolls off and raises up on one elbow. In the dim light, he smiles at me and strokes my cheek. "Wait for me, my beauty. I will bring your wine."

While he's out of the room, I decide to gather my dress and panties, which are still in the living room. As soon as my foot hits the floor, squish. *What is this? Is this what I heard drop when he was messing around in the condom drawer? A tube?* I pick it up and squint. *Sterile Personal Lubricant.* Right on the floor where Miguel dropped it. He had to use lubricant on the condom. Because of me.

Seventeen minutes later—after declining his sweet invitation to sleep over—I ride a cab home with Burt in my head. "Jenny, I could never have loved Desdemona. She's a freak. She...she...she even fakes orgasms."

4

At home I fill Eleanor's food bowl and turn on my phone. *What was I thinking—having sex with Miguel? What must he be thinking now?* My phone powers up to connect me back to reality, and all the horror of yesterday crashes back. At least twenty messages, mostly from Kari and one from a piano student. None of my missed calls are from unknown numbers, so Hunter hasn't tried to reach me. I knew he wouldn't. I wish Mom hadn't given him my number. That tiny glimmer of hope she raised is futile. He hasn't contacted me in nine years. It's stupid to think he'll ever speak to me again.

Before I can listen to voice mails, my phone rings—Kari. "Desdemona? Are you OK? I've called a thousand times. What happened to your phone?"

I don't know where to begin. She's my best friend—someone I tell everything. Almost.

"Desdemona, say something, or I'm coming over there."

"I'm OK. Just don't want to deal with..." I can't make myself say it.

"You can tell me anything. You're my best friend. I won't judge."

So for the next hour, I lie on my sofa, with my chocolate-stained throw clutched to my chest, and unburden all the sins committed during my reign as Queen Fake It, including the interlude with Miguel. But in spite of this purging, I can't make myself tell her about Hunter—how much I love him, how I ruined any chance we had of making it together, and how our lives have brushed past each other for the first time in nine years. Hunter is in a different plain—too deep and too tender to be polluted by conversation, even with my best friend.

Kari doesn't seem shocked by my confession. "Maybe you need professional help. Listen, I've never talked to Miguel, but I've seen him perform. He's one of the sexiest men alive. I almost come just sitting in the audience watching his hands, hearing his music. And when he speaks, that smile, that accent. He makes me feel totally..." She seems to be floundering for her next word. Finally she purrs, "Erotic."

I sigh. "I'm de-rotic."

"Is that a word?"

I suddenly feel exhausted—doesn't matter if it's a word or not. It's me. "Should be."

"Hmm—maybe the word would be un-rotic or a-rotic."

My phone beeps an incoming call. "Gotta go—it's Ross—we have a lesson scheduled for tomorrow."

Ross, my only adult student, is a sweet, handsome systems engineer who's actually my age. He took up piano about five years ago. The first words out of his mouth hit my alarm button. "Are you OK?"

Crap. I sit up, instantly tense. "I'm fine. How are you?"

Long silence. "Look, I want to level with you. I saw the clips of your asshole-ex." Ross and I have kept up with each other's dating stories over the past five years. He knows all about Burt.

"No comment."

"If I could get my hands on the sorry bastard, I'd probably rack up an assault charge." He pauses—I guess to let me speak. Then he gives up and goes on. "Or I could practice my castrating technique on him. I cut quite a few stock-show pigs when I was in high school. I could use a refresher."

"Gross." I laugh in spite of myself.

"This is none of my business, but I had a girlfriend before I moved to Austin who couldn't get off, and we figured out a way that worked for her."

"Ross, I don't want to talk about this." But I'm actually curious. *What did they figure out?*

"I get that—and I wouldn't even bring it up—except I'm sure I could help you."

Ross has always been a straight shooter—never tried to BS me. I think he really believes what he's saying. Sometimes I think Ross and I might have dated each other, but the timing never worked—when I was free, he was in a relationship, and vice versa. Now, he's practically married. Still, I'm too embarrassed to ask for details. "Thanks, but I'm not comfortable with this whole conversation. Are you coming to your lesson tomorrow?"

"Yeah, and it will probably be my last." His voice drops an octave lower the way it always does when he's sad or serious. "Dell offered me a spot in a new plant in China."

"You're kidding. That's so exciting." What I wouldn't give to go to the other side of the planet where no one has heard of me.

"Yeah, and all the more reason to let me help you out." He speaks very slowly, still in that low, personal sounding tone. "Last chance."

"Thanks, you're thoughtful, but no thanks." His offer to help is sweet, but I can't switch from our friendly, student-teacher connection to orgasm talk with him. "See you tomorrow."

I barely have a moment to pick up Eleanor, who's just strolled in through her pet door, when my phone rings again. Burt. Chills skitter across the back of my neck. Eleanor escapes from my lap to check out her dinner. I could let it go to voice mail. But now that I've been totally humiliated in front of the entire civilized world, and I've had unplanned sex with Miguel, my regular social filters are clogged. *What have I got to lose? Privacy? Pride? Nope—already lost it all.*

I stand up, square my shoulders, and take a deep breath—determined not to let him know how much his TV announcement bothers me. "Hello, Burt." I keep my voice calm as if I were not remotely impacted by anything about him.

"I'm so sorry." He sounds as if he really means this. "I mean it. I never intended to say that about you. It sucks being in front of an audience, trying to calm your wife." He zips through words as if he has this speech memorized and wants to get it all out before a timer goes off, and I'm frozen as if breathing might make me miss a word. "But I know that's no excuse. I don't want you to think that I deliberately told her about you. We were at Zilker Park one night when you were playing. And she'd seen your name in my Facebook friends list, so she started asking questions. I told her we were together a year. I didn't go into details, but she couldn't stop talking about you—how beautiful, how talented. I didn't realize until after we got married that she's insecure." He's almost breathless. "And then she gained weight—she'd lost fifty pounds right before we met. I never knew her as overweight until after we married. Then she lost her job. Then she started obsessing that I don't love her anymore, and for some reason she fixated on you." He stops fast and takes several quick breaths. *Why doesn't he say how he knew I was faking? Why doesn't he say when he figured it out? Why doesn't he say how I was different from women who don't fake? Why is he barraging me with his marriage issues?*

"Des, baby, are you there?"

I squirm like a worm trying to get off a painful hook. Instead of asking him the questions that are crowding my mind, I bark, "Don't call me that...that pet name."

"You're mad at me, right?" I visualize his squinting expression, the one he uses when he knows he's screwed up.

Too loudly I say, "How I feel or don't feel is none of your business." I can't believe how cold and direct I'm being.

He's quiet for a moment. I'm about to hang up when he says, "You're right, and I don't blame you for not wanting to tell me anything—not after what I said on the show."

I'm silent.

He asks, "Still there?"

"If you're done, I'll hang up now." Feeling drained and defeated, I walk toward the kitchen cabinet where there would be a bottle of wine or a bag of chocolates if I had any, which I don't.

"Wait. I need to tell you something." He's back in the hurry-get-it-out mode. "You see, the audience that day went apeshit over you, and the show got more hits and e-mails about you than they've ever had be-fore." I linger in a trance in front of my bare cabinet. "And you weren't even there in person. The producer wants us to do a show together. They're even talking about maybe doing a two-part—one with you, me, and Jenny. Then a second one with you and a psychologist who will talk with you about why you fake it." I thought no greater humiliation could assault my being, but at this moment I'm in agony. I cannot be in this conversation. "They'll pay us good—I think they'll offer as much as they do to celebrity guests, and I bet you could get them to let you play the piano on the show. This would be great exposure for you. That program has a good following in Austin."

I should say something. The notion of talking on TV about my or-gasm issue has me choked. The hardened armor I wore at the beginning of our conversation crumbles. I force out a feeble whisper. "No, thank you." I push *end* and stand there, listening to the silent phone and star-ing into the empty cabinet until the phone rings again.

Ugh. Burt's name flashes on the screen. I let him go to voice mail this time. *OK,* I assure myself while I wait for his message, *things can't get any worse. I'll just wait out this nightmare and get back to normal.* Wrong. I'm wrong. His recording takes the nightmare to a new level. "You've got to reconsider. We need the money, and we're going back on with or without you. Uh, I gave them...I wanted to ask you first, but they were persistent...and your Facebook page is gone...and they had no way to check with you, so I sort of uh...gave them your...uh...phone number."

As if on cue, my phone rings again. Why bother to check the caller ID? My life is over. I'm powerless to do anything about anything. Not only can I not orgasm, I can't control the circus building around my lost privacy.

I accept the call, and Miguel says, "I want to be sure you make it home safely."

"Thanks." Drained of energy and my cabinet being bereft of choco-late and wine makes me want to cry.

"I wish you were still here. I wish I could have convinced you to stay."

"Thanks." I drag myself back to the sofa and plop down.

"It was beautiful. You are beautiful. I hope we can be together again soon."

"Thanks."

"Can I see you tomorrow, my beauty?"

I lose track of what he says. "Thanks."

"This means yes? Shall I come to you?"

I've got to pull myself together and disentangle sweet Miguel from my mess.

"Desdemona. Are you there?"

"I can't see you tomorrow. What happened tonight was wrong of me. I've got issues that you'll hear about soon enough." I talk as fast as Burt did. I have to get this out before I cave. "I'm a freak. I don't do relationships. I thought maybe I could change. And I'm sorry that I let the whole thing happen tonight. It wasn't fair to you. You're a sweet, kind, gorgeous man, and any woman who gets to be with you is so very lucky. But I can't be with anyone. Ever."

"Desdemona. I worry for you. You must not say these things. You must not think them."

"Thanks."

"When can we meet to talk about this?"

"Thanks—nothing else to talk about."

"No. We must meet. I will come to you."

This snaps me back to alertness. I don't want him to come over. "No," I say. "Don't come, please."

"Tomorrow then. We can meet?"

"No—I'm busy—lots of students tomorrow."

"Then I come tonight."

He doesn't seem to give up, so I name the most public, unromantic place I can think of. "Tomorrow morning meet me at the Whole Foods juice bar at eleven."

The next call is from a strange number. Now that I'm notorious for sexual ineptness, I'm besieged with calls.

"Desdemona Lorents, please." It's not Hunter. But, of course, I knew it wouldn't be. Why does that perverse hope keep prodding me?

I mumble something.

"I'm Jake Rawls, producer with *Marriage Exposure*."

"Yes." I get good at monotone.

"I guess you know you rocked our show yesterday." He's upbeat—like a Santa spurting *Ho, ho, ho! Merry Christmas!* "Everyone wants to hear your story. We'd like to meet with you to discuss when you can come on and give your side."

"No, thank you."

"I can see why you might be hesitant, but give it some thought. If you come—heh, heh, no pun intended—you can set the story straight. Make sure the true version is out there instead of Burt's."

"No, thank you." But little snippets of mean, evil retorts I could make to Burt pop into my head. If I were a bold blabber like him, there's plenty I could talk about on TV. *The way he could only get it up in the mornings. His no-cuddling-afterward and must-shower-immediately rules.*

"Believe me, you'll be well received. We've Googled your interviews, photos, performances. You're photogenic and have a powerful presence. You'll get more free publicity out of this than you could pay for—even if you used a top firm. This is gold."

In spite of the mean digs at Burt flying through my head, there's no way I could bash him on TV, and revenge wouldn't undo what he has done to me. "No." This time without the *thank you.*

"We'd pay you ten thousand dollars for a one-hour show, plus all your travel expenses. Ten thousand for one hour. Then there's the possibility for an increased fee for a second show."

The new sound system I've been coveting comes to mind, but I hold firm. "No."

"Could we meet and talk about this in person? I'd like to show you our publicity plan and a summary of the great feedback we've had about you so far. You should let yourself weigh the facts before you make up your mind."

What the hell—why not meet him in person?

He jumps on my pause. "Name the time and place. I can be in Austin as soon as Tuesday to talk to you." Eleanor, finished with her dinner, stretches lazily against my legs. "Or if you'd prefer, we can fly you to LA. You could see our studio. Meet the other producers and staff. How does Tuesday sound?"

No. I can't go on TV and talk about faking orgasms. I can't—not even for ten thousand. "I will never be on the show. Please don't call me back."

He squeezes in, "But Tuesday—" I disconnect.

Monday morning Miguel waits for me at the Whole Foods juice bar. He jumps to his feet and offers me a stool.

Reggie, the red-haired, bearded juice master, waves his towel at me. "Hey, Des. Your regular?"

"Sure. Thanks, Reggie."

Miguel says, "And I'll have the same, thank you."

We watch while Reggie loads in celery, lemon, ginger, parsley, and spinach.

Miguel's skin tone transforms to match the green that forms in the juicer. "You have this beverage regularly?"

"Yes—love it."

He nods slowly. When Reggie serves our drinks, Miguel sniffs at his and watches while I drink. He takes a cautious sip and nods. "Hmmm. Not so bad."

I don't want to drag this out. "Miguel, please listen. I'm sorry about last night." I want to say all of this before Kari comes—he doesn't know I invited her. "It was reckless and thoughtless of me." He looks at me kindly with perfect stillness. "I'd had some bad news earlier in the day, and it gave me such a lift at the Hilton when I saw you that I lost my head. You were wonderful last night, but I'm not ready for anything but a friendship. I want us to go back to what we had before last night—just a casual friendship."

"I am sorry to hear this, because I have hoped for a long time that we might—"

"Kari. Hi." I interrupt as Kari approaches us. "Miguel, this is my friend Kari. Kari—Miguel."

Miguel gives me a long, knowing look. Can he tell that I staged this? To his credit, he stands up like the gallant gentleman he is and offers her a chair.

Kari plops down and waves Reggie away. "None of the health junk for me." She pulls a Diet Coke out of her large bag.

Miguel laughs at her. The tension between Miguel and me that weighted the air moments earlier dissipates.

Kari is on—her long, chocolate hair crimped and glowing, her purple tights showing off the muscle tone in her legs, and her clingy, sleeveless tunic features a floral pattern hinting of South America. In a quick aside to me, she says, "Check your texts." Then she turns her full attention to Miguel. "I saw you perform at the Long Center last month. I love your technique."

Miguel easily flows into conversation with her. I read my text from Kari. "U can go."

I text Kari back. "Soon."

She ignores her phone and me and everything else while she laughs at something Miguel just said. After a couple of minutes of listening to their chatter, I finish my drink and stand up. They both stop and look at me politely, and I think, expectantly. Kari, at least, is ready for me to leave.

"I'm going—have a lesson to—"

"Bye," Kari says.

Their heads are close together, eyes locked. She nods about whatever he tells her—they speak Spanish now. Looks like he's recovering from his disappointment over me. *Thank you, Kari.* I'm glad not to feel guilty about Miguel. I have enough guilt about Hunter to keep me mired in regret for the rest of my life.

I glance back at them before I exit. Kari's hands shape a circle in the air as she excitedly describes something. Miguel smiles and nods politely and looks past her animated face toward me. In the instant our eyes meet, he has that same sad, knowing expression that he had yesterday at the hotel when he said, "Tell me, beautiful Desdemona, do you really think I joke? Or do you choose to receive my heartfelt declarations as jest?"

5

At home I try to focus on planning Ross's lesson. I want to put together some pieces that he can take with him, music that will challenge him to keep progressing but not overwhelm him. I pull a file box out of the closet and search through the volumes of musty sheet music left from my own lessons. Of course, all the songs are from high school and those lonely years afterward. Every piece I touch takes me back.

— ⁓

The police showed up at school a few weeks after I found out about Mrs. Johns embezzling the money.

Cash flow had escalated in the office because the football team won the district championship. And the first bidistrict game was at our stadium. The event drew bigger-than-average crowds, so concession and gate incomes were at least double those of regular season games.

On Saturday after the big Friday-night game, when I went to school to practice, I saw Mrs. Johns through the glass wall of the front office. She was at her desk with stacks of money all around her. My stomach clenched. I knew that she could be in the act right now of stealing, and

I could be witnessing it. My feet couldn't keep walking past. I swung the door open, stepped into her office, approached her desk, and took a deep breath. I had to be sure she understood the seriousness of the amount of money she'd taken. I'd looked up Texas theft laws online. Under fifteen hundred dollars is only a misdemeanor, but anything over that is a felony—prison time.

She glanced up at me. "Hi, Desdemona. Trying to get a head start on this for Monday."

"Mrs. Johns, I—"

Swish. The door behind me swung open. I turned to see Emmitt Straus, president of the new computer club, walking toward us. As usual he looked steamed about something—his pudgy face, covered with straw-colored freckles, flushed a rosy red. Even his scalp was pinking through his thin, straw-colored spikes.

Mrs. Johns's glance boomeranged from Emmitt to me and back again.

I backed toward the door. "Never mind. Just stopping to say hi, and let me know if you need any help. I'll just be practicing for a couple of hours—nothing out of the ordinary."

Emmitt took my place in front of her. He placed both his splayed hands on the edge of her desk and crouched low to tell her something as I slipped out the door. I watched them through the glass for a moment, thinking he might leave and I could go back in. Emmitt's back was to me while he talked, but I could see Mrs. Johns's face clearly. She turned pale, stared at her computer screen, and shook her head. I couldn't hear what she was saying, but her blue eyes, locked on her screen, were horrified, frantic. Emmitt pulled up a chair beside her so he could see the screen. When he plopped himself down with his arms folded, he spotted me watching. He gave me a single backward nod and arched one eyebrow as if he'd just uncovered some dark secret. I backed away.

I planned to practice an hour or so and then go back and try again to talk to Mrs. Johns. But while I was playing, there was a knock on the door. I stopped as the door opened and a police officer came in. He introduced himself as he approached the piano. "How did you get in? Did the secretary let you in?"

I had started to stand up during his introduction, so I was halfway up and frozen by the accusatory tone in his questions. "No, sir." I sat back down, reached into my purse that was on the floor beside me, and pulled out the keys. "The band director gave me a key to the front door and to this room last year. I come all the time to practice."

"Do any other students have keys?"

"I don't think so. Just me."

He picked up the keys. "Do these fit the office?"

"No—just the door of the main hall and this room." He glanced down at my hands, which were clutched together in my lap.

"What do you know about the seven hundred dollars missing from the club?"

"What club?" I unclutched my hands and put them on the bench beside me. "I mean, I didn't know seven hundred dollars is missing, but there's a lot of clubs." I was talking too much—too fast. "That's a misdemeanor, not a felony, right? When did it go missing?" Why did I ask these stupid questions? "Ah. No. I don't know anything."

"Emmitt Straus reported he left cash in the office, and it hasn't shown up in the account." Emmitt—I wanted to strangle him. He'd been a whiney baby since kindergarten. When he didn't get his choice of red, not green, Jell-O the first week of school, he pitched a fit. We had been stuck in a class together almost every year, and he'd called foul about something every day since kindergarten. "You're here a lot. Know anything?"

"When did he turn it in?" My hands of their own volition had defaulted into the lap clutch. I jerked them back to my sides. "There's a lot of cash in the office right now with the game last night." I sounded false even to myself. "Does he have his receipt? If he does, then why is he worried? Maybe when it's all counted, his money will turn up." It's hard to lie to an officer.

He stood there looking at me with a blank expression. For a long time. Never taking his eyes off me, he pulled a business card from his wallet and laid it with the keys on the piano bench next to my hand. "If you think of anything, call me."

I meant to nod causally as he started to turn away, but instead my muscles were so tense, I jerked my head once—hard. The jerk, as if a physical tug, stopped him. I froze. My mouth went dry, and my heart raced.

He leveled me with his gaze. "If you're not comfortable calling me, call Crime Stoppers. There's a sign with the number in the entryway of the school."

He slowly turned and left the room.

I was shaking so much I could hardly play. I made myself do scales until I figured he might have left. Then I headed up the hall to the front door, hoping no one would be there. I needed to go home and phone Emmitt. Some kids had cell phones then, but I didn't.

Mrs. Johns and the officer were still in her office. She was going through a file—looked like receipts. And the stacks of cash were still on her desk. They both watched me leave.

I ran all the way to the shop, and on my way up the stairs to our living quarters, I saw Mom in her walk-in refrigerator culling old flowers. *Good. She won't hear me.*

My fingers trembled as I looked up Emmitt's number in the student directory and dialed. "When did you turn your money in?" Rage surged up in me. I should have confronted him when he was with Mrs. Johns instead of slinking away. "And who did you give it to?"

"Why do you want to know? This is police business."

"Emmitt. It may just be a mistake. Why are you assuming someone stole it? It may be misplaced. The police asked me about it. I want to know when and who you gave it to."

"Oh." This was the story of Emmitt's life. He always overreacted about some perceived injustice and later saw the error of his way. "Uh. It was Thursday. It was seven hundred and twenty from donations, and we're going to have an Internet café in the—"

"Who did you give it to? Who signed your receipt?"

"Alex, I think his name is, the fifth-period student aide. But he gave it to Mrs. Johns—I saw him with my own eyes, and she signed the receipt."

"Then your money isn't missing, Emmitt. If you turned it in, and you have a receipt, it's not missing."

"Yes, it is missing. I have access to our online account, and it is not there."

I gritted my teeth. None of the other clubs that I knew of tracked their accounts online, but it made sense that computer groupies would be into that. My mind was racing. Surely Mrs. Johns wouldn't steal from such a small account. "It's too soon for the money to be deposited." I didn't know if this was really true or not. "They're extra busy with the bidistrict game. Your deposit will get done Monday or Tuesday. You need to tell the police that you only turned it in on Thursday."

"Sure," Emmitt said coolly. "I'll wait, but nothing will change. The money won't be there. You don't understand how online deposits work."

My stomach sank. He was right. I didn't understand the online part, but I did know that if Mrs. Johns had taken the money instead of depositing it, maybe by Monday, she'd put it back.

In homeroom on Monday morning, Hunter, who now sat in the desk in front of mine, was leaning over my desktop, telling me about the next play-off game when Mr. Phelps, the principal, came on the intercom. "Students and faculty, I have important announcements today—good news and bad news. First the good. Congratulations to Hunter Johns!" Hunter grinned and cast his eyes downward. He always took praise with a genuine smile, blended with almost bashful humility. The guy in front of him turned around, and the two high-fived. "We've received word that he'll be offered a full, four-year football scholarship to A and M." A couple of guys came up and slapped him on the shoulder. "We are proud of Hunter, our whole team, and the coaching staff for all the work that made this happen."

The teacher walked to Hunter's desk, shook his hand, and offered the traditional fist-and-thumb-up gesture and the Aggie fight words, "Gig 'em."

Hoots rang out around the room. I reached up and palmed the back of his head. I loved rubbing his buzzed hair.

He turned back toward me, and the hooting fans receded. Hunter gazed into my eyes, and his hand covered mine. His touch made the rest of the world fall away. "Wanna be an Aggie next year?" Warmth flooded my body at the thought of going away to college next year with Hunter. Hunter leaned closer and pulled my arm so that we were close enough for our lips to meet. He broke our kiss long enough to whisper, "You'll be hot in maroon." PDA was forbidden at school, but I guess as seniors we were pushing the limits on a lot of the rules.

Mr. Phelps droned on. "Now, I am very saddened to make this next announcement. A large amount of money is missing from the office." With a jolt Hunter pulled back. His eyes, when they met mine, looked pained and hurt. He turned quickly away from me. Things had been awkward for us since I found out about the money, but he was even more closed off at this moment. His mother must have told him about the police coming on Saturday. "This was cash donated for an Internet café. If anyone has information that could help us locate this cash, please let me know as soon as possible." In spite of my conversation with Emmitt, the investigation wasn't going away, and the search for the missing $720 might expose the thousands that Mrs. Johns had taken. Might result in her going to prison. I couldn't bear this happening to Hunter. "We are hoping this was a mistake and that we will be able to clear it up. If you know anything, come in and talk to me. I want to get the money back where it belongs. Even if you're not sure about your information, please let me know. You may know something that will help us get to the bottom of this."

As I looked at the back of Hunter's head and saw the tension in his shoulders, I wanted to hug him—take care of him. Suddenly a peaceful feeling settled over me. Serendipitously, I actually had $775 saved from years of gifts and commissions. I could fix this.

At lunch I walked the three blocks to the bank and withdrew $720 in twenties from my savings account. This left $55 in my account. I had been saving to buy a $1,200 used piano from my old piano teacher. My parents split when I was ten, and Dad took only one thing with him when he left—the piano.

I wasn't sure how I would do it, but I was determined to slip this $720 into the office so that Emmitt could get his deposit made, and the police would quit sniffing around.

When I came back to school near the end of lunch break, Hunter was in front of the main building looking for me. "Where were you?"

My face turned hot. "I had to go home for a few minutes." I couldn't look at him.

"But—" He was probably going to point out that I came from the wrong direction.

I cut him off and rushed into the building. "I have to go into English early."

I felt his eyes watching me as I walked away.

All afternoon I looked for opportunities to get into the office and find a place to put the money. I even thought of giving it to Emmitt and telling him I found it, but I knew he'd know the denominations of the bills he'd collected—and they probably weren't all twenties.

After school I went to the piano room and was surprised to see Hunter already there waiting for me.

I asked, "Why aren't you at football practice?"

He came close, wrapped his arms around me, and pulled me to his chest. "I'm going. Just wanted to see you for a minute first."

My head lay against his heart, and I listened to the thudding I loved. Tears welled in my eyes as I thought about how unfair it was that his father had been injured and that the donations and insurance ran out and that his mother had to support Hunter and his little sister alone.

He lifted my chin and started to kiss me but stopped and frowned. "Hey, what's wrong?" He thumbed away the tears from under my eyes. "What's going on?"

I shook my head and tiptoed up to kiss him. He pulled back after a moment and asked again, "What's wrong?"

"I love you, Hunter. I love you so much. And I worry...worry about... everything."

He put his hands on the sides of my face. "I love you, Desdemona. I always have, and always will. What's wrong?"

"I...I...don't know how to begin. I want to fix everything, but I'm not sure how..." The custodian came in with his dust mop and garbage can. We pulled apart, and I said, "I...let's talk after practice."

Hunter released me. "It's about the money, isn't it?"

I was shocked that he had figured it out. Shocked that he was admitting it. I couldn't look at him. I couldn't make the love in my heart OK with their stealing.

His voice dropped so low that I could barely hear his words. "I promise you I'll fix it. I'll get the money if it's the last thing I do. You don't have to worry."

How? More stealing? I felt as if a part of me were going with him as he walked out the door.

I played until I thought the halls would be clear. Then I walked toward Mrs. Johns's office. Luck was with me. No one was in sight. I rushed to her desk and grabbed a school envelope. Keeping an eye on the hallway and making sure no one was watching, I stuffed the money into the envelope and slipped it under some papers on her desk.

I went right back to the piano room and started playing.

Yes.

The $720 was there waiting for someone to run across it, and *voila*— the mystery would be solved. Emmitt's club would get its deposit. There would be no more searching, and no one would ever find out about the thousands in Mrs. Johns's little, pink, happy-face book.

I just needed to make sure she found it quickly. *Maybe I can go in and help her—I can notice the envelope and say, "What's this?"* I walked back down the hall and glanced into the office, but Mrs. Johns was on the phone, and a teacher was standing next to her desk as if waiting for the call to end. I made three more strolls down the hall, and each time it wasn't the right moment to go in and help her find the envelope. On the third stroll, Hunter's sister was sitting in the waiting area coloring. Someone must have dropped her off. She spotted me and ran out into the hall. "Look, Desimoni. Look what I drew."

"Hi, Clara." I bent down to see her picture. "Daisies. And is that a bee? You did a good job."

Above her chatter about drawing, I overheard Mrs. Johns's answer on the phone. "No. We haven't found the money yet...Yes, officer. I'll be here until five thirty or six."

I glanced up and saw Mrs. Johns put both hands to her face and look down at her desk as if she were defeated. Inches from her elbow was the envelope with my $720.

I pulled away from Clara. "Thank you for showing me your picture."

In an adrenaline rush, I knew I had to do something fast. *Crime Stoppers*—I mentally recorded the number from the sign as I rushed out the main door. I didn't go back to lock the piano room or get my purse and books. I ran all the way home. Mom, as usual, was occupied in her shop. I ran upstairs and dialed Crime Stoppers. "Just now I saw some-one leave seven hundred and twenty dollars on the secretary's desk at the high school. This person stole the money and returned it."

Mom, who rarely noticed whether I was home or not, made a sur-prise entrance as I hung up. "Mija, done for the day? Could you help me? I have to get a load to the Methodist church." She was frazzled. "Lulu came in and kept me tied up for hours figuring out what she wants to send her daughter-in-law. One bouquet—took her all day to figure out."

"Sorry—I left my purse and books at school—need to go back."

"If you could just help me get them into the van. It will only take a few minutes."

"OK. OK. Let's hurry."

The police car was parked in front of the school when I returned. Hunter stood next to the car with his hands cuffed behind him.

"No!" I screamed. "No!"

I ran to Hunter and put my arms around him. He lowered his head to mine and whispered, "It's OK. We'll get this all figured out. It's going to be OK."

"No, we have to tell them you didn't take the money. It wasn't you."

The officer put his hand on my shoulder. "I need for you to back away, miss."

"But he's innocent. He didn't steal the money." Through my blur of tears, I could see confusion on Hunter's and the officer's faces. I was crying so hard that I don't know if they could have understood what I was saying. "You can't arrest him. He's innocent." I jerked from the officer and flung my arms around Hunter again.

This time Hunter got closer to my ear. "Listen to me. I want your promise that you won't say anything to anyone. Don't talk to my mom or the police. I'll go to juvie awhile—not a big deal. This is what I want. It's easier for a guy than it would be for—"

Hard arms gripped me from behind, lifting and moving me backward and away from Hunter. Even as we were forced apart, our gazes stayed locked. He whispered, "Promise me. Promise me." This time an officer held onto me while another one pushed Hunter into the car. After the door was shut, Hunter watched me through the window. "Promise me," he mouthed again.

For a moment I stood frozen, watching them drive away—Hunter taking the blame to keep his mother out of prison. Then I dropped to my knees on the hard sidewalk and covered my face with my hands. Something broke inside me. Seeing Hunter arrested hurt far worse than the time my father left us. My father wanted to go away from us, but Hunter was going only to protect his mother. My whole body shook with sobs.

Warm hands on my shoulders pulled me to my feet. I didn't try to uncover my face or open my streaming eyes, but I recognized Georgina's voice. "Des, what's wrong? Why are the police here?" My eyes flew open. There was a second, empty squad car parked a few feet away.

I couldn't bear to say the words—*Hunter's been arrested.* And Hunter had asked me not to talk to anyone about it. I just shook my head and pulled away from her. By now Emmitt and several girls coming from cheerleader practice gathered around, whispering about cops and watching me curiously. I straightened and shook my head. "Nothing. It's nothing," my voice scraped out. "I have to go."

I headed back into the school to get my things from the piano room. When I passed the office, Mrs. Johns was at her desk, shuffling through papers. Even in my fast walk-by, I could see that her face was tortured. Next to her an officer, the same one who had questioned me in the piano room, stood stiff and calm, watching her frantic hands.

For the rest of the evening, I honored Hunter's request and spoke to no one about what happened—least of all Mom. She was still oblivious to my and Hunter's connection. She barely knew the names of any of my classmates. After my dad left, my world narrowed to a single focus— piano. I stopped connecting with other kids, stopped bringing friends home. Dad's disappearance became a barrier between Mom and me. I loved her dearly, but we just didn't share our stories with each other. I played, and she worked her flowers.

I slept maybe an hour that night, hoping all night long Hunter would call me and let me know that everything was straightened out. That somehow his arrest was a mistake.

The next morning everyone at school was talking about Hunter spending the night in jail. When I walked into homeroom, the gossiping students went silent. They all knew Hunter and I were an item, and probably Emmitt, Georgina, and her friends had filled in the details about what they saw after school. Plus, when everyone saw me this morning, they could tell by my puffy face and bloodshot eyes that I was in bad shape. I felt sick—in a daze. Too sick to be at school, but too scared to stay home and risk missing news of Hunter. I slid into my desk with my backpack clutched to my chest and stared at Hunter's empty place.

As soon as the first bell rang, the principal came on the intercom. "Students, your attention please." For once all the students were already quiet, and their stillness this morning added a whole new depth to the silence. "The money that was missing from the office has been returned, and the guilty person confessed. I want to give a special thanks to the courageous person who reported it." His voice went flat. He paused, sighed, cleared his throat. "Because of this person, the computer club will be able to move forward with their plans."

I stood up, still clutching my backpack, and walked out of the classroom.

"Desdemona," the teacher called after me. "Where are you going?"

Ignoring her, I made a beeline for the office. Mr. Phelps was standing at the intercom making more announcements, so I stood inside the waiting-room door until he finished. I looked around for Mrs. Johns but realized she was absent because the white-haired substitute, a retired secretary named Betty, was at Mrs. Johns's desk. Hunter's last words to me stabbed at my heart. "I want your promise that you won't say anything to anyone. Don't talk to my mom or the police. I'll go to juvie awhile—not a big deal." I was about to go against his request.

Finally clicking off the mic, Mr. Phelps said, "Desdemona, do you need to see me?"

"Hunter didn't steal that money."

"Come into my office."

— ⁓

6

oss rings my doorbell at 6:30 p.m. sharp, always precisely on time. He's an interesting mix—a systems engineer by trade and a pianist for fun—the exactness of a computer nerd with the sensitivity of a musician. I shake off my mood and put on my teacher face. He pays well for his lessons and deserves the best.

"Whoa," I say as I open the door and he thrusts a bottle of Malbec at me. Ross is the only student I teach at home—the others meet me at a studio or school. "This doesn't look like your sheet music. Yum." I glance at the label as I take the bottle. "Argentina."

"Yep. Almost five years of lessons—I figure for this last one, we'll just kick back and theorize instead of play." He strolls in and plops onto my denim sofa instead of the wide piano bench I use when there are two people playing.

"Ah. Hello." I put my hands on my hips. "Who is the teacher here?"

"After tonight you're no longer my teacher, so your authority is running thin." He grins. Blue eyes cut up at me through sandy hair that has fallen across his forehead. "It's always been kind of weird anyway, considering we're the same age"—he throws his black corduroy jacket across the back of the sofa and stretches his legs out in front of himself—"and I make way more money than you do." His warm smile makes the remark a friendly bond.

"Well, I give up." I set the bottle on my bar, which also serves to divide the kitchen from the living room. "You've turned into a sassy student." I glance around my kitchen. "Oh, we're in luck. I have two matching, clean wineglasses and..." I drag out the *and* while I search through a drawer for an opener. "Yes. A corkscrew—that I'm actually able to find."

"Let me." He stands up and takes the corkscrew. "Please, maestro, be seated and allow your student to serve you."

"Only if you tell me every detail about China." I wonder when his girlfriend and her son will join him in China. "Are Sarah and Aiden excited? Will they get to go when you do? Or later?"

At first I think he doesn't hear my question because he's silent, working the corkscrew. I wait while he pours and hands me a glass. "Oh," I say after the first sip. "This is the most mellow, complex Malbec ever."

He sits beside me on the sofa and nods. With his elbows on his knees, he looks down at his feet, and by now his silence gets awkward. He runs a hand through his hair and takes off his black-framed glasses and puts them in his shirt pocket. I don't remember seeing him without glasses before. He somehow looks younger. "Sarah and Aiden aren't going. Ever. That's one of the reasons I took China." He takes a deep breath. "We broke up." Now that he does not smile, the laugh lines around his eyes are pronounced, sad.

"Oh gosh—I'm sorry to hear that." I put my hand on his shoulder. "I thought she was the one." I never noticed before, but he has faint freckles on his temples.

"I did too." He turns toward me, and I discover streaks of gray in his blue eyes.

"Aiden must be taking this hard." Three-year-old Aiden is the child of Sarah and her ex-husband, but Ross has been in the child's life more than the biological father.

He nods, looking again at his feet. "Sarah's going back to her ex."

My hand is still on his shoulder, and I give what I hope is a comforting squeeze. "That totally sucks. And she's an idiot—certifiable—to let you go. What is she thinking?"

"I've known about it for a few weeks but haven't wanted to talk about it."

I rerun our last few lessons and realize there have been changes in Ross. He's been quieter, more somber. I want more than anything to take his pain away. "Well, China will be a great diversion from all of this." I take my hand off his shoulder and lean back. "Tell me everything—where you'll live, what your work will be like, everything."

One hour, one bottle of Malbec, and one China scoop later, Ross steers the conversation to *Marriage Exposure.* "Let me tell you about the girlfriend I had in Houston."

"Ross." I shake my head and shoot him a warning glare.

He meets my eyes. "Why not listen?" He touches my hand. "You can say no if you want." He squeezes my hand and grins. "And don't worry if it's embarrassing. You may never see me again. I'll be on the other side of the globe—for years, maybe."

I take a deep breath, another gulp of the wine, and stare straight ahead so we're not making eye contact. "Say it."

He sets his glass on the coffee table, releases my hand, and gestures as if he's explaining an engineering design. "So she was never able to get off—no matter what we did. And I very carefully analyzed her anatomy— did massive research—had the G-spot—"

"OK. OK. Mr. Engineer, I don't need the analytics. I'm sure you were excellent. Just tell me—in general terms—what worked." I can't believe I ask him this.

"Simple. She needed to be in control. Once we made that happen, everything worked. Something about not knowing what I was going to do kept her from getting off."

"I don't get it—control?"

"Yep. She blindfolded me and tied me up, and I agreed to be completely passive." He glances down and reddens. "Well, as passive as I could be—there's one muscle I can't control."

I can't stop myself from glancing at his crotch—*a vision of a naked Ross tied up with a huge erection.* "Uh," I gasp as if he can read my mind. I feel my face go hot.

But he laughs—takes away my embarrassment. "Yeah. Pretty funny." His face becomes serious, his honest eyes connect with mine, and he covers my hand again. "So here's my offer. We've had a respectful relationship for five years. You know I'm not a weirdo who would hurt you. Let me be your teacher for once." He releases my hand, reaches for his jacket, and pulls a roll of slim black cord and a blindfold out of a pocket. "I'll strip. You tie me up, blindfold me, and do whatever you want. Just think about what pleases you. If it works, you're cured. If it doesn't, we're still buds—and I'm leaving in three weeks. You won't see me again. Honest—no strings."

My stomach shifts—even with the numbing Malbec buzz, chills run over my whole body. "No. Ross. No." I stand up and step back from the cord and blindfold. "It's not in me to do that." I can't look at him—can't believe this conversation happens.

He stands up. "I've made you uncomfortable. I guess it was presumptuous of me, but I'd like to help you." He looks disappointed. "You've done a lot for me."

"Thank you for that." I'm in full teacher mode now. "But you've paid well for your lessons. You owe me nothing."

He shoves the cord and blindfold back into his pocket. "Right." He steps to the door.

"But thank you for the offer and the wine and the years of friendship." As he opens the door to leave, I suddenly feel as if I might cry. "I'll miss you."

I step toward him, and we hug. My breath catches as I say, "I guess this is good-bye."

His solid arms surround me as if he doesn't want this connection to stop. For long moments we breathe together. Finally, he says, "Maybe not."

I don't want to let him go. Somehow knowing that I could have chosen to be in bed with him this very second makes his departure unbearable.

Should I change my mind? Bring him back? He feels warm, sturdy, safe. He's familiar on so many levels, and now that he's opened the possibility of a new level, I tingle with wonder about what sex with this old friend would be like. While I struggle with my decision, he whispers close to my ear—I can feel his lips move as he speaks. "If you change your mind—remember you've got three weeks." He turns and leaves, without looking at me again.

My apartment is desolate without him.

I wander to the piano and look at the sheet music I had set out for him to take. The loss of him stabs anew. I should practice one of my own pieces for my next gig, but nothing appeals. The computer is off. I've been avoiding Internet like I avoid the bathroom scales when I eat too much. I don't want to see anything else about *Marriage Exposure* or Burt. Ever. I reach for my phone—which is still off, as it always is when I'm teaching—but I drop it back onto the counter. No reason to turn it on.

I pour the last drop of Ross's Malbec into my glass and plop down on my bed. On the bedside table is Hunter's first book—I bought it today. I had read his two most recent ones before I knew who Des Amone really is. Now everything he's published is a massive lure that keeps me reading every free minute.

The deeper I get into his stories, the more I agree with a book-cover blurb by a literary critic who talks about the underlying anguish that tortures the hero in Amone's books. The main character in each novel solves a crime mystery, but beneath the action is a greater story of a man struggling with his connection to a woman who has some deep, dark flaw. In one book she embezzles money from a bank in order to get false identities for undocumented immigrants. In another story the woman has a drug addiction, and she steals money through a complex Internet scam. Hunter's hero is always trying to fix a woman who has a sinful secret. And in each book I've read so far, the hero never achieves peace.

I'm no psychologist, but, hello. Hunter's struggle with his mother's stealing is driving him to constantly create these flawed women.

He sacrificed everything for her—his integrity, his freedom, and me. And I heard she died a few years ago of cancer, so now he'll forever be tortured by his need to fix her in his stories.

— —

The morning after his arrest, when I had charged into the principal's office to spill about Mrs. Johns's journal, my mission was derailed when Mr. Phelps closed the door and said, "Hunter told me you'd come in here and claimed that he didn't do it."

At first I was too stunned and choked up to speak.

Mr. Phelps handed me a box of tissues and nudged me toward the chair that was facing his desk. I wasn't even aware that my face was wet with tears until I touched my cheek. He dropped into his chair behind his desk, sighed, and shook his head. "I never would have suspected Hunter to do something like this. Never. And what puzzles me even more is why you reported it to Crime Stoppers. If you're so upset that he's been caught, why did you report it at the time when the police could walk in and catch him red-handed? And why didn't you just come and talk to me? We could have gotten it squared away without Hunter having to be dragged away in cuffs and put in jail overnight. He could have turned himself in—it would have made things so much easier for him legally." My stomach twisted. I couldn't believe the bad luck of my timing. I thought Hunter would have been in athletics when I called. "The police came immediately when you called, and there he was with the cash."

"But I didn't give my name." Clearly I was a pathetic liar. I shook my head at my own stupidity and confusion. "And I didn't say Hunter did it. I said someone was trying to put it back. And how do you know it was me who called?"

"I figured it had to be you. The police asked if you might be involved. They've seen you around too much. And you tried to get Emmitt to withdraw his complaint."

"But none of that proves anything." *I have to tell him I put the money there. I have to tell him Hunter is just covering for his mother.* My chest tightened, and I squeezed my eyes shut as I remembered Hunter asking me to promise not to tell. "Hunter is innocent—"

He cut me off. "Let it go." His patience turned to anger. "Hunter admitted it—the money is back—story is finished." He leaned forward and glared at me.

"No, Hunter did not—"

He cut me off again. "And now I want to know where you got the keys to the school." I flashed back on the police officer asking me about having my own key to the building. It had never occurred to me that Mr. Phelps would care that I had keys. "Is Hunter involved in that, too?"

"No. It was Mr. Fox." I was horrified to think that Hunter could also be blamed for stealing keys.

"Well. That's convenient, since Fox no longer works here." He shouted, "Betty!"

The door opened instantly. She must have been standing there waiting. "Yes, Mr. Phelps?" Her voice wavered weakly.

"Look in the personnel files and find a number for Melvin Fox. I want to talk to him."

"Yes, sir, I'll find it, but I need to tell you some bad news." I turned and looked at her red-rimmed eyes. She brought a tissue up to her face. "Mr. Johns passed away early this morning." Hunter's dad was dead.

The air sucked out of the room. I lost track of all the teachers and other staff who came in and out of the room during the next few minutes. Everyone in our small town either knew Mr. Johns or one of his children or his wife. Mr. Johns had graduated from this very high school. Mr. Phelps's face sagged. Then slowly his head drooped downward, and he covered his face with both hands.

Some teacher who had wandered in said, "Do you want to make an announcement to the students?"

He stayed silent.

I was so shocked by the death news that things were confusing for the next few minutes. Suddenly Mrs. Sanchez, the guidance counselor, was in the room. "Desdemona, go to my office. Betty, there'll be an announcement shortly—go back to your desk." She shuttled us out of the room while she continued her directives. "You teachers need to go back to your classrooms—even if you don't have a class. Grieving students may want to come in and talk with you." She closed the principal's door, but through the thin walls I could hear her as I walked away. "Mr. Phelps, take a moment to compose yourself. Deep breaths. Deep breaths…"

I wandered into the counseling center, which was just a small office and waiting room on the other side of the main-office entry area. Betty drifted around like a deperched bird looking for a safe place. She wandered past me and patted my shoulder. "There, there, dear. Death is a fact of life. It will be OK."

I forced out a scraping whisper. "Where's Hunter?"

She didn't seem to hear me and drifted back to her desk, which was really Mrs. Johns's desk. I put my head down into my hands, but the next thing she said jerked me to alert. "I'll just put Sue's personal things together. I told her I'd do that for her. She's not going to want to come back for a while." Betty opened the drawer where I'd found the plastic happy-face journal. "Let's see—some of this must be personal. And she'll want her photos." She held up a picture with Mr. Johns and the whole family. She froze for a moment, and then dropped into the chair crying.

"Let me help." I moved toward her.

"Yes, dear. Find a box for her things. Maybe a stationery box by the copy machine."

When I returned with the box, she was sniffling and rummaging through the desk drawer. She already had a small stack of Mrs. Johns's things collected on the corner of the desk. But in the open drawer, I could see the journal that could send Mrs. Johns to prison.

The counselor stuck her head out of the principal's office. "Betty, please come in here."

Betty disappeared behind the closed door without a word. I set the box on the desk and put all the personal stuff into it. Among her pictures was one of Hunter and me holding hands and walking away off the football field at the end of a game. I didn't even know she had taken this picture. She had written our names and the date at the bottom.

With my heart pounding and my hands trembling, I lifted the little journal out of the drawer and started to drop it into the box. But my hand froze. *Dozens of people are in and out of this office all the time. Someone could look in the box—see the page listing the stolen money. Someone could add prison time to the horrors that are already pounding Hunter's family.* Mrs. Sanchez's voice was getting closer to the door again. I couldn't leave the incriminating secret in that box. The moment the principal's office door opened, I slipped the little book up under my sweater and clamped my arm down to hold the secret in place.

I never wanted to keep it.

I tried to tell Mrs. Johns about it that very day—to let her know she didn't have to worry about someone seeing it. As soon as I got home from school, I dialed their number, thinking there would probably be a crowd of people at their home. Maybe I wouldn't even get to talk with her or Hunter. Maybe they'd be too sad to think about the journal. But I had to try.

Amazingly, Mrs. Johns picked up on the second ring. "Sue Johns." Her tone was soft but clear—and rocked me because she sounded normal.

For a moment I was too surprised to speak. "Hi...it's Desdemona. I'm so—"

"You." Now her voice sliced through me like a cold blade. For an instant I thought someone else had taken the phone from her. This didn't make sense. Mrs. Johns would never sound so mean. "Desdemona." Hate dripped from my name. She started breathing hard, talking fast and loud. "Don't you ever call here again. Don't you come near my family." The fury behind her words went all over me. "You ruined us. You ruined my son. You caused this trouble."

Voices in the background—someone said her name. It sounded as if she moved away from the phone—talking with other people.

I stood there stunned, sensing that someone else was now holding the phone and had moved to a quiet place. All the background chatter was gone. Hunter said, low and calm, "I asked you not to talk to anyone—including my mother."

"I'm so sorry, so very sorry." I was gasping and crying, sick about their pain but determined to make him know the truth. "I didn't want to upset her. I didn't realize you meant not to talk to her forever about anything. I thought you just meant about the seven hundred you got blamed for. I just wanted her to know that I have the little journal with all the entries—the twenty-six thousand. I don't want her to worry that someone will find it. Hunter, I love you. I'm so sorry about your dad. I just want to help. I'll do whatever you ask. I only called Crime Stoppers to get them to stop sniffing around. I was afraid they'd find out about all the other money she stole." I waited for him to say something. Waited until I realized he had already hung up.

— ◦ —

Did Hunter hear my explanation? Or did he hang up as soon as he finished his final words to me? I don't know. For years I hoped he'd heard, and after things were settled, he'd contact me—he'd say he understood why I called Crime Stoppers and that he forgives me and we're OK. But now, after nine years of silence, maybe it doesn't matter whether he heard me or not. For whatever reason, he and his mother decided to shut me out.

And to this day I still have the journal in a lockbox in the drawer of my bedside table. I pull the key out from under the shelf paper in the drawer and unlock the box. The pink plastic cover has cracked and the happy faces are dimmer. The first few pages are filled with Clara's childish crayon drawings. The last few pages are blank. But there in the middle is the one page with the list of dates, accounts, and amounts. The last date entered is a few days before the computer-club $720 went missing. I guess she didn't have time to enter that one. And folded in the back is the old insurance statement. I've looked at this a million times.

7

$\mathcal{I}$ love Tuesdays. I always do an early-dinner gig at Uncle's, out in the hills west of Austin. Even though there's nothing as slamming as Austin's downtown scene, Uncle's has its own special pace. Some of the customers are retirees who've been coming for years. Others are professionals—usually still dressed in business clothes from their workday. Sometimes there are families with children. All in all, not the type of people who would watch *Marriage Exposure.*

Going to Uncle's each week is comforting for another reason—this is where I had my first job in Austin, waiting tables for two years while I attended a nearby junior college. I'll never forget my first day on the job, working a noon-to-eight. shift.

❧

An old upright piano sat silent in one corner. I was dying to play it—I love the honky-tonk tone of an upright. But even though I'm at ease playing music for people, talking to the same people is always a challenge.

Toward the end of my shift, I edged up to the owner as he walked a couple of customers to the door. I checked out my five tables, and everyone looked fine for the moment. As I expected, after the two customers were outside, the owner turned back into the entryway. I was so nervous I practically hopped up to him—overestimating and nearly bumping him.

"Mr. Jenkins, may I ask a favor?"

His thick white eyebrows raised in surprise. "Ah, sure."

"The piano—" My mind froze as he looked over at the piano curiously. I took a deep breath, and words spewed out with energy of their own. "Would you mind if I play it after my shift? I'd just like to practice until you lock up, if no one minds. I don't have access to a piano at night—only at a church during the day. But if you'd rather I not play it, that's OK. I understand completely—just thought I'd inquire in case you wouldn't mind."

Now his gaze of curiosity shifted from the piano to me. He gave a short, single nod. "OK—just not too loud."

The rest of my shift whizzed by, and after I passed my last customers to the final shift waitress, I sat at the piano and raised the key cover. The ivories were yellowed with age. I did a slow, soft, looping run from base to treble and found that all the keys worked—only a couple of sticky high trebles. And the tune was good. For the next hour, I lost myself in my old favorites.

Playing was like getting a breath of air after being underwater too long. Songs had been a part of my life as far back as I remembered. Throughout my school years in Garcia, I was never as social as most girls, maybe because I connected to music more than people—except for Hunter. But after he went to juvie, and I came to Austin to live with my aunt, the piano was my life. I had no friends in Austin—no social life. All I did when I wasn't in class or at work was practice.

That first night at Uncle's, I played until a tap on my shoulder stopped me. Mr. Jenkins smiled and nodded. "That was nice, but I'm locking up now. You can do this again—any time."

～ ～

Fast-forward to today—Uncle's has a permanent display stand by the piano with my photo: *Desdemona—Tuesdays—6:00–9:00 p.m.*

The cashier, Edna, smiles when I enter. "Hi, Des. How you doing?" *Is she smiling bigger than usual? Looking at me funny?*

"Great. How are you?" I pause for a moment, even though all I want to do is rush to the piano and play. A reddish hue creeps beneath her makeup. She blushes.

She tugs at her long, gray ponytail. "Oh, I'm just fine." She avoids eye contact.

I move to the piano and brace myself with self-talk: *Even if she saw the show, she can't know for sure I'm the person they were talking about. None of the staff or customers here ever saw Burt. He never wanted to come out here. Don't be paranoid. Shake it off.* It's way more crowded than usual. The waitresses hustle to keep up. I settle at the piano and warm up with my favorite measures from Beethoven's Fifth.

My trademark-unique-pianist feature is that I never forget someone who makes a request. Anytime I see a familiar face in the audience, I can play the song that person asked for. Tonight there's a table full of regulars, Aggie baby boomers in one corner, and three new men in Longhorn orange in the opposite corner. So I launch into the Aggie fight song, and when the room is lively with hoots, I spring into "The Eyes of Texas." Amid the good-natured "Hook 'ems" and "Gig 'ems," a familiar little girl waves shyly at me. She loves "It's a Small World," and she breaks into a huge smile when I switch to her song. As I play for her, I scan the new faces. A loud-talking group of twentysomethings, whom I've never seen before, have three pushed-together tables in the center of the room. That group seems oblivious to music right now. *I'll think about them later.* An elegant looking, middle-aged woman sitting alone near the piano picks at a salad and watches me closely. She's dressed in a dark business suit, and her brown hair is swept up in a sleek twist. *Hmmm... Maybe something classical for her.* As I continue to think about what she might like, I spot a couple dressed in Wrangler jeans and western boots. Next song is "Today I Passed You On the Street"—a classic any country-western fan appreciates.

I've almost forgotten my moment of paranoia with Edna when I notice there's a slip of paper under the tip bowl on the piano. At the end of Hank Williams, I pause and reach for the note. It's folded over four times. At first glance I think it's blank.

"Shush," one of the twentysomethings hisses loud enough to quiet the whole noisy group. I can't help glancing toward the sudden silence in the center of the room. Every pair of eyes at the three pushed-together tables is glued on one spot. Me. I self-consciously glance down at myself. *Is my shirt unbuttoned, stained? No. Nothing's out of the ordinary. Surely they really aren't gawking at me?* I peek back at the group. *Yes. They are. Every last one of them.* And one by one, the heads of the other diners, as if puppet-skulls pulled by strings, swivel between the muted twentysomethings and the shocked-shitless me.

My stomach drops, and hair skitters across the back of my neck. I look back down at the note in my trembling fingers. It's not blank. In dull pencil, in the lower right corner is a tiny print. Four words: "Play *Marriage Exposure* theme."

Run to the bathroom. Run outside. Rip the paper to shreds and toss it at the twenty-somethings. Cry. Fake it—pretend I don't get the significance of the request. Maybe for a split second or maybe for long minutes, these possible reactions spark through my brain. I look down at my hands, lay the slip of paper next to the keyboard, stretch my hands for a moment to control the trembling, and place my fingers in position with thumbs on middle C.

I close my eyes, and for the first time in my life while in front of an audience, I play for myself. The notes I love. The measures that touch my soul. The melodies—some whole, some fragments, some contemporary, some classic, some of my own compositions—that carried me through the years of loneliness after my dad left and after I lost Hunter. The music that takes me to the only place where I can be myself. No pretending. No performing. No words. Tears stream down my face, and I note their wetness and the way they slowly dry. A whimsical note lifts me and I chuckle. I feel like embellishing, so I hum softly, communing with that which defies language.

Time passes. People come and go, ordering and eating. They disappear to me until after I play a rendition of "Always on My Mind," which has the full base that is found in most sheet music versions, but also has my adapted melody that captures some of the nuances that Willie Nelson uses when he sings the lyrics. The burst of applause from a roomful of customers and waitresses cracks the barrier of my private zone. Austin is a Willie Nelson town—his music rules even when it's played by only a piano. Usually I'm hypersensitive to my audience, wanting to be aligned with them. Tonight I'm annoyed by their approval. I played this song for myself, not for this audience.

Mr. Jenkins taps me on the shoulder. "Take a bow, Desdemona." He grins and claps with the rest of the restaurant.

On autopilot from years of recital training, I stand up, place my right hand on the piano, and without making eye contact with anyone in the room, bend at the waist. Chairs shuffle and slide. People stand up as they clap. Even though I avert my eyes from faces, I can tell that all the twentysomethings have gone. I suspect they left after they figured out they weren't getting a raunchy style of *Marriage Exposure* reaction from me. I sit and place my hands on the keyboard. Mr. Jenkins leans down and says, "You can take a break now. You haven't stopped for almost two hours."

"Thank you. I'd like to play until nine—don't need a break." I begin "Always on My Mind" again, but this time I add in some trills and try to twist the heartrending melody into something mocking and satirical. Suddenly I hate this song with its message that being on someone's mind makes up for shunning and deserting. Several people, who had been on their way out, gather around the piano as if reluctant to leave. Their rapt attention tells me that this one time that I have played for myself is my finest hour of artistic expression. And it's the only time I have received a spontaneous standing ovation. I close my eyes and play on, flowing from my bizarre rendition of "Always on My Mind" to Chopin's Nocturne 15 in G Minor. I can hear the people moving away with the advent of this calm, predictable piece. But I don't care. I'm finished with my incessant need to please the audience and to please men—to fake orgasms—to make relationships work even if they aren't right.

And most of all, I'm finished with Hunter. I fucked up royally by making that frantic Crime Stoppers call, but he helped his mother steal. He let her kick me out of their lives. Their family tragedy was heartbreaking, but they chose to steal $26,300. I've held my breath year after year, trying to make myself stop hoping that somehow we'll find our way back together, but I've ignored the reality: I wouldn't be happy with a liar and a thief no matter how beautiful our stolen moments together were. I've been stuck in the memory of gooey, teenage make-out sessions. I'm done.

Done. The moment this thought hits my consciousness, an eerie sense of foreboding forces my eyes open. In my peripheral vision, a waitress with a load of dirty dishes falters on a collision course with a customer who steps backward as he wildly gestures to the bored-looking lady walking with him. Before I can gasp, the waitress's arm bangs discordant notes on the piano as she breaks her fall, and her tray of dishes hits the floor.

I give her a hand with the mess and then check the wall clock. *A quarter after nine.* I quickly close the piano, dump the surprisingly stuffed tip jar into my purse, and head toward the door.

"Desdemona," a woman's voice stops me. It's the elegant-eating-alone woman who was watching me closely when I first started to play. *She's still here.* "Please, may I speak with you?" She stands at her table, with one hand outstretched to an empty chair.

I pause but don't move closer.

"Your playing was amazing. Remarkable, actually. I enjoyed every moment."

Something tells me there's a catch to this. I freeze and wait for the ax to fall.

"My name is Dr. Gloria Rhymer." She speaks with a gentle confidence. "I'm a clinical psychologist. I've been contracted by *Marriage Exposure* to explore relationship issues that have triggered widespread viewer response." I shake my head and take a step backward. I expect she'll speed up her sales pitch in reaction to my retreat, but oddly she holds still and nods almost imperceptibly. Even more oddly, I stop in my tracks.

Psychologists always throw me off. I instantly flash on the Dr. Phil show, with all the smug guests who get annihilated by his reality checks.

His unsuspecting visitors are always oblivious to how stupid they are until he cleverly leads them into a trap and illuminates their failings. *Is she about to blindside me? She's already somehow tricked me into listening a little longer. If I run out the door, is that a sign of psychological weakness—denial? But if I listen to her, will I give her the upper hand and enable her to manipulate me? Grrrr! Clinical psychologists are too tricky. Have I just weakened all the resolutions I made during my piano-playing epiphany?*

"Desdemona, please pardon my intrusion into your environment." I glance around the room. Waitresses back near the kitchen count their tips. The last two customers pay the cashier. No one listens to us. At least she has waited until this conversation can be private. "We know that you don't wish to work with a regular producer or to appear on a show with your former partner. We respect your decision." She pauses as if she wants me to acknowledge her consideration. I'm frozen—staring at her, waiting for the trap to spring. I force my eyes to blink. "I'm here to ask you to review my research and my proposal for future exploration—and then to consider if you'd like to have a role in next steps." She points toward a thick, black folder on her table.

At the same moment, the waitress comes to the table and picks up the wineglass and tip. Dr. Rhymer stands calmly until the waitress is out of hearing range. "I think if you'll consent to review this information, you'll appreciate how many women struggle with comparable issues. The executive producer is planning to develop programming that takes a less sensational and more constructive approach to issues that concern viewers."

I step to her table and pick up the folder with its quarter inch of papers inside. "Thank you, Dr. Rhymer." Her card is stapled to the outside of the folder. "I'd like to read this material, and I'll contact you if I'm interested." I turn and quickly move toward door.

"Thank you, Desdemona," she says to my back. "I hope to hear from you."

I push the door to go outside, but again I'm stopped. "Wait, Des." This time it's Edna, the cashier. Finished with her last customers, she steps from behind the cash register and wraps her warm, rose-lotion-scented arms around me. "Thank you for your beautiful music. Thank you." This is the first time she's ever touched me in all the years I've been coming here.

Strangely, I feel myself tearing up. "Thanks, Edna."

As I turn to leave, she stops me again. "Here. A family left this card and asked that you contact them. They're planning an event and want to talk to you about playing. They didn't want to interrupt and couldn't stay until closing."

I glance at the card—don't recognize the man's name, but according to his title, he's CEO of one of the biggest tech companies in town. *Nice.*

The night air is fresher than usual. Or maybe my resolution to truly free myself from mourning over Hunter has enlivened my senses. I'm moving forward—getting unstuck.

As soon as I get into my car, I text Ross. "If your offer still stands, and you're free tomorrow evening, please come over at seven thirty with your rope and blindfold. Don't bring wine. Don't wear cologne or deodorant, and don't shave. Dress comfortably, because we won't be going out. And thank you in advance for being a good friend."

I can't imagine anything more appealing than an evening with a naturally smelling, unshaven, naked man. Especially one as nice and handsome as Ross. And I want to experience him without the blurring effect of alcohol.

Before I pull out of the parking lot, my phone buzzes with a response from Ross: "Yes! I'll be there! Can't wait!"

Less than a second later, another text from him: "Thank you!"

I smile all the way home—except during the ten-minute conversation with my mother. "Hi, Desdemona, how was Uncle's tonight?" She has my schedule memorized now that I live in Austin and I'm an adult. When I lived with her, she hardly knew where I was most of the time. Her world was her flowers; mine was the piano. Maybe because Garcia was such a small town, she felt I was safe. But now that she's tracking my every moment, resentment nips at me from time to time. Where was she when I was lonely for Dad? Where was she when I couldn't understand why he took the piano but left all the pictures of me—left the plaster handprint I made him for Father's Day? Where was she when I was the odd-outcast-piano girl, who never fit into the giggling cliques? Where was she when I fell hopelessly in love with Hunter? Where was she when my whole world crashed after Hunter was arrested and his mother exiled me from their life? The answer was always the same. *Con sus flores.*

"Great—nice crowd."

"Guess who's in Austin!"

"Who?" She must mean Hunter—his book tour. *Please don't let it be Mom at my duplex for one of her surprise visits!* Visions of my derailed orgasm plans for tomorrow flash before my eyes.

"Hunter—he'll be at three different bookstores, doing a local television interview, and at a couple of book clubs this week. Isn't that exciting? I'll e-mail you his schedule so you can go to a signing."

"Thanks, Mom." Confusing feelings wash over me. A hard core in my gut clenches—I am finished with my Hunter fantasy. But colliding with that knot are soft, elusive waves of memory—*the night during our sophomore year when he rescued me and I fell in love with him; later in our junior and senior years, his body straddled behind me on the piano bench, his exploring hands making me melt, his warm brown eyes. No.* In the same hour that I unstuck myself from the gooey high-school memory, I'm letting those feelings trap me again. *Remember, he and his mother embezzled. He's dishonest.*

She rattles on about his schedule. I promise to try to swing by one of his events.

She laments about her orchid virus and finally yawns. "Good night, mija. I love you with all my heart." And she means this. We do love each other more than life itself, in spite of our rocky, distant relationship after Dad left.

"Love you, Mom. Good night."

As soon as I get home, I throw off my clothes and slip into a soft, long T-shirt. Hunter's book waits on my bedside table. I toss it into the trash and fill the empty tabletop with the black folder of orgasm research. I flop onto my bed and plunge in, reading about my new focus.

I'm seriously tempted to scan Mom's e-mail about Hunter's schedule, but I force myself to ignore it. He's the past. This research is my step into the future.

A hundred or so single-spaced, data-dense pages and three hours later, I realize that even though no girlfriend has ever mentioned faking to me, and no one, male or female, has ever complained about elusive orgasms, I'm not alone. Apparently, 25 percent of women fake all the time, and 80 percent fake sometimes. Even more surprising, 25 percent of men fake sometimes. Reasons for faking range from wanting to please their partners to arousing themselves. And some women, bored with their partners who take too long to finish, fake to get the act over with. Causes for lack of orgasms, which seem to be rampant among women, range from physical to psychological, with 10 percent of women never having orgasm.

I should already have known this stuff. It must be on the Internet. Everyone has seen the funny restaurant scene in *When Harry Met Sally.* But coward that I am, I've never mustered up the nerve to Google about my faking-orgasm issues because I'm afraid someone, even a computer repair person, might see my search history and guess my secret flaw. Or what if I had an accident and was in a coma and people had to organize my records? How mortifying if anyone saw that I had been researching fake orgasms!

Well, my days of being frozen with self-consciousness are done. I'm stepping out—finding answers. I'm not worrying any longer about my secret being exposed. I fall asleep a little irritated about all the novels I've read with heroines howling about wetness and comings—again and again. But I also tingle with anticipation about my date with Ross.

8

Wednesday is my official day off—no students, no gigs. I decide to do everything possible to reap the benefits of the research, including some shopping. I'll stock up on supplies to defeat my secondary anorgasmia. I'm a tiny bit smug after reading the research, because I don't have primary anorgasmia—the condition of never having had an orgasm ever. At least I've had three, almost four.

I don't want to be spotted making my purchases, so I pin my hair up and cover it with a black Spurs cap. I pull on faded jeans with a long, loose denim shirt, slip on large sunshades, and drive across town to an area where I don't know anyone.

After scoping out the parking lot of a drugstore for familiar cars, I park backed in with a straight shot into the exit lane. I want to be able to get away quickly with my scandalous purchases. I nonchalantly enter the store, keeping my shades on and cap down. First I pick up a little carrying basket and stroll around the store, browsing in numerous departments. I grab a *People* magazine that I'll use to camouflage my goodies. When I reach the aisle of personal-pleasure aides, I casually peruse the products and make my decisions, without putting anything into my basket. *Uh oh.* I freeze in front of the condoms. There are no vibrators.

Vibrators are a must, according to the research, for shaking down orgasm barriers. The cheap one I won years ago as a gag at a bachelorette party died during the fourth use, and I've been too embarrassed to purchase a new one, until now.

A young woman wearing the store's ID badge and smock approaches me. She looks twelve years old. "May I help you find something?"

"Oh, no, thank you. Just checking my list." I dig into my purse and pull out my phone, squinting at my notes. I stroll to another aisle.

They must have vibrators for massaging aches and pains. I find the bandages and muscle-rubbing creams—all kinds of vibrators. All shapes and sizes. I grab a small battery-operated one with four screw-on attachments. One attachment has a round nub on the end—perfect for my objective! The package fits neatly under my *People.*

I amble through the store again just to make sure no one looks familiar. I zip back to the forbidden aisle and quickly drop my three preselected items into my basket: lubricant, feminine arousal cream, and condoms labeled *guaranteed to give her pleasure.* As an afterthought I grab a couple more boxes of condoms just to have different types to experiment with.

With the items tucked under the magazine, I rush to the checkout counter, which was blissfully lonely until now. A gray-haired lady checks out with about a thousand items and a million coupons. After the cashier, a young man with thick glasses, finally figures out her total, something doesn't work when she swipes her credit card. The cashier comes around to the front of the counter to help the lady push the right buttons on the screen. I face forward and act nonchalant, but I screech inside. *Hurry. Hurry. Hurry.*

Finally, she gathers her bags and turns to me as she steps toward the door. "Sorry for taking so long, dear."

I nod and force a smile.

The cashier reaches for my basket, which I've placed on the edge of the counter. I realize I'm still clutching the basket with both hands. He tugs. "Ma'am, did you find everything all right?" I clutch. He tugs again. "Ma'am? Would you like to check out now?"

I force myself to let go of the basket. He scoots it toward himself and lifts the magazine off the top of my secrets. I glance around, praying that no one is standing behind me. The coast is clear; if he'll just hurry and check me out, I can get out of here. His hand freezes as he reaches for the vibrator, and his eyes scan over the other items. His eyebrows shoot up above his thick glasses, and his gaze flits across my face with his hand still hovering above the vibrator. Although this bleep probably takes less than a second, it feels like hours. He recovers himself and places all the items on the counter and sets the basket on the floor. "Will that be on your super-savings card today?"

"Oh. No. Visa." I kick myself for not having my card ready. All the time I was waiting for the coupon lady I could have used to get my card out and ready to scan. I dig into my purse. *Where is that card?* A phone rings—a strange-sounding ring. Stupidly, I stare at my phone, which has conveniently fallen into my searching hand. But it's the cashier's phone ringing.

"Hello." He listens, and I take a deep breath. *Card. Just find it. It's in here.*

"Ah—here's my card." I hold it up and swipe.

The cashier, who still has my magazine and four items displayed on the counter, is focused on his phone call. "Yes, the regular light bulbs and the aspirin are still on sale." He unfolds a sales flier as he listens to the caller. "Next week the lemon-scented ones will be on sale."

Can't he scan my stuff and talk at the same time?

"Desdemona?" The deep, rich voice from behind me sends tingles through my body faster than my brain can process whose voice it is. I turn to find myself face-to-face with Hunter. The new bearded Hunter. Some subtle essence of his breath fills me and makes me want to suck in more, just like the scent of dark chocolate makes me salivate. His dark-brown eyes are the same, but his skin has textured and matured, and his grown-out hair touches his shirt collar. His neck and shoulders are thicker than I remember.

"Ma'am." The cashier has finally finished his phone call. "Did you find everything you need?"

On autopilot, I pull my eyes off Hunter and back to the cashier and nod as he finally picks up the vibrator and scans it.

I turn back to Hunter and wave my hand weakly toward the counter. "This stuff is not what you think. It's for—" I want to say "someone else" or "for a joke," but the lies freeze in my chest. "Congratulations on your writing."

A slow smile lifts his lips. "Thanks. How are you?"

I have my mouth open to say something, but nothing comes out. My head swivels—counter, Hunter, counter, Hunter. In spite of my best efforts to act normal, I suck in more air as if my body is trying to inhale him.

Now the cashier has scanned all my items and has them stacked on the other side of his register. "Would you like these in a bag today, ma'am?"

"Yes."

"Did you bring your own today, ma'am?" My eyes bounce from my orgasm supplies to the cashier to Hunter.

"No."

"Would you like paper or plastic, ma'am?"

I glance down at Hunter's purchases, wondering if his could possibly be as embarrassing as mine. He has bottled water and organic trail mix in his hands.

A new voice enters our conversation. "Hunter, there you are." She's tall and gorgeous with curly, vibrant red hair like Little Orphan Annie— only on this girl it's sultry and sexy. She hands Hunter two huge bags of peppermints. "Let's get these, too."

Somehow I manage to steady my hands enough to grab my vibrator, condoms, lube, arousal cream, and *People* and shove them into my purse. They peep out like too-large baby birds trying to escape the nest, but I no longer care who sees them. It couldn't be as bad as who has already seen them. I have to get out of here.

Hunter drops his stuff on the checkout counter. "Desdemona, wait."

Sultry, sexy red gasps. "Desdemona? *The* Desdemona?" She looks from Hunter to me and back to Hunter.

I no longer feel my legs, but somehow they sprint me out of the store and into my car. Luckily I'm reverse parked and no cars are in the exit lane. I squeal out before Hunter can catch up with me. In my rearview-mirror glimpse of him, he stands just outside the doorway of the drug-store with his gorgeous companion next to him. She talks with her hands flying, and he watches me with a sad and worried expression.

By some miracle I make it safely home. I race to my computer to find my mother's e-mail detailing Hunter's schedule. I click it open. Ah! The twisted irony of the universe led me to the very neighborhood where his first book signing is scheduled today. He'll be in Austin five more days. I pace in circles around my living room-kitchen combo. Eleanor eyes me nervously and goes outside. Whirls of emotions churn through my body: shock at the feelings he awakened in me when I heard his voice and looked into his eyes, fury at myself for planning my clandestine shop-ping in the very neighborhood he's in today, and shame beyond belief that not only did they recognize me as "The Desdemona" but also they caught me buying orgasm aides.

Pacing into my bedroom, I realize that the one saving factor in the whole situation is my piano-playing epiphany last night. Even if my body still goes bonkers over Hunter, my head knows there is no future for us. I would never be happy with a liar and a thief. Never. Thankfully, I figured this out before running into him and his girlfriend or wife or significant whatever she is. I notice I'm clutching his book to my chest. In my pacing I must have lifted it from the trash basket by my bed. OK. I can't throw the book away any more than I can obliterate the memo-ries of Hunter. But I can put it out of sight. It fits nicely into the small drawer with the lockbox containing his mother's embezzlement record. I shut the drawer with a sharp bang. Done.

The rest of the day I get ready for Ross—candles, music we both love, fresh sheets, long hot bath, a white satin wrap that stops at mid-thigh and falls open with one tug of the sash. I change outfits a dozen times but keep going back to the white satin wrap—simple and purposeful. Late afternoon my doorbell chimes. I fly into my bedroom and throw on my faded jeans and denim shirt. Two more chimes ring out before I'm dressed enough to open the door.

An older man leans against one of the porch columns, and he holds a huge bouquet of white flowers—hydrangeas, roses, lilies, carnations, orchids, anemones, and yarrow. The vase, a classic ivory white, is wrapped in a wide ribbon, embossed with a subtle black and white pattern of piano keys. It is truly a piano bouquet. "Delivery for Miss D. Lorents."

I take them from him. "Thank you." My eyes skirt through the array of white flowers. And before I look up or have a chance to find the deliveryman a tip, he's gone.

The flowers are perfect on my piano. Their carnation fresh scent fills the room. My fingers tremble as I unhook the card. *Could Hunter have sent these? Will the message say, let's talk...let's clear things up? Sultry, sexy red is just a friend.* My idiot brain runs wild even though I command it to stop. I rip the envelope open.

Dear Desdemona,

There aren't enough flowers or ivories in the world to add up to how much our years together have meant to me. Thank you for your music and your friendship. Remember, this night is about you.

Your friend,

Ross

His thoughtfulness brings tears to my eyes. I text him. "Just received your beautiful flowers. Thank you—you are the best friend in the world."

The rest of the afternoon is too long—gives me time to get nervous. To kill time, I call the CEO of the tech company who left his card last night. I'm surprised when his secretary says he was hoping I would call. She puts me right through. I chew my bottom lip while I wait for him to pick up. *Please don't let this be some twisted thing about* Marriage Exposure.

"Desdemona, thank you for calling me." His voice is warm and positive.

"You are welcome." I try not to sound as if I'm suspicious. "How may I help you?"

"I'm having a three-day retreat for some of my staff—mostly the creative teams—at a hill-country resort next month." Relief flows over me in waves—this sounds like a legitimate gig proposal. "I'd like for you to come and play—just like you did at Uncle's." He speeds along—clearly a businessman getting to the point. "You would play during breaks and as background during some of their work sessions. You were great last night—your mix, your passion, your range. I think your music will be a perfect trigger point for the goals of the retreat. We have one thousand dollars per day budgeted, so you'd get three thousand plus food and lodging and any other expenses you incur. Would you be interested?"

"Yes. And thank you for asking me—and for your comments about my playing."

"Great. I'm going to transfer you back to Jane. She'll get the dates squared with you and ask you for the info she needs to draw up a contract."

Jane comes back on and efficiently works out the logistics with me. "Good-bye, Miss Lorents. Your contract will be e-mailed in a few minutes."

Yes! I squeal, jump up, and twirl around the room. This is affirmation that when I do what I know in my heart is right, things go well for me. I played my way last night, and now I've got an awesome gig—first time ever that I will play for a corporate retreat. Maybe this will be the beginning of greater things for me professionally.

But as the hour of Ross's arrival draws nearer, I morph into a sieve, and my brave high from Uncle's dribbles out of me minute by minute. I'm shocked at myself that last night I asked Ross to do this.

I force myself to focus on the research—I must calm down. Anxiety and stress are leading causes of secondary anorgasmia. An hour before Ross's scheduled arrival, I decide, as one study suggests, to prep myself with the vibrator, so I'll already be in the flow before Ross arrives. I rip it open, read the instructions, and click it on. Nothing. I reread the instructions and find the tiny disclaimer, "Batteries Not Included." Of course, I don't have any batteries.

I insert lube into my vagina so I won't have to worry about whether I'm wet—a tip from a different study. I pace awhile, change clothes, and then put on the white wrap again.

At 7:30 p.m. sharp the doorbell chimes. I have the lights dimmed, the music playing, and candles everywhere. I open the door. Ross takes two steps into the room, and I quickly shut the door behind him in case my landlady is out watering her flowers as she often does in the early evening.

Ross freezes. "Hi..." He trails off as if there would have been more but it has slipped his mind. His eyes rake over me from head to toe and back again. He glances around the room, taking in the dimmed light and candles. Then his gaze locks on me. His eyes widen. I have worn the white satin wrap around, with nothing underneath. I'm sure that even in the dim light, it's clear that I'm nearly naked. "Oh, this is going to be harder than I thought." He steps toward me and stops himself, wadding the small paper bag that he carries in one hand and fisting it against his other hand. He seems to be having a battle with himself. "But I promised I'd be passive, and I will."

I approach him and reach for the small bag.

He hands it over. "It's taking all the willpower I have to keep my hands off of you." His voice grows husky. "You're beautiful. Desirable."

I peek inside the bag at the black blindfold and satin ropes. I let my eyes drink him in from the top of his head to his feet. The bulge at his crotch makes me smile. I point him toward the bedroom. In all his years of lessons, he's never entered this room. It's small—the double bed and bedside table practically fill the room. My bed has four wooden posts that will be perfect for tying him. I still haven't spoken a word to him. Being silent makes me feel sexy. With him standing next to the bed, I slowly circle him, letting my hand drag across his body. He stares at me hungrily. When I caress his bulging crotch, he growls deep in his chest. I circle him again, this time more closely. I roll my body over his, letting my nipples brush against him through our clothes.

Seeing him watch me is exciting, but it's also inhibiting. I pull the blindfold out of the bag and slip it over his eyes. He stands perfectly still.

I run my fingers over his face and settle on his lips. The muscles in his lips flex, begging to be touched. I place my own mouth over his, sliding my tongue across his teeth. His tongue meshes with mine. I chuckle about his inability to keep his mouth passive, and I pull away.

I unbutton his shirt slowly, starting at the top. Each time I open a button, I kiss the newly exposed skin. He's pale under his clothes where the sun doesn't touch. Pale with black springy hair, unlike the sandiness of his brows and head. The hair is thick across his chest and narrows to a line that points to his navel and below. I remove his shirt and move to his back. He's only a few inches taller than I am, so I can kiss the tops of his shoulders and the back of his neck. He takes deep, slow breaths as if he's trying to calm himself. I wrap my arms around him, enjoying the feel of his naked stomach and back against my body, still covered by the satin wrap. His skin smells fresh and masculine.

I move to the front of him and lick his lips. Then I make a kissing, licking trail down his neck and chest, exploring with my mouth while I caress his back and sides with my hands. He has not worn a belt, so his jeans come open with one quick snap and zip. I slide them down, letting my hands squeeze his butt and thighs while my face nuzzles his crotch through his boxers. He moans and breathes heavily. His fists are clenched.

I push him back toward the bed and lower him until he sits. I pull his jeans and sports sandals off. I guide him into a lying position spread eagle in the center of the bed. I decide to tie his hands first with the plan to fool around, taking off his boxers before I tie his feet. I hit my first snag. There are four black satin ropes, and it seems as if tying each of his hands to a post would be easy enough. But I've never been a knot expert, and my first attempt slips right off before I move to his second hand. I tie again with a double knot, which I realize, from his bulging wrist veins, is cutting off his circulation. After several failed attempts, I solve the problem by simply tying a loop around the bedpost and putting his hand in it. He can easily escape, but the whole tying thing is only symbolic anyway.

By the time I get his hands in the ropes, his erection is gone. Tension buzzes through me. It really bugs me that I'd flubbed with the tying so badly that his erection has gone. "Wait," I say before I can muzzle myself. Rats, I just broke my sexy silence.

Ross flinches and raises his head. "Are you OK? What's wrong?"

Somewhere in the research folder, I'd read about how the ankles are an important zone for increasing arousal. I scoot to the foot of the bed and massage one of his ankles. He raises his blindfolded head and tilts it as if confused. I switch to the other ankle. Still no erection. I trail my hands up his legs, softly kneading the flesh of inner thighs, working up under his boxers. Ah, erection returns. On my hands and knees, I nuzzle his crotch with my face while I rub his inner thighs with my hands. He arches his back and growls. This is fun. I straddle one of his legs while I continue to play under his boxers, slipping my fingers up to the soft folds of his testicles. I rotate my clitoris against his thigh just above his knee. I tongue his navel. His erection pushes through the flap of his boxers. OK, big guy, time to come out of there.

Maybe I'm a bit of a voyeur, but having complete free reign to explore this beautiful man puts me over the moon. As if opening a long-awaited Christmas gift, I slowly edge down the waistband of his boxers. The hairiness around his navel increases the lower I go—rich, black, and springy. I gently lift the band over his stiffness, which is pale and pinker than the rest of his skin. With my cheek I rub his organ all the way to the base where it morphs into vulnerable folds. Then upward back to the enticing smoothness of his erection.

Its shape and strength beckons me. Unlike Burt, who was more pointed at the tip and wider at the base, Ross has a solid girth all the way to the tip. A bulk pumped and ready to plunge into me. I want to taste him. I want the full organ in my mouth. I want to run my tongue up and down the shaft and then circle the opening in the tip. I want to gently suck until I can taste his precum. Dr. Oz's voice warns in my head that human papillomaviruses make such intimacy impractical. I sigh with regret.

I slip my hands under his buttocks and slide the boxers off. I quickly make loops around each of the bedposts at the foot and slip his feet into them. I love the sight of him, arms and legs spread wide, penis pumped with excitement, his chest rising and falling erratically, depending on where I'm touching him.

I crawl up the bed on my hands and knees until I can reach his lips. I kiss him long and deep. I use one arm to hold myself up, and with the other I pull my sash and let the satin softness drop onto Ross as the wrap falls open. I slip one arm out and let my breast swing across his chest. He's so turned on, his face turns red and his chest starts heaving. I switch arms so I can drop the wrap onto the bed. I stretch and lie flat against him—not centered but angled to one side so that I can straddle his leg and rub myself against his thigh. At the same time, I massage his erection while I blow gently onto the tip. Each time my warm breath strikes, he flinches and shudders.

I want him inside me. I want to feel fully connected to him. I grab a condom from the tabletop, tear it open, and roll it onto him. I straddle and guide him inside. I lie forward so that my breasts rest on his chest and my mouth finds his. My hands are in his hair. The willpower he's been garnering weakens, and for several moments he rocks his pelvis into me. Then his whole body stiffens, and his breathing slows down. I think he wills himself to be still, passive—to let me lead.

I take several moments to enjoy the stillness, the fullness, the strength of his chest and shoulders and arms. Then some primitive calling guides my pelvis—gently side to side at first. My gentle side-to-side movement graduates into circles—slow and deliberate.

This connection reaches into my soul as surely as any music or laughter or tears I've ever experienced. What a sublime gift to humans this is!

And then as surely as Ross went limp when I fiddled with the hand ropes too long, I lose the sublimity. I still feel warm and close to Ross. I still adore his solid masculine body. I still love having him inside me. But the special, orgasmic melting feeling is gone. And I know that nothing he or I can do will bring it back. So I do what I always do, because this loving, precious man should not be deprived of his moment just because I can't get there.

I ease one of his hands and feet out of their ties, and pull him over on his side. Within moments he's on top of me, and his body is lost in its primal rhythm. He plunges deeper and deeper. I like the way he holds still after each plunge, giving us both a moment to savor the depth and closeness. I like the way he starts to twitch inside me and his breathing speeds up and his tongue plunges deep into my mouth and a helpless growl vibrates in his chest. I like feeling his final surrender and his collapse on top of me.

I stroke his hair and push the blindfold off his head. "How lucky the woman will be who gets to share your bed every day."

His blue eyes with their secret streaks of gray peer into mine. His laugh lines deepen. His smile always begins up at his eyes. "So now you're going to talk."

I return his smile, happy to be in this close, afterglow with him. He tightens his arms around me and rests his chin on top of my head. I could easily fall asleep in this warm, solid nest of him.

He sighs. "I know you didn't come, but I have another idea." I pull back in surprise and gape at him. He grins with excitement. "Want to hear it?"

9

He sits up, reaches to the floor for his jeans, pulls his phone out of his pants pocket, and checks the time. "It's early—not even nine." Even though we've finished with sex, I love looking at his nakedness as he pulls himself up straighter. He slips off the condom, and with a tissue from the bedside table, he blots himself and wraps the condom in one quick move. "We could do it tonight." He sits up straighter, looking for a trash can, spots it on my side of the bed, and leans over me to toss the condom and tissue.

I'm astonished and clueless. "What? We could do what?" I sit up, since it's clear that his cuddling moment is over.

"Try the other extreme." Now he's in his pumped-analytical mode—excitement energizing his face. "So you didn't make it tonight when you were in control—the dominant one—and when you had no viewers." He uses his hands as he talks, as if he were teaching a class. "Even I was blindfolded. Maybe you need to be dominated or observed." He pauses thoughtfully. Then his face lights up. "You're a performer. You do your best playing for an audience. Right?" He doesn't give me a chance to respond. "Maybe you need an audience."

"Whoa. Oh, no, I don't know what you're getting at." I pull the sheet all the way up to my chin. "But no way would I have sex for an audience. Good grief, Ross."

"Of course not. You don't have to do that, but let's go to L and L. You could at least get a feel for the roles of dominant and submissive. And a look—"

Alarms go off in my head. Is this my old friend, Ross? "What's L and L?"

He slows down and makes eye contact with me. And in that instant my shock seems to register with him. "OK. Let me back up. L and L is Lashes and Licks. It's—"

My jaw drops. "Lashes as in eyelashes?"

"No, as in lashes with a whip. It's a private club where people go to relax—be kinky—like being dominant or submissive. You don't have to actually do anything unless you want to. Some people just go have a drink and take in the atmosphere. There's sex toys—whips, ropes, a spanking sofa, f-beds, kink room—stuff like that."

"You..."—I have to stop and swallow before I can ask the question—"go to L and L and have sex?"

His blue eyes connect with mine, and a flash of sadness washes over his face. "Yeah. I did. It was Sarah's thing. I guess it's what led to our breakup." He slumps back against the headboard as if defeated.

Now I'm the one sitting up expectantly. "Don't stop now." I must have the whole story.

He folds his arms across his chest and looks down. "Guess I never mentioned L and L before, did I?"

"Ah. No. You did not."

He sighs. "Sarah and her ex were big into dominant and submissive stuff. They broke up when he went too far—got too rough—and hurt her. When she and I first got together, we didn't go to L and L. But she missed it, so I gave it a try. And it was OK, but she got into group stuff, and that didn't work for me—especially when her ex was in the group. So I told her to choose L and L or me. She dumped me."

Crazy images ricochet through my head. "You whipped her—with a whip."

"Yeah. It's funny sitting here talking about it—it all seems unreal. But I got into it little by little. She liked to be whipped and ordered around. She liked to be tied up and to pretend that she was being forced. And she liked having other people around."

I'm speechless. I remember seeing Sarah, an engineer like Ross, at a few gigs. She's a petite, librarian-looking girl—glasses, no makeup, limp brown hair usually in a low ponytail. I can't picture her playing sex games, period, much less in a public place.

Ross seems to shake off his moment of sadness over Sarah. "So what do you say? We can just go have a drink—check out the place. My membership is still active. We can leave the minute you want to."

"But what if Sarah's there?"

"She only goes on weekends—when her parents keep Aiden."

I'm not able to answer. The notion of going to Lashes and Licks is so removed from anything I've ever considered.

He lounges back into a lying-down position, still beautifully naked. "I won't push it if it sounds too weird to you. But sometimes it's good to see extremes—to explore. You know?"

I still clutch the sheet to my chin. "What should I wear?" My voice squeaks midquestion.

He cuts his eyes up at me and grins. "Same thing you'd wear to any bar in Austin."

I ease myself toward the edge of the bed, pulling the sheet around me.

"Desdemona." His voice is low, personal.

I look over my shoulder at him.

"The way you made love to me was beautiful. It was beyond anything a guy could hope for." I feel heat crawling up to my face. "You're a natural, and you deserve to get off—all the way. We'll figure it out."

The distance between our faces closes—I guess we both move forward—and then the distance between our lips closes. His kiss is warm and sweet.

I slip on a black tank top, a short denim skirt, sandals that lace up to my knees, and peachy lip gloss. I run a comb through my hair, blow out the candles, and we giggle all the way to Ross's car.

L and L is in a tiny strip mall with a pastry shop, dry cleaners, and laundry. I've been here before and never noticed the black entry door, recessed between the pastry shop and laundry. The dull black door has shiny black letters: L and L—Members Only.

The closer we get to the door, the more I have second thoughts. *Do I really want to go to this place?* "You promise we can leave anytime, right? And I don't have to do anything?"

Ross takes my hand and squeezes. "Promise."

He pushes the buzzer—also black. A voice over an intercom says, "Card."

Ross swipes a plastic card into a slot sort of like those on hotel-room doors. After a couple of minutes, the door opens, and a bearded guy with a long ponytail and wearing a gray T-shirt and jeans steps back to let us into a small, bare, dimly lit entry room. "Hey, Ross."

"Hey—this is my guest, Desdemona. Gilbert."

He does a mock salute. "Welcome—make yourself at home." We follow him down a dark hallway that opens into a bar area. It has the typical ten-foot bar, with stools and some booths and small tables around the room. The dominant color is black, but on one wall there's a red, fury rug covered with a display of whips, handcuffs, blindfolds, and some other metal and satin items that I have no idea what they are. There's a couple in their thirties sitting at the bar, and another couple in a booth—too dark in their corner to guess their ages.

"Wine?" Ross asks when we pause at the bar.

"Sure—you pick—you always get the best." And the truth is I'm too nervous to even think about looking at a list. He says something to the bartender.

"Ross!" a high-pitched voice rings out. A woman, at least forty, comes into the bar from a connecting room, wearing nothing but a black thong and a boatload of makeup. "I haven't seen you in forever." Her large, firm breasts are perfect and must have cost thousands. There're little tattoos—maybe flowers—all around her nipples, but I don't want to stare long enough to decipher the art. She lays her hand on his shoulder. Each of her fingers has a little silver talon-like cover over the nail. "I was so sorry to hear about you and Sarah."

"Hi, Rita. This is Desdemona. Rita."

I nod and pretend I'm fascinated with the huge snack bowl on the bar in front of me. I stick my hand into the bowl and come out with a handful of condoms and miniature tubes of lube. I instantly drop them back in with a gasp.

She smiles at me. "First time, right?" I nod and accept the glass of red Ross has just put in my hand. "Want a tour? I'll be happy to show you around."

"Oh." I clutch Ross's arm with one hand and my glass with the other. "I ah…" It's crazy talking to a topless woman and even crazier to think of walking around with her.

I taper off and Ross rescues me. "I'll take her around later. Going to have a drink first."

"Oh, of course. I'll leave you two with your wine, but just let me know if you need anything." She winks at both of us. "Sometimes girls like to get info from girls, you know."

She leaves, and I gulp my wine. I glance around quickly to see if there are any other scantily clad people in the room and to check out the other doorways. Aside from the one we came in and the one Rita came through, there's one other closed door with a big, black K on it. The one Rita came from stands open; strobe-light reflections and slow, pulsing blues come through—there may be dancing in there.

Ross guides me to a booth and slides in next to me. "Should have warned you about Rita. She and her husband are here a lot. She seems to take it on herself to be the welcome wagon. Harmless. But annoying."

"Ah, do a lot of the patrons wear so little?"

"Nah—at least not out here. She and her husband both wear thongs a lot. They work on their bodies big-time. Guess they like to show them off."

The wine on my empty stomach mellows me. "She's in great shape."

"When you're ready for the tour, we can go to the music room first. Then"—he points toward the closed door—"if you're game, we'll go into—"

Sarah plops into the seat across from us. "Well, well. Ross and Desdemona, never thought I'd see you two here." She's dressed the same as always—a plain button-down white shirt, jeans, and sports sandals. Actually, her clothes look a lot like Ross's. She lasers in on Ross. "Why haven't you returned my calls or texts?"

Ross stiffens up straighter, squaring his shoulders. "Hello, Sarah."

I feel like an intruder. "Where's the ladies' room?"

Sarah gestures toward the music room.

I nudge Ross to get him to let me out, and I head toward the music. There's a small dance floor under the strobe light. Three couples, all fully dressed, move slowly to blues. In one corner I spot what must be the spanking couch. Rita is on her knees on the cushiony seat, and she leans over a large, fur-covered tableau with metal rings that her hands are tied to. A perfectly muscled bald guy in a black thong rubs her butt with one hand and flicks a little whip with the other. The whip has a thick bundle of soft-looking brown leather strips on the end of a black handle. Each time he flicks, it makes a little snapping noise that sends chills of dread all over me.

Rita twists her butt. "Oh, Franklin, spank me, spank me." He flicks the whip again but doesn't make contact with her skin. As if some magic signal alerts them, they both look at me at the same instant. "Oh, please, Franklin, let me have it." She ratchets up her butt twisting and gasps. "Please, I'm so wet for it."

Franklin drops his brown leather whip and picks up a red one with stiff-looking strips of leather—each strip has a shiny silver bead on the end. *Ouch—that one must really sting.* He pops her butt with the beaded strips, but his eyes are on me, and his lips slink into a grin.

Rita gasps. "Yes. Yes. More. More. I'm so wet. Please more." She, too, gazes at me.

I could teach her a few things about faking.

I avoid their begging eye contact and look around for the restroom. Curtains cover most of the walls. I grab the nearest one and squint into the darkness. I hear before I see the definite rhythm of cohabitation. *Oops.* As my eyes adjust, I see a large bed with four naked, entangled legs. "Excuse me—looking for the bathroom."

I do an about-face. Never mind. I don't really need the bathroom anyway. But as I head back, I spot the ladies' room right next to the door that leads back into the bar. Before I shut the bathroom door, Rita increases her volume. "Oh, baby. I'm so wet." *Sheesh! Someone should give her a diaper.*

I collapse against the door and just breathe for a few seconds. I decide to do a few cleansing breaths and yoga stretches to give Ross and Sarah time to work out their issue. Then I'll tell Ross I'm ready to go home.

But when I escape back into the bar, averting my eyes from Rita and Franklin who moan and flick louder than ever, Ross has moved around to the side of our booth where Sarah sits, and he has his arm around her. She has her face buried in her hands. Her shoulders shake.

OK. Still not a good time to interrupt. I make a ninety-degree turn and head toward the bar. A barstool with a strategically located booster step is vacant. I back up to it, thankful that my five-foot-four body doesn't have to struggle unnecessarily to get seated. I ask the bartender for another glass of the red that Ross ordered.

A man sitting a couple of stools down from me sighs loudly. I ignore him and pick up a little stuffed bunny from the row of about a dozen perched along the bar. I know better now than to rummage through the big snack bowl. The man sighs even louder. I pretend to be absorbed in the bunny, but in my peripheral vision I can see that he has worn a black satin shirt tucked into black leather pants. He has black, slicked-back hair, a thin mustache, and a short goatee.

He mumbles, "Torture. I'm in torture."

I feel very nervous. But I remind myself that Ross is just across the room. Eight steps away. One hop off the barstool. Eight steps.

I hear Ross's low voice saying something in soothing tones. Sarah's louder voice says, "But you don't understand."

The tortured man is suddenly on the barstool next to me. He points to the bunny I'm holding just about the time I notice a complex series of knots in a cord tied around the legs, arm, and stomach of the toy. The man leans too close to my ear. "That bondage wrap is good, but"—he picks up a different bunny—"this one is the best."

I gasp, and before I can execute my hop-down-eight-steps plan, Ross is beside me with his arm around my shoulders. "Ready?"

I drop the bondage bunny and hop off the stool. He drops some cash on the bar, takes my hand, and we hoof it to the door. Sarah, her eyes tracking Ross, stands next to the booth with her hands hanging limply at her side.

As soon as the heavy black door slams behind us, we both say almost at the same time, "Are you OK?"

Then we stay silent until we get into his car. He turns to me, and I can see pain in his eyes. "That was a bad idea. Sorry. Didn't think Sarah and Brock would be there. She used to only go out on weekends, when Aiden was with his grandparents. I didn't want you to be alone there."

"That's OK. It was interesting. I wasn't scared until tortured guy at the bar moved next to me, but then you showed up. I'm glad I got to see the place."

He gives me a sideways glance as he pulls onto the street. "That guy was Brock—Sarah's ex. Well, I guess I'm Sarah's ex now. He's her present."

"She's an idiot to give that guy the time of day. He was weird—mumbling that he was tortured. Is he always like that?"

Ross sighs and nods. "He has some horrible history of being sexually abused as a child, and he works out his torment in weird ways. Sarah told me that he has a room at his house that is full of torture gadgets and costumes. He spends most of his free time figuring out his next sex-play scenario."

"She was upset?" I pry, but Sarah is the elephant in the room. Maybe he needs to talk about her.

"Yeah."

The silence waits for one of us to fill it. After a couple of miles, Ross changes the subject. "We should eat. Want some tacos?"

We do a drive-through and take the food back to my place. While we eat, I give him a play-by-play of Rita's moans, Franklin's whipping, and the entangled legs.

He laughs at my tale. "Wow—you saw a lot of action for weekday night. Too bad we didn't go into the kink room." I widened my eyes for more info as I stuffed a huge bite of chicken-fajita taco in my mouth. "That's the place for the group activities. Like sometimes everyone goes in blindfold-ed—well, except for the ones that just go to watch. So there's one big bed and all these blindfolded people doing whatever. It can get really raunchy."

"Oh. Let's go back and do the kink room."

His eyes meet mine with momentary shock. Then he grins and squeezes my hand as he realizes I'm seriously kidding. "Yeah, right."

After we eat, we wind up lying on my bed—fully clothed still—just thumbing through the black folder Dr. Rhymer gave me. It's cozy, com-panionable. I like having him next to me. I like having someone I trust that I can talk about my anorgasmia with. He's quiet for a while, lying on his back with his eyes closed, holding my hand on his chest. He turns to face me and looks into my eyes as if he needs to say something but strug-gling to make it come out.

Finally I ask, "What is it, Ross?"

"Sarah wants me back. She says she made a mistake."

"Oh." I wait. *Has he made a decision? Is he considering going back to her?*

"If tonight—you making love to me—hadn't happened, I would have said yes to her. It's what I've been hoping for—hoping she'd come to her senses and want me back. But when I looked up and saw you at the bar, I knew that I didn't want to go back to her. She's still under my skin, but I know she's not right for me."

"Ross, I hope I'm not confusing things. I don't want to mess up any-thing with you and Sarah." I don't want the guilt of thinking that some-thing I'm doing is keeping Ross from Sarah. And I don't want Ross to think of us as having a future. Our deal from the beginning is he's leaving for China in three weeks. "You two were together a long time."

"She'll never be free of Brock. I don't want to be with someone who's stuck on someone else."

She's like me. I'm stuck on Hunter. "Yeah. I get that."

The next morning, I wake with Ross still in bed facing me, as if he hasn't moved all night. My back is to him—spooned up against him. I roll over and watch his sleeping face and think how lucky a woman would be to wake up with him each morning.

I wish I loved him.

As if he can hear my thoughts, he opens his eyes. "Could get used to waking up with you."

I smile. "You think."

His face stays serious. "I mean it. Come to China with me. You'll be my full-time project. I'll figure out what it takes to get you off." He grins. "I have lots of ideas."

I hug him. I can't bear to look into his eyes and say no. "Thank you, Ross. That wouldn't be fair. I can't do it."

He pulls back and looks at me again. "You mean because of Sarah. You don't have to worry about her. I won't get back with her—ever. You can trust me."

"I do trust you. But you have feelings for her. And I'm in love with—" *Hunter* was on the tip of my tongue. I was saying *love* out loud to Ross even while I denied it to myself.

"Who?"

"Someone I knew in high school." Sadness washes over me. I've never said this out loud before. "I can't get over him. I want to, but I can't." I tell Ross the whole saga.

He listens intently—never rushing me—asking from time to time, with his engineer's need for exactness, a few clarifying questions as I go through those disastrous high-school events.

His eyes stay locked with mine after I finally stop. "You should come to China with me." He takes both my hands in his. "You've got Hunter to forget. I've got Sarah to forget. We like each other and have fun together. Maybe together we could get over them and build something."

Saying no to Ross is the saddest thing I've ever done on purpose. Something is dying—the possibility of a safe future together. I wonder how many people settle. I wonder if not settling for a safe future with Ross is leaving me with no future with anyone forever. Even if being alone is my fate, I can't let Ross settle for me. He would be cheated out of his chance to meet someone special. Someone he can't live without. Someone who gets under his skin, as he put it, like Sarah. "You're going to the other side of the planet where you'll be a free, hot bachelor. You'll meet so many people, and maybe *the one* is there right now, waiting for you. If I came with you to China, you'd miss your chance to meet her."

"Maybe you're her. And I just haven't seen it until now."

I shake my head.

Ross sits up. "Yikes. Gonna be late for work." He grins at me. "Good thing I'm already dressed."

I show him where supplies are in the bathroom, and while he's in there, I make a blender smoothie and coffee. When he comes out, I point to both cups on the bar. "Here you go—breakfast for the man on the run."

He approaches the bar, but instead of taking the drinks, he wraps his warm, strong arms around me. I love his masculine scent, even though now it's blending with a whiff of my lavender-scented deodorant. He kisses me softly, and then pulls back and peers into my eyes. "I'm not accepting your *no* yet. We've got two and a half weeks—seventeen days. Come to China with me."

10

I shower, straighten my apartment, and marvel at all the changes ripping through my life since *Marriage Exposure* last Saturday.
Hunter resurfacing...sex with Miguel and Ross...piano-playing
epiphany...three-thousand-dollar gig coming up...a visit to L and L...
Ross's China question. I lift the black folder of orgasm research from
my bedside table and fiddle with the card stapled to the front. Dr. Gloria
Rhymer. Her office address is less than a mile from my duplex. I'm familiar with the quaint area of older homes on the edge of downtown—
I've actually taken long walks there. The neighborhood blends residenc-
es and small offices in restored homes.

I call her number to see if she wants her folder back, and she says
I can bring it by this morning. She explains that she has patients in
the afternoons, but in the mornings she's in her office doing research
and writing. I'm relieved to return it to her—I don't want to have to
worry about her showing up again at Uncle's or somewhere to retrieve it.
Wearing sneakers, lightweight sweats, and a T-shirt, I set out to jog over
there, drop off the folder, and be done with her.

Her office is in a small, white, wood house, with lacy-looking wood
trim along the front porch and windows. The trim has been carefully painted yellow and turquoise. Wicker chairs and a small glass table

cluster on one side of the front door. Everything about the house makes it look like a home instead of a business except for the discreet, brass plaque above the doorbell: Dr. Gloria Rhymer, By Appointment Only. Cute place, but I'm not going to be enticed to go inside.

She answers almost as soon as I buzz. Today she has worn a loose, natural-fabric pull-over shirt and trousers. The casual straw color contrasts to the business black she wore at Uncle's. But her dark hair is the same—sleeked into a twist. She opens the door wide and steps back into a homey-looking entry hall with a gleaming hardwood floor. "Please come in, Desdemona. I'm so happy for this opportunity to thank you properly."

Why does she want to thank me properly? I step into the house, puzzled, and as usual, intimidated by her psychologist credentials. "Thanks."

"May I offer you tea?" She gestures to a small sitting room that adjoins the entry hall. A brocade-covered sofa sits in front of a rustic, copper-top coffee table. An aluminum shelf behind the sofa holds three large, colorful blown-glass pieces. The house is an eclectic blend of traditional and modern. In spite of my hackled-up psychologist wariness, I feel at home here.

Enveloped by an inviting eucalyptus scent, I sit, even though my plan had been to drop the folder and scat.

She lifts an oriental iron teapot. "This is tulsi—one of my favorite antioxidant herbals. But I can also make you a cup of green jasmine if you prefer."

"Tulsi is great." Wait. This is one of my favorites too. *Is this a spy trick so she can win me over? Or am I paranoid?* Having my orgasm secret blasted on TV makes me suspicious of everyone. Maybe I shouldn't drink her tea. I set the black folder on the coffee table with a curt snap to clarify my errand.

She pours with a focused expression as if she's enjoying the sound of the tea trickling into the tiny white porcelain cups. I decide to pretend to take just one sip. But the aroma is too tempting. It really tastes good. I wonder how she brews, but my nerves are too jangled to ask.

She settles back onto the sofa. "I owe you a special thanks, because even though you didn't purposefully become the focus of a TV program, your situation resulted in the producers discovering my research and contacting me. I've published a few articles on anorgasmia, and for years have sought funding to conduct qualitative focus-group research. However, resources for that kind of work are scarce." She pauses as if offering me the opportunity to chime in.

I keep my face blank, my voice mute, and I nod once, determined that I'll listen but not give her anything. She smiles gently as if my blandness is perfectly fine. "They contacted me and asked for a draft overview of how I would prepare for a series of programs exploring the issue. So I pulled a proposal together based on the one that I already had done for group research." She flips through the black folder I placed on the table. "Here's the proposal."

I had skimmed the pages she points out, but I'm more interested in the actual recommendations and case studies.

She pauses again. I stay silent again. "May I review it with you?"

I nod and pour myself more tulsi.

"I will begin with a series of one-on-one interviews with approximately twenty women. From that group, based on predetermined criteria, I will offer approximately ten of those women the opportunity to proceed and expand their sessions to include their partners. After that series of interviews, I will target approximately five women to work together in a focus group. Likewise, we'll have focus groups with the five partners. I expect this phase to take six to eight months." I gulp down the tiny cupful of tulsi. She's going to totally get into these people's heads. "By the time we actually do the television programs, the participants will be well-grounded and experienced in talking about their situations. My hope is that the program will open this subject and help millions of women and their partners." She refills my empty cup. "Would you be interested in being one of the first twenty?"

I gulp my tea and shake my head. *I need to get out of here.*

"Desdemona, do you have any questions or suggestions?"

My mind darts around. *How can I get information out of her professional, expert brain without revealing anything about myself?* I tilt my head and raise one brow. "I like your case studies."

She nods, smiles, and waits.

I clear my throat. "I bet you've had a lot more cases. Right? Cases you haven't published?"

"Oh yes. I've been in practice for seventeen years, but I've published only a few articles. That's why I'm so happy to be funded to do this project."

"Do you ever have patients who only get turned on by certain types?" She nods.

"How about patients who only get turned on by one certain person?" I remember Hunter in the practice room. No one since has come close to having his effect on me. Was it teenage hormones? Was it something about him?

She nods again. "That's probably more unusual, but not unheard of."

"How about patients who only get turned on by a guy who is bad?"

She wrinkles her brow and tilts her head as if fascinated by my question. "Bad? Can you explain?"

I sit up straighter and look around the tops of the walls where they meet with the ceiling as if I'm thinking of an example. "Such as a guy who broke the law—stole something—like money—from someplace like... like say a school, for example—and whose mother, hypothetically, was in on it with him—" I pause and pretend to think of more factors. Dr. Rhymer listens intently and waits, as if my example is fascinating to her, so I act as if I've suddenly created more. "And it happened back in high school—and he told her to never call him or his mother again—and for nine years she never got over him—and she had two lovers—but nothing worked right for her—and then, hypothetically, her faking secret got exposed—and she had sex with two different men—and—" My face gets hot. I open and close my mouth a couple of times like a goldfish, but no sound comes out. In spite of Dr. Rhymer's polite, attentive expression, I realize I've blabbed a few too many hypotheticals.

I'm a performer, and the show must go on, in spite of my few extra notes. I lean back calmly and pose my face in what I hope is an academic expression. "What would you recommend to such a patient, Dr. Rhymer?" I meet her gaze.

She fills my cup again as I recall my plan not to drink. "I would need more information. May I ask a few hypothetical questions?"

I reach for the cup. "Of course, hypothetically."

"Has she seen him during the nine years?"

Uh oh. *Is this a trick question?* "Hmmm. Well, let me think." I gaze up at the ceiling as if imaginatively fleshing out the scenario. "Well, let's say hypothetically, that she never saw him for nine years, and then she accidentally runs into him while she's doing something totally humiliating that she would have never wanted him to see, but even though she knows she'd never be happy with a thief, he still has the same effect on her that he did in high school." I bite my bottom lip hard to shut myself up as I scan the ceiling, which by the way has lovely old wooden cornices, and pause as if figuring out if there's more to the scenario. "So, what is your opinion? What should she do?"

"If he's not dangerous—"

"Oh no. He's not dangerous. He's kind and considerate—takes care of his mother and younger sister—or at least he did in high school. That was part of his problem—he went to juvie for stealing seven hundred and twenty dollars instead of letting his mother go to prison for stealing twenty-six thousand, three hundred. He's protective—not dangerous." I gasp. "Hypothetically, of course." *Why does my brain turn to mush when I'm thinking about Hunter? Or is she using psychological tricks to make me talk?*

She watches me thoughtfully and sets her teacup on the copper-top table with a light clink. Then she takes a deep breath. "If he's not dangerous, I would suggest she spend time with him and explore her own feelings. Does she love him? Does she really know him? Or is she stuck in a fantasy? A high-school fantasy from nine years ago could be just that—a fantasy. If she spends time with the real person, she may see that in reality he's not as dreamy as he is in her memory."

"See him? How would she do that?"

"I would need more specifics to answer your question—about his life, profession."

"He's a—" *Wait. She is definitely trying to trick me into giving her facts about Hunter.* "Ah, I don't know—guess my hypothetical ran out of steam." I set my empty cup on the table and stand. "Thank you for letting me read your research, and good luck with your project."

"You are most welcome." She stands and extends her hand to shake mine. "Please drop by any morning if you have other questions or suggestions. And, again, your music at Uncle's was remarkable—there was an element of truth that stays with me. I loved it."

Truth? "Thanks," I mutter, thinking a little shamefully that she just nailed it. My conversation with her has been tainted by my pretense, but my playing that night was truth.

I replay our conversation on my walk home. She's right. I need to see Hunter. I need to get him out of my system. Two blocks into the walk, I kick it up to a hard run. The pounding on the pavement, together with the oxygenation of my brain, blasts away my idiotic denial. *Dr. Rhymer knows I was talking about myself. She knows the Hunter hypothetical was real. Oh well, I'll never see her—*

My phone interrupts my thoughts. Kari. I take the call and slow down to a fast walk.

She doesn't even say hello. "I'm totally, madly in love with Miguel. He's the most wonderful man I've ever met."

"Wow, that's great. So things are going well for you two?"

"Yes and no."

"What does that mean?" There's a long silence. "Kari, are you still there?"

"Yeah. I don't know how to say this. I don't want to get serious with him because I think he still has a thing for you. Or maybe it's my imagination. But I think our relationship won't go anywhere unless we're all sure that there won't be anything between the two of you."

I hate that I had that one-night thing with Miguel. "I've already told him that he and I are just friends—end of story. The one-time hookup was a mistake."

She groans. "I know. I know. Maybe it's all in my head. I'm just so afraid that he's carrying something for you."

I don't know what to say. Before I can come up with something, she races ahead. "You're playing tonight at Tank, right?"

"Yeah."

She pushes out a loud exhale. "OK. Miguel and I are going to come there. I think I just need to see how he acts around you. And I think it's like that old saying, 'Absence makes the heart grow fonder.' I think he needs to see you in the flesh so he'll get over you." Kari is usually so in control. It's not like her to be flustered. "And if he gets mushy over you, I'll be able to face up to the fact that he's not over you."

This all sounds a little weird to me. "Well, whatever you want." By now I'm on my street. "Guess what." I decide to tell Kari about Hunter. "My old high-school flame is in town."

"What old high-school flame? Have I met him?"

"No. I haven't seen him in nine years—well, until yesterday—accidentally."

"Oh my gosh! Were you two serious?"

"Yeah." I take a deep breath. "I loved him—we loved each other."

Kari pauses. I can feel her forming the orgasm question. "So—how was it with him? You know—the sex?"

My voice goes flat. "We never did it."

"What? Why not? You loved each other but never did it? What happened?"

"We were going to, but it got screwed up." I reach my front door.

"What happened?"

"Neither of us had a car, and we were hardly ever alone except in the piano room at school. But finally there was a Saturday night—the last night we were alone together. He had his mother's car and keys to a house he'd been working on—he did part-time construction repairs. So we were going to be alone in this vacant house—all night." Inside my duplex I sit in front of my computer and search for Mom's e-mail with Hunter's schedule. "But when we got to the house, a bunch of kids showed up, and everything went south." I scan Mom's list of his events.

"Why? Had he invited them?"

"No." Hunter has a book signing this afternoon at a Barnes and Noble in a suburb north of Austin. I can go before I head for my gig at Tank tonight. "Garcia is a tiny town—everyone knew he was working on that house. Kids were always looking for a place to hang out—drink—party. Someone saw us park in the back, and word spread."

Kari groaned. "So what about later—after they all left?"

I sighed, remembering the disappointment. "Hunter made everyone leave right away. He was totally immune to peer pressure. But there was this one gross guy—Emmitt Straus—who was so drunk that when he tried to get in his car, he fell down. So Hunter made Emmitt hand over the keys, and Hunter drove him home. I followed in Hunter's car."

"Wow," Kari says. "That's a pretty significant thing for a horny high-school guy to do."

"Yeah. I guess. So we drove to Emmitt's house and left him asleep in his car."

"OK—sounding better."

"Yeah—it was feeling better. But we had to pass Hunter's neighborhood on our way back, and every light in his house was on. We knew something was wrong—his dad had been in a hospital for a brain injury for a long time. So we stopped—his mom wanted to go to the hospital. So Hunter stayed at the house with his little sister, and his mom dropped me off at my house on her way to the hospital. And that was the end of it."

"End? You mean you broke up after that?"

"Yeah. I guess we did. A couple of days later, Hunter was arrested for stealing money from the school. It was really his mother who stole it, but he took the blame. Then his father died, and his mother...he told me to leave them alone. That's when I moved to Austin."

"Just like that? You never saw him again after that night?"

"I saw him at school the next day...the day he was arrested...getting into the cop car...in handcuffs."

Kari immediately assesses my Hunter hang-up. "Well, this all makes total sense." I listen and peel off my sweaty clothes and drop them in the washer. "Your first love had a tragic, twisted ending, so you've never been able to move forward and relate like a mature woman." While she wraps up her amateur psychoanalysis, I strip the sheets off my bed to make a load. *Rats.* Ross must have dropped one of Dr. Rhymer's articles that's lying under the edge of the bed. "Anorgasmia Indications and Determinants." I lay it on top of my bedside table.

"Well, thanks, Dr. Kari." I drop the sheets into the washer and start the load. "I'm going to see him while he's in Austin—get myself over my dreamy, nine-year-old, high-school fantasy. I'm going to explore the 'Absence makes the heart grow fonder' idea myself."

11

As I drive out to the bookstore, I rehearse what I'll say to Hunter. "Mom said I must come to your book signing—honoring our Garcia background." No, that sounds too fake. "I love catching up with old Garcia friends." Gag. I'll just buy a book, get in line, and ask him to sign. Just like Mom did. Just like all customers do. And I'll play it by ear. He'll say something about us both being from Garcia. I'll say, "Yes, good old Garcia." And then one thing will lead to another, and he'll bring up his troubled, dead mother and say it's too bad her issues caused our abrupt split. He'll introduce Sultry to me. He'll say they didn't even notice what I bought at the drugstore. I'll say, "Oh that—long story!" I'll wish them both well and leave with a clear, clean conscience ready to move forward with my life. I'll be finished with comparing every man I meet to Hunter.

But the more I rehearse our closure, the more the flashbacks crowd into my thoughts. And the more I resolve that I'm finished with him, the stronger that one memory becomes—the moment that I knew I loved him. It was during our sophomore year—long before we became a couple and started having our piano-room interludes.

I was driving home alone down a country road after playing at a wedding. I came upon four cows in the road—a pasture fence along the side of the road was pushed to the ground, leaving an opening big enough for a car to drive through. A van was parked inside the fence, and a young woman, standing in front of the van near the gap in the fence, was urging the cows back to come back into the field. A little boy, about three or four years old, was inside the van, standing on the front seat, peering out of the window. The cows simply gazed at the woman as if she were an annoying fly. One cow proceeded to slowly sit down in the middle of the road.

I cut my engine, left my headlights on to light up the scene, and eased out the door, trying to think of how I could help her. Unlike many of my classmates who'd worked on ranches or raised calves for stock shows, I was pretty much out of my element with livestock. But even in my ignorance, I could see the young mother was getting herself in deeper and deeper with those four cows.

I decided to approach the beasts from the opposite direction—the mother seemed to be trying to lead them to the gap. I would chase them toward it instead. I made a wide circle and came up from the other side. At about five feet away, I clapped my hands together, and yelled, "Shoo! Shoo!" The cows paid no attention, but I was feeling braver. Even though they were huge, they seemed totally submissive.

I was wearing a ridiculous outfit the bride had insisted on. She was in love with yellow tulle, and had ordered me a floor-length, full, fluffy skirt with layers and layers of ruffles—she wanted the skirt to pouf over the piano bench while I played the wedding march. The bodice of the outfit was a strapless, chartreuse tube top. I was an upside down, hideously dyed carnation. Anyway, I clutched the layers of tulle into a wad and made a couple of jumping motions toward the cows. They slowly took notice of me, and the lying-down cow pushed herself up to a standing position. *Yes!*

The young mother ratcheted up her herding efforts, and I *shooed* louder and edged closer, even daring to nudge the nearest cow on her shoulder. But instead of moving toward the gap, the cows lumbered closer to me. *Crap!* "Shoo, shoo, shoo! Please shoo!" I shouted again, dropping the wad of tulle and clapping my hands repeatedly.

One cow lazily stretched out her neck until her nose was touching my ruffles. She opened her mouth and grabbed a bite of tulle. With a slight snap of her head, a chunk ripped off the skirt, and she calmly chewed as if it were a perfectly tasty bite of hay. At the same moment, another cow slowly pressed the front of her head up against my back and began a nodding motion as if wanting to scratch herself on my butt, but her head motions became more energetic, and she literally lifted me off my feet. I had to grab the still-munching cow's furry head to keep balanced as my body moved up and down.

Panic gripped me. *I must get away from these cows—back to my car.*

The little boy called, "Mama, mama."

The young mother's herding calls rose to a frantic but useless volume.

All four cows surrounded me, munching at my dress, edging closer and closer, with their huge heads boxing me in. My heart pounded. I envisioned being crushed between their heads, or worse, stumbling and being trampled by their feet.

The loud diesel engine of a truck rumbled up close. Doors slammed. "Heeyah!" A new, deep voice was nearby—another person helping! And something wrapped around my waist from behind. At first I imagined it to be a cow's long tongue, but I quickly understood it was a strong arm— lifting me off my feet and away from the cows. Other men moved among the cows, transforming the unresponsive giants into sheeplike clumps, lugging submissively toward the gap in the fence.

Hunter's voice close to my ear asked, "Are you OK?"

Before I could answer, he hoisted me roughly into the back end of the truck. I landed on my butt, my face covered with yellow tulle. Just as I managed to get myself to my feet, the truck started moving with a jerk, and I landed on my butt a second time. This time I held onto the side and pulled up cautiously to see that two men were herding the now-orderly cows back through the gap in the fence, and the driver of the truck I was in inched along behind them as if planning to use the vehicle as a temporary blockade at the gap in the fence. *Where did Hunter go?*

"Hunter?" I asked softly—more to myself than anyone else. *Did I just imagine him being here?*

"Oh my God! Seth! No!" the young mother screamed. She shoved herself in front of the truck and through the gap. In the beam of the truck headlights shining into the pasture, she hurried into the field. Well ahead of her, Hunter ran directly toward a bull that was galloping hard toward us and the four errant cows. *What is Hunter doing? Running headlong toward a bull?* Even I knew enough about cattle to know that no one should be between the cows and the bull.

Hunter stopped and stooped down. When he stood, he was carrying a little boy. That's when I realized the boy who'd been in the van was gone.

The mother caught up with Hunter, and he handed the boy off to her.

The bull stopped and looked toward the cows, and then toward Hunter and the mother and child. The bull's head rotated from one group to the other. He turned toward Hunter, who had stepped out in front of the mother and child. The bull scraped a hoof in the loose dirt. Hunter slowly walked toward the bull. My heart stopped.

Hunter's dad standing near the truck chanted under his breath as if he were praying, "Easy, Hunter. Easy."

The bull continued his scraping, and it snorted loudly as Hunter moved steadily forward.

"Shit," one of the men said. "Chase the cows in—distract him from Hunter." The lazy cows stood still as if wondering if they might get a chance to slip out the gap again.

Hunter's dad said, "We have to wait until the mother and kid are clear."

I couldn't breathe as the mother ran toward us and Hunter continued his slow approach toward the bull. *Hunter. Be safe.* Finally, she made it to the truck, dropped the little boy into the bed with me, and climbed in herself. At the same time, the driver blared the truck horn and Hunter's dad started slapping the cows on their rears, making them trot into the pasture. The bull took one last look at Hunter, snorted again, and turned toward the cows.

"Seth, what were you doing?" The young mother had him by the shoulders. "You could have been killed."

The little boy had on a pull-up diaper and a superman pajama top. "Puttin' Oscar in the barn like Daddy does." He answered as if it were the most common-sense thing for anyone to do.

As Hunter approached us, one of the men slapped him on the back. "How in the hell did you see that kid?"

There were several minutes of the mother thanking Hunter over and over. Then the men and Hunter, who had been driving home from a construction job, began pulling tools from a toolbox and repairing the fence.

After recovering from the shock, I felt utterly stupid because of my futile efforts to herd the cows, my ridiculous outfit, and my paranoid fear that the others—in spite of their crisis engagement—might have seen my clumsy butt flops in the back of the pickup. The mom, wearing jeans, had already hopped out of the truck. I tried to climb down from the pickup without looking more ridiculous, and Hunter, as if he had radar tuned on me, rushed over and lifted me out.

As he lowered me to the ground, he asked, "Are you OK?"

"The bride made me wear this." I shivered—maybe from his proximity, maybe because the night air was chilly on my bare shoulders.

He tilted his head as if puzzled. His hands lingered on my waist even though I was now firmly on the ground. "The bride?"

"I played at a wedding, and her color scheme was yellow and chartreuse, and she wanted everyone to be color coordinated, hence the yellow tulle and chartreuse tube top..." I plucked at the stretchy bodice—sputtering in my default, blab-when-nervous mode. "And she wanted the ruffles to drape out around the piano bench during the wedding march, and even the groomsmen had yellow tulle trimming and chartreuse ribbon on their dyed-yellow carnation boutonnieres, and I should have changed clothes before driving home, but I was in too big of a hurry to—"

Hunter put his warm hands on my shoulders. "Whoa. It's OK. Everything's fine."

His warmth surged through me. I wanted to collapse against him and wrap my arms around him. I took a deep breath to calm my voice. "How could you walk toward that bull, and how did you even notice that little boy, and how did you get to me so fast?" Heat crawled up my face. Hunter was far more than a hot high-school jock. He was a confident, heroic man—a cut above most others.

He shrugged, and his hands slid from my shoulders to my upper arms. "Just kept the bull guessing until the boy was safe. Bull probably thought I was bringing him a snack." He squeezed my arms. "You're shivering." He glanced back at the men still working on the fence.

I figured he wanted to get back and help them, so I pulled away from him. Every cell in my body wept when his hands released my arms, and I turned toward my car. "Oh, thanks. I'm fine. Thank you for every-thing—for getting me out of those cows and everything."

He followed me to my car and started to open the door for me. He paused. Then he took his hand off the handle and rested it against the top of the car—his naked arm inches from my face. He was wearing a sleeveless T-shirt, and warmth radiated from his skin. The scent of him intoxicated me. I felt an urge to lay my face against his arm. "Would you like me to drive you home?" His breath was warm on my bare shoulder, and his voice triggered a longing deep inside me.

One of the men called out, "Hunter, can you give us a hand over here?"

I found my voice and tried to act nonchalant, as if being up close to the hottest boy on the planet was no big deal to me. "Thanks, but I'm fine. I can drive." He opened the door, and I slid in.

He motioned for me to roll down the window. Leaning into the win-dow, he said, "Buckle up."

I buckled, nodded, and smiled. "Thank you again for everything. I owe you."

"Hunter?" one of the men called again.

Hunter reached in, unhurried, and lightly brushed my cheek with his hand. He gazed at me for long seconds. His mouth slowly lifted on one side, and his dimple, the one that creases for an instant right before his full smile, flashed. "You don't owe me." His gaze slipped to my lips and then back to my eyes. "But OK if I call you? Maybe we could go out next weekend?"

"Sure—I'd like that." I wondered if he could see my heart doing flip-flops in my bare chest. *The most slamming dude I know is asking me out.*

His dimple disappeared, and his full grin flashed. "In the meantime, try to stop feeding cows your dress—they'll have indigestion."

His hand dropped to my shoulder and he gently squeezed. His smile faded, and our eyes connected. That was the moment—after the danger was over, after everyone was safe, after he brought it home with his touch and his humor—that was the moment I knew I loved him.

When I drove away, I was a different person—a person in love with Hunter.

Maybe he would have called me, and we would have gone out the next weekend. But a few days after the cows, Hunter's dad had his accident, and everything changed. Hunter stopped being just a high-school boy and became the head of his family. He kept his mother going, parented his little sister, and helped with the care of his brain-injured dad. And he seemed to forget about me. We didn't find our way back to each other until our junior year in homeroom.

— ◦ —

I spot the Barnes and Noble a few blocks away. Questions bombard me. What if I had talked to Mrs. Johns about her stealing as soon as I discovered it? What if we had fixed things so that Emmitt Straus got his money? What if I hadn't made that stupid Crime Stoppers call? What if the police hadn't come and found Hunter with the money? What if Hunter had never been expelled and sentenced to finish high school in juvie? What if he had wanted to stay with me?

There's a huge photograph of Hunter and his new book on the marquee above the front door. I want to look at his strong, perfect face and say, "What-ifs don't matter. I don't want to be with someone who covers for embezzlement." But I'm kidding myself. My deepest core can't let go of the hero in the field who touched my heart with his courage and his humor and his flesh. Even though he embezzled with his mother, and even though he never looked back for me, and even though he's with gorgeous Sultry...I don't want to finish my thought. This makes me so mad, but I have to be honest with myself or I'll never stop wanting him. Even after all those things, I still love him. But I'm a strong woman now. I step out of the car and march toward the store. I'm facing down my need for him. Digging it out of the past and exposing it to the light of reality.

The store is crowded, but I quickly find the big display of his books, grab two that I don't already have, and pay for them. Then I follow the signs toward the stairs leading up to the event section. There in the center of the room, Hunter sits at a table, signing a book. For a moment I freeze, just taking him in. He says something to the couple standing in front of the table, but his eyes are cast downward toward the book he's autographs. He raises his gaze toward the couple, but some sense causes him to shift his eyes toward me. Our gazes lock for a moment. Then he shifts away from me and hands the book to the lady.

This is the reality. The high-school fantasy is finished. *He's an author leading a busy, full life. He's with Sultry. I'll greet him, get my books signed, and start a new life with this realistic image of him. And I'll forever kill the impossible, immature, romantic dream.* I step to the end of the line, ready to face him.

Sultry appears and dumps a bag of peppermints into a big bowl on the signing table. Then she comes walking down the line, counting people. I'd rather she not spot me, so I turn my face toward a rack of local papers, grab a copy of *Austin Lights Lights*, open it to a random center section, and try to shrink behind it. And there right in front of my face is a picture of me taken at a concert a couple of months earlier. Next to my picture is a shot of Burt and Jennifer. "Austin Musician Gets Sour Notes on *Marriage Exposure*." I slap the paper shut and open it to a different page. There are at least twenty copies of the paper left on the rack. Maybe no one would notice if I buy them all. I steal a peek back in Sultry's direction. She's gone. I could grab them all, pay for them, take them out to my car, and come back in. The line I'm in has moved forward a little, and now there's a group of women behind me, so I've moved a couple of feet away from the rack. I slither between the women and the rack, working my way back to the offending section. *Am I in these other local publications?*

I grab another paper and quickly skim through the pages. Thank goodness I'm not in this one.

"Are you in line?" A lady stands next to me holding one of Hunter's books.

"Yes. No. I mean go ahead of me. I'm waiting a bit."

She nods with raised eyebrows but moves into the line. I'm about to grab another local when a new voice makes my heart stop.

"Hey. Glad you came." It's Hunter.

I put the paper back on the rack. "Oh. You left your table."

"Yeah, I left my table."

"Yeah, you did."

I'm about to spiel one of my inane rehearsed lines when a woman up ahead in the line holds up the *Austin Lights Lights*, open to my page, and shows it to the man beside her.

I have to get out of here. Someone is going to spot me. I have to say everything to Hunter now—have closure now. This may be the last and only chance. With my books and paper clutched to my chest, I step a little closer so I can whisper. "I'm sorry for everything that happened." There's no time to list all the awful events—the stealing, the brain injury, the missed chance for our love, the Crime Stoppers call. "I'm sorry for what I did that made things worse."

He puts his hands on my arms—just like he did that night in the field. And the warm energy of him surges through me as strongly as it did when I was fifteen. "I never thought you'd say that."

Why did he say that? What does he mean?

I start to ask. "Wait." But I pause, suspended between escaping from the store, asking him for clarification, and snuggling closer to his body.

The movement around us stills. We stand here too long, too obviously. His hands squeeze my arms gently, and his eyes skate over my face. *Is he going to kiss me?*

"Des, there you are, baby." Sultry takes his arm. For a nanosecond I think she's calling me Des, but then I realize she's using his pen name. We're in public. "Break's over." She's almost as tall as he is. She puts her cheek next to his and beams at me.

Now everyone in the area is watching us, including the couple up ahead, who still have the *Austin Lights Lights*. I pull away from Hunter's hands. "So sorry. Look at the time. I have to go." I step backward willing that no one connects my face with the paper. I hold up my books. "Mom said I must come to your book signing—honoring our Garcia background." Sultry, tugging hard, almost physically drags Hunter. The couple with the paper watch me now with gaping mouths. "I love catching up with old Garcia friends. Good old Garcia." I turn, race down the stairs, drop the *Austin Lights Lights* on some shelf so I don't have to stop and pay, and run all the way to my car without looking back.

12

ank, in spite of the rustic name, is the most elegant place I play. It's a high-end bar that caters to classical music lovers. I'm on almost every Thursday. Miguel, their top draw, plays on Saturdays. Miguel and I met at Tank. He saw me perform and tipped me with a free pass to watch him play on a Saturday. It was my first exposure to a classical guitarist of his caliber.

I always take a cab to Tank because parking is challenging, and it's only a couple of miles from my duplex. This night, because of my post–Barnes and Noble crying jag, I dash in just in time for my first set—a program of classical and semiclassical selections.

I don't have time to look for Kari and Miguel, but I suspect they're at his regular table in a recessed balcony on the third level. Tank is a blended, three-story-high structure with one large open area in the center of the main floor and lots of little nooks and balconies at different levels. It's a place where customers who want privacy can spend hours unseen. But those who like openness can lounge in the main area.

The piano, a black grand, is on a midlevel recessed balcony, with the keyboard side facing the audience. Tonight, as usual when I play here, I wear a rose-colored, backless cocktail dress with my hair cascading down my back. I rarely see the audience because my back is to them and many of the patrons sit in the dimly lit private coves. Requests and gratuities are delivered to me by the waitstaff. On nights I play, the manager turns on a graduated light that peaks to almost white on the keyboard and fades into a deep rose circle around the piano and me.

Before my first break, Kari sends a note. "Miguel and I are in the top balcony. Join us." I don't relish the idea of talking with them, but I get her need to confront the whole situation. I get it that she wants to see Miguel and me together—just as I needed to see Hunter and Sultry. Hopefully, for Kari's sake, the notion of a connection between Miguel and me will dissipate after we three spend time together. If Miguel has any delusions that there's something between him and me, he'll get over them.

At my break I go to their dark little balcony nook.

There's one small table with fresh yellow lilies and a low candle. A third, empty chair waits for me. Miguel stands and pulls out my chair. I sit and lean toward Kari for a cheek brush.

Kari glows. I've never seen her this elated. "Your playing was so beautiful." She squeezes my hand. "I ordered you tonic water with lime." She pushes a glass toward me, almost toppling it. "OK?" She talks fast and high pitched—so unlike her. "Or we could order you something else. Are you hungry?"

Miguel watches us. His dark, calm eyes unwavering. His guitar case stands in the corner. Sometimes he plays a couple of songs with me on Thursdays. Or, I should say, he plays and I accompany. The manager likes to tempt the Thursday night crowd with little teasers of Miguel's high-dollar, Saturday-night performances.

I put my hand on Kari's fluttering fingers. "I'm fine—this drink is perfect."

Miguel, his gaze shooting past me at someone entering, stands up. "*Como estas*?" He shakes hands with the manager, who is dressed as always in an immaculate black tuxedo.

"Miguel and Desdemona." Max leans down and kisses my cheek. "Our most talented, beautiful, magical musicians." He pauses and reaches across the table to Kari. "Welcome. I'm Max Wafford."

Miguel says, "Max, may I present Miss Kari Jalisco. My beautiful companion this evening."

After obligatory small talk, Max gets to the point. "Miguel, would you please play with Desdemona in her next set? Just two pieces, 'Sabia' and 'Melodia Sentimental?'?"

I see a look of concern flash across Kari's eyes. This is probably not what she hoped would happen this evening.

I stand up. "Excuse me—I'm going to the ladies' room before my break ends."

The small table scoots forward dangerously fast as Kari pops to her feet. "Me too. I mean, not before my break ends." Miguel steadies the table and holds Kari's wineglass as she wiggles out of her corner. "I'm not on a break, but I'm going with Desdemona. You know—girl-talk time— well not—"

What has happened to my cool, in-charge Kari? I pull her with me to the little stairway. "Bye, everyone—see you later." We quickly reach the ladies' room, and I take her by the shoulders. "Kari, breathe."

She nods her head, forces a smile, and blinks her eyes quickly as if keeping back threatening tears.

I hold her shoulders and shake her a little for emphasis. "Everything is going fine. You are a beautiful woman. Miguel is totally into you. This business of him playing with me is routine. Max puts Miguel on stage at every opportunity. He's the draw that keeps this place in business. It will be two songs, and Miguel will be itching to get back to you."

She nods and hugs me. "Thank you."

I send her back to their nook, and before I go up to the piano, I find Max. "Max, while Miguel plays, would you put a spotlight on Kari?"

He grins. "I was thinking the same thing. A little romance there? People love to see that."

"Yeah, and turn the light off of me completely. I can see well enough without it."

Max nods. "You got it."

By the end of my second song, Miguel has set up about four feet away from me. He caresses his guitar while sitting on a tall stool looking out over the balcony. His slight, muscular form dressed in black makes a striking picture. As Max promised, the light on me blacks out. A soft blue light circles Miguel, and another one shines up to the top balcony and catches Kari's head and shoulders. Miguel, as I had hoped, looks toward Kari and strums the first notes of "Sabia." A hush falls over the entire bar. I play minimal pianissimo chords, so that my accompaniment is barely noticeable.

When he ends the song, applause breaks out, and Max's voice booms over the sound system. "Thank you, ladies and gentlemen. 'Sabia' played by Tank's own Miguel San Felipe Rodriguez." Miguel bows his head slightly. "He will be here Saturday night beginning at eight, performing an array of classical pieces. Tonight his songs are dedicated to the lovely Miss Kari Jalisco." Miguel raises a hand toward Kari, who's beaming. "And now, one final piece before he rejoins his lady—'Melodia Sentimental.' May you enjoy."

Miguel plays his next piece, and at the end, he stands up and throws a kiss to Kari. Amid the applause, the blue lights click off, and the white-to-rose graduated light opens onto me again as I play the opening of a new song. *Yes, this is awesome. Let this be a happy beginning for Kari.*

During this set, a waiter delivers four notes to me. I read them while I play, using measures when I have a free hand to unfold and open each paper on the piano. The first one is from Kari. "That was magic! We're staying until you finish—we'll drive you home." Ride sharing is protocol among musicians. We help each other out to avoid parking and cab fees whenever possible. Miguel has dropped me off many times, but I'll beg off tonight—let the two have more time alone. Two other notes are requests for the standard classical pieces that I play here.

The last message stops my breath and speeds up my heart. "Always on My Mind." Something in my core responds to the bold handwriting before my conscious brain assimilates. The fine hairs all over my body stand and twist. I've received the "Always on My Mind" request before over the years, but never, never at Tank. Hunter is here.

I crane my neck to peek over my shoulder down into the main bar area. Many of the tables are not in my line of view, but at least a dozen people sit at tables I can see. No Hunter. But, holy hell, Burt and Jenny are perched at a table right in the middle of the open area. I can't believe this. For the first time ever, my training fails me. My hands freeze for four beats, and when I hit the next chord, it's way too loud. I grit my teeth and turn back toward the piano. Burt never came to one performance the whole time we were together—said it was silly to pay when he heard me at home all the time. Now here he is.

I can't stop myself from glancing toward the bar, I gasp and hold a chord two beats too long. There's Ross, hulking over a drink, flashing onto Burt a full-on, hate-filled glare that I can read even from this distance. It's not unusual for Ross to be at my performances, but he usually shows up at the more relaxed venues—only at Tank occasionally. Now I play way too fast—completely out of rhythm. *What are the chances, statistically, that three out of the four people I've ever had sex with are in the same room? Please don't let spring-break Victor be here, too.*

While I sneak peeks, Burt sneers at Ross. Animosity sparks between the two men. I remember Ross's castration joke when he called me the day after the *Marriage Exposure* show. Ross and Burt met only a few times, but obviously they recognize each other. Sweat breaks out all over my body.

Where is Hunter? I scan the note again—no signature. But I know Hunter's handwriting. Our relationship predates texting, so we passed notes daily between classes. Hunter is here. I keep looking over my shoulder, squinting into the nooks and balconies. I butcher my sonata. Each glance down into the bar area ratchets up my alarm about what Burt and Ross might say to each other. I wish Burt would use his brain and take his wife out of here before a scene erupts.

The moment the spotlight on me goes off and my break begins, I zip down toward the bar, checking out every nook and table along the way, searching for Hunter and Sultry.

Max, with a worried frown, waits at the foot of the stairs. "Are you OK?"

"I'm so sorry, Max. It won't happen again. I'll be back on track after the break."

He doesn't look convinced, but luckily a group of customers approach him with questions, and he shifts his attention off me.

At the bar I grip Ross's arm. "Ross, why are you here?"

He stands up, kisses the side of my hair, and offers me a stool. "I thought I'd see if you need a ride home." He looks past me, narrowing his eyes at Burt.

I hiss. "Don't look at him."

Ross pulls his worried focus back to me. "Would you like a drink?"

"No, thanks." I back up to the barstool but realize it's one of those unbelievably high things that my stilettos and short, tight dress will prevent me from settling onto without an awkward climb. So I just lean against the stool.

Ross runs his hand across the top of his head as if shoving off a hat that isn't there. "What is he doing here?"

"I don't know. But it's a public place. Anyone can come. Please don't start something with him. Stop glaring at him." The embarrassment of the TV show expands into a huge knot in my chest. I don't want anything to happen here that will resurrect talk about it.

"OK. You're right." Even as he agrees, he continues to glance Burt's way. "I'll move somewhere else and wait until you're done."

"No. Kari and Miguel are driving me home. Thanks for the offer, but I don't want you to wait." Normally, I'd accept his ride, and I would rather not invade Kari's time with Miguel, but I've never seen Ross as angry as he is right now, and I'm afraid he'll get into a scene with Burt.

"I'm not leaving with Burt here. He won't try anything as long as I'm around. He knows better."

"Ross, think. He's with his wife. What can he try?" Except, I don't say out loud, that they want me to go back on the show with them. "He's not remotely interested in me. And if he were to say anything to me, I can handle him. You are not my protector."

Ross peers past my eyes. Kari has approached from behind me. "Desdemona, what is Burt doing here? Are you OK?" Miguel stands next to her. From his angry scowl at Burt, it's clear that Kari has filled Miguel in on the scandal.

Now Ross, Kari, and Miguel all glare at Burt, who squirms in his chair. Poor Jenny, her face turned away from us, fills her glass with white wine and gulps it down.

In a commanding whisper, I hiss, "Ross, Kari, and Miguel. Stop. Staring. At. Them."

They all cast their eyes down toward their shoes.

"Look at me," I order. When I have their full attention, I whisper. "He won't dare approach me. I do not need all of you guarding him. You're just drawing attention to the whole"—I can't make myself say *Marriage Exposure* or fake orgasms—"issue."

They lower their eyes like scolded children.

"My break is almost over. Kari and Miguel, please go back to your table. Ross, please go home."

Kari squeezes my arm. "OK, but we'll watch him. Ross, would you like to sit with us? Unless you're leaving."

Ross nods to her. "Yeah, thanks."

I spin on my heel and click-clack back to the piano balcony, still trying to figure out where Hunter and Sultry are. I reach my balcony before time to begin playing, so my area is pitch black—invisible to the audience. I collapse onto the bench, rest my head on my arms, folded on the piano, and try to calm my pounding heart. My life has been a circus since Burt's announcement on the show. Will this ever end?

"Desdemona?" It's Burt. He must have slithered up here while my three guards were on the other stairway going up to their balcony.

I jerk myself to my feet. "Burt, get out of here. Customers are not allowed in here."

"I know. I'll leave, but I wanted to apologize in person. Jenny and I both do. And we still want to do the show with you, but if you're not willing, we won't bother you."

"You're bothering me now." My voice trembles. "How dare you come to my place of work?" I grip the side of the piano to steady myself. "Turn around, and walk out now, and never, never approach me again."

He moves closer with his hands reached out. "OK. But can I just—"

Hunter steps up behind Burt. "I think Desdemona's instructions were clear." Even though his volume is low, the force of his deep, strong voice vibrates throughout the area. "You need to leave."

Burt shuts his gaping mouth. Opens it again. Shuts it. Like a fish giving up on a handout, he backs away and almost stumbles when he reaches the stairway. He pauses for an instant—does the fish mouth again. His eyes dart from Hunter to me and back to Hunter.

Hunter edges closer to Burt with clenched fists. "Don't even think about saying anything else." Although his beard covers his lower face, I know that the muscles in his strong jaw are flexing. "She said, 'Turn around, and walk out now, and never, never approach me again.' And that's what you're doing."

Burt turns and leaves.

The balcony is dark, but I can see Hunter's eyes glittering at me. It's good that I'm still gripping the piano because otherwise my jelly knees would buckle. Being near him triggers the ancient humming he caused in my body nine years ago. My very core melts, and I tense to keep from wrapping myself around him. It's as if the pull of gravity that previously came from the floor now comes from his body. Battling the force of nature that pulls me toward him, the voice in my head says, "Get a grip. We're grown-ups now. This man lied, stole, and dumped me. This man is so hung up on his mother's sin that he's written novels about it. Now he's with Sultry, and I need to get him out of my system once and for all, so I can grow up."

His eyes, burrowing into mine, quiet the voice in my head. Desire to touch him gushes through my body and churns with the logic from my self-lecture. Somehow my voice squeaks out. "Hunter, we need to talk."

At that moment the graduated spotlight flicks on. Break time has ended. My performance training takes over. I turn and drop onto the bench and begin the rippling opening of Chopin's first Nocturne. I angle my face toward Hunter, who's standing just outside the rose circle of light. "Will you meet me downstairs in an hour?"

"Of course." He backs away.

For the next hour, I let the music explore and probe the depths of my feelings. My playing feels stilted. Usually the classical selections that Tank clientele enjoy are a nice change of pace for me. But my fingers itch to play "Always on My Mind." Nine years of separation from Hunter, and the attraction to him is still strong. The key to unsticking myself from the high-school fantasy still eludes me. But tonight I will speak with him and Sultry. I'll lay it all out. Be done with it.

I'm not surprised as I descend the stairs at the end of my last set to find Hunter, Miguel, Ross, and Kari all standing at the base. Burt and his wife are gone. *No Sultry?* Kari's animated chatter has all three men spellbound. She's clearly introduced herself to Hunter. In spite of her bubbling, the three men look off-balance, as if standing on unsteady ground.

Ross steps forward, hugs me, and kisses the side of my head. "Are you OK?"

His concern touches my heart. His clear blue eyes pierce mine and assure me of the purity in his caring. I kiss his cheek. "Thank you, Ross, for coming tonight. I'm fine."

Kari hooks arms with me. "We'll take you home, Desdemona."

I switch my hug to her and suddenly feel choked up. Her friendship tugs at my heart. "Thank you, but I'm going to talk with Hunter before I leave. I'll take a cab. You go home with Miguel."

Miguel says something to her in Spanish about me being OK and making sure I have my phone turned on. They know it's off during performances.

Ross still has an arm around my waist, and his face is full of concern.

"Excuse us a moment," I say to Hunter, Kari, and Miguel. I pull Ross a few steps away and look into his worried eyes. "Hunter is under my skin. I'm not over him. I'll love you until the end of time for what you tried to do for me. But I want you to go to China with a clean slate."

He shakes his head and whispers close to my ear. "No. I'm not giving up yet. You need to spend time with him—like I spent time with Sarah. Then I'll take your answer. For now, my offer stands—come to China with me." He squeezes both my hands and leaves.

Kari, now quizzing Hunter about his books, interrupts herself when I return. "Des, are you sure you don't want to come with us?"

"I'm sure. You two go ahead."

She points to my purse dangling from the strap looped over my shoulder. "Turn on your phone first." She cuts her gaze to Hunter and adds with exaggerated loudness. "We'll be a call away if you need anything."

She won't leave unless I follow her directive. I snap open my small clutch and power on my phone. Kari waits until it beeps its little in-service signal. She glances down at the face. "Looks like your mother left you a message."

Mom will have to wait. They walk away, and I turn to Hunter, whose dark eyes lock with mine. "Buy me a glass of wine, Hunter?"

His serious expression flows into the smile that I loved in high school. The essence of his eyes is the same after all these years. "This way." He gestures toward a table with a bottle of something red and two glasses.

As my luck would have it, our table is one of those tall ones with tall chairs. I back up to the chair and reflect briefly about how to get my butt on the seat without a major grunting session. There's a horizontal bar at the base of the chair on which I gingerly plant one of my feet. Suddenly, I'm lifted up and landing gently on the seat. Hunter, without a word or seemingly a strain, has clasped my waistline at just the right point to lift me.

His hands around my waist make my breath catch and unleash that wild curl of sensation that I haven't felt since we were alone in the piano room nine years ago. Without thinking, I place both my hands on his. Our eyes meet. Time stops. Everything in me wants to close the distance between our lips and taste him—love him—if only one more time. *Sultry*, I remind myself. *And Dr. Rhymer's caution that a nine-year-old memory may be more fantasy than reality.* I stiffen, drop my hands, and pull back. He holds my gaze for a moment, and a flicker of disappointment crosses his eyes. He drops his hands from my waist, and every cell in my body mourns the loss of connection with him. He quickly slides my chair closer to the table.

"Is that OK?" he asks.

I nod, expecting he'll step back now—sit in his own chair.

Instead of moving away, he stays still and moves his lips close to my ear. I inhale the breath of his whisper. "You're even more beautiful than you were nine years and four months ago." His touch, his breath, and his words obliterate all the speeches I had rehearsed for the past hour. I lose myself in his deep, dark-brown eyes. My body does that convulsive inhale as if my lungs are trying to draw him in. I want to touch his arms, his thick beard, his hiding lips, his strong back.

He backs away and sits in his own chair. "Does this look OK to you?" He holds up the bottle of red Spain something. "Would you like something different?"

"It looks great." I force myself to inhale and exhale as he pours. "Where's Sultry?" My anchorless feet dangle in the air. Why do they make these chairs that fit only tall people?

He fills my glass. "Sultry?"

Crap. "Oh, I mean the red-haired lady you were with at the drugstore and Barnes and Noble." My face gets hot at the memory of my drugstore purchases and her "The Desdemona" exclamation. "You know, she has red hair like Little Orphan Annie, except your lady is sultry and sexy, so I've been mentally calling her sultry, sexy red." Even my ears are flaming. "Then I shortened it to Sultry. Therefore, I'm calling her Sultry." His eyes never leave me, and he fills his own glass. "Which is totally a complement. She's so pretty and tall, and you two are gorgeous together." I bite my lip to shut myself up and drink half a glass of the red-Spain-something wine. My feet swing to and fro, as if they might propel me off the stool at any second. I halt my feet and gulp more wine.

"She's Zoe Lynch, my literary agent." His voice, his body, his everything jerk me back and forth as if I'm a slinky. Swish—he's the boy who stirred me in the practice room. "I think tonight she's with another author she has in the area." Swish—he's a hot, mature, muscular, seasoned man I've never seen before. "She's based in New York—just here for the week."

Swish. I gape at him. He stopped talking moments earlier, but I still swish. I'm glad that Sultry is not his lover but torqued that even she—his business associate—recognized me as "The Desdemona" of *Marriage Exposure* fame. I've got to keep him talking, so I can squelch my nervous habit of blabbing too much and get used to this new mature Hunter. "How did you become a writer?" I sound like a TV anchor person conducting an interview. "I never knew you wanted to do that."

His gaze holds mine for long seconds. Both his hands are touching the base of his wineglass, but he still hasn't tasted it. He moves one finger slowly, back and forth, across the base of the stem. "At first, I wrote... to you...long letters." I jerk forward—shocked. He reads my expression.

"Hunter." My voice is thick. "I never received any letters."

He nods, sadly. "I guess I'm not surprised. Mom was opposed to us communicating. When I was in juvie, she was the only person I could give them to."

I whisper. "What did they say? The letters."

"All the things we'd talked about—what I hoped for the future—now that I wasn't going to A and M."

Relief that he hadn't stopped caring about me, regret that we lost so much time, and anger that his mother sabotaged our chance ricochet through me. But all those discordant feelings are drowned out by a crescendo of joy that we're face-to-face, and at least back then, he still cared about me. "I didn't know."

"I was in juvie until the end of my senior year. Then Mom moved us to El Paso to be near my grandparents. I got a job working on a large ranch—had lots of time alone, lots of time to think. Took writing courses at a local junior college. Wrote my first book in about two years. Got lucky—got an agent right away, and she sold the movie rights and chewed my ass to make me write more books." He pauses and shifts his gaze down to his glass. "Mom was diagnosed with breast cancer about that time, so for a couple of years I moved back in with her and Clara." He meets my gaze again. "After she died I started managing the same ranch I'd worked on earlier and kept writing."

"Clara? How is she now? Where is she?"

"Living with my grandparents—just started high school—doing great."

"I love your books." I'm blown away by all he's been through and by the elephant-in-the-room question—*Do you still care about me now?* Somehow the logical portion of my mind keeps pumping out prosaic comments. "I've read the literary criticism about your incessant need to save a sinful woman. That must be painful for you." *Good grief—that was tactless—he just told me about his mother's death and I'm bringing up her crimes.*

His lids drop for a moment. He studies the glass in his hand. He slowly raises his eyes to meet mine, and whatever I was about to say disintegrates. I hear nothing from the other people in the bar. My dangling feet no longer annoy me. The wineglass in my hand disappears. All I'm aware of are his deep, brown eyes burrowing into mine. "I'm done with that." His low, intense voice fills places inside me that I didn't know were empty. "I realized today when you said you're sorry that it doesn't matter"—he tapers off, and his voice becomes deeper, almost tortured— "what you did in high school. I want to know you now. I want to move forward."

I breathe deeply, sucking in his words. But my head won't let me go with this flow. "Wait." The intensity of the feelings he stirs churns with the illogic of his words. "What I did in high school? What do you mean?" *My Crime Stoppers call?* The tone he uses sounds as if I committed a murder or something—not that I just made a stupid phone call.

A streak of sadness and disappointment crosses his eyes. I want to stop the pain that I see there. But at the same time, he must acknowledge the truth. His mother was embezzling, and I was only trying to solve her immediate $720 problem and save him and his sister from being parentless. *How can I criticize a dead woman?*

He fills my glass again. "Are you involved with anyone now?" *OK. He's not answering my question, and he's changing the subject.*

I take a quick gulp. "Well, that depends on what you mean by involved. Burt ended over a year ago. I can't believe he showed up here tonight with his wife—they just want to be on that horrible TV show. You know, he's the one you scared off the balcony." I pause to make sure he knows who I'm talking about. He nods, so I rush on. "Ross is trying to help me, and he's really a dear friend, but we don't love each other. You also met him." He nods. "Well, we do love each other—but as friends only. We had sex once. He'll be OK in time, but Sarah right now has him tied in knots, just like you've done to me." I ignore Hunter's shocked expression and take another gulp. I didn't want to get into our clearing-up-the-past conversation like this. "I think he'll be better after he gets to China. And Miguel was seriously only a one-night mistake that I would never have done if I hadn't been reeling from Burt's announcement. Especially since now he's with my best friend, Kari. And other than that, there was that one guy, Victor, on spring break my last year of college. By then I'd waited for you to get over the high-school fiasco for almost five years, and I figured I needed to move on with my life. But it was a huge mistake." I notice that his glass is untouched. "Don't you like the wine?"

"The wine is fine." His hands stay still, and his eyes stay locked with mine.

I take another gulp.

A small grin starts to sneak onto his face. His lips curl upward on one side. His dimple would be showing if he didn't have that beard. "Does your long answer mean that you aren't involved with anyone right now?"

I open my mouth to explain about Burt and Ross and Miguel and spring break again but realize I'm babbling too much. I shut my mouth tightly and straighten on my stool. With a curt nod, I say, "Yes."

"Yes. You are not involved with anyone right now."

"No."

His chest goes up and down as if he's chuckling inside. "No. You are not involved with anyone right now."

I take a deep breath and say way too loud—I should never gulp a glass of wine on an empty stomach during an emotional interlude. "Hunter, I am not involved with anyone right now." *Wait. Maybe I should clarify that although Ross is a dear friend and we had seriously intimate relations last night, we both know we're not involved.* I open my mouth, ready to explain again about Ross and to assure that Miguel was a one-time impulsive mistake and that—

Hunter leans across the small table, puts one hand under my chin, locks his gaze with mine, and lowers his lips closer to mine. There's no mistake—he's going to kiss me.

"Wait." I blurt with gut-level knowledge that I'll be lost if he kisses me. I must clarify everything now. He pauses with his lips one and a half inches from mine. His eyes, with a language of their own, question me and wait.

My carefully planned interrogation takes flight and disappears. His eyes hold me. His lips, so close, pull me forward. "Wait." I say this time to myself more than to him. The only question I can remember is the same one he asked me. "Are you involved with anyone right now?"

"Just you."

I inhale his two words and close the distance between our lips. I stop feeling my body—just the magic pressure of his lips against mine. Slowly his lips part, and my own, as if they've become enmeshed with his, also part. I don't even know what lip, tongue, and teeth parts intertwine in those moments, because my whole being levitates until every part of me is one intoxicated sensation melting into him.

I'm so off-balance I don't realize when he pulls away. The next thing I know, he leans back, grinning at me and pouring more wine into my glass.

"Wait," I say. I reel from the kiss but still hear my logical mind surround-sound the fact that he never answered my question about Crime Stoppers. I jiggle my head and my shoulders, trying to understand what he means about wanting to forget what I did in high school. "Wait." We need to have a clear, clean conversation about his mother's embezzlement, and I need to hand over her journal once and for all.

He watches me closely, giving me time to complete my thought.

My thoughts jumble, but somehow I force out a coherent sentence. "Hunter, will you come to my house? I have something of yours that I've held onto for nine years and four months." With his mother's journal in hand, it will be her own record that sites her crime and not me criticizing her. I'll lay everything out in the open and deal with his nine-year-angst over his mother's sin.

"Yes." He reaches across the table and puts his warm, solid hand on top of mine. "I have something of yours, too. But it's not with me."

His touch unravels me again, but I manage to ask, "What do you have of mine?" I backtrack about all our moments together. He couldn't have anything of mine, unless he saved notes I wrote him in high school. There's nothing.

His hand continues to cover mine. "It's something you forgot." Only our hands touch, but the effect ripples through my body. I melt and pull toward him—as if he were a pulsating magnetic force attuned to the frequency of my body alone.

I shake my head, fighting to make my thoughts gain clarity in spite of my surging emotions. "Let's go."

Before I can execute a graceful, safe hop down from the stool, Hunter's hands again circle my waistline at just the right place, and my feet drop safely on the floor. He throws some cash on the table and leads me to the door.

13

The crisp night air clears my head as we cross through the parking garage. For some reason we're both in a hurry. He guides me to a black Mustang and opens the passenger door.

Inside the cocoon-like enclosure, the knowledge of his impending closeness triggers a dancing sensation on every inch of my skin. He opens his door, and I give up diverting my rebellious eyes from him. He removes his jacket as he slides into the car and is down to a cream-colored dress shirt. He unbuttons the cuffs and rolls the sleeves up. I would recognize his hands anywhere, but nine years have enlarged and roughened them. My heart stutters back to the moments when those hands caressed my secret lips and awakened sensations I hadn't even dreamed about yet.

I force myself to inhale and exhale slowly, and I command my attention to stay on the brick wall in front of the car and my mind to articulate the questions Hunter and I need to settle. Instead, my eyes track his skin up to his now-rolled-up cuffs. Then I linger on his neck at the V-opening of his shirt. His skin is lighter there, as if naked. He's outside a lot with a shirt on—not tanned like someone who lies in the sun. Dark-brown chest hair, lying flat against his body, peeps out. The skin on my fingertips tingles as I think about putting my hand there and pushing the shirt open.

He starts the car, puts it in reverse, and faces my direction as he swivels to check behind the car before backing out.

His movement ceases. His breath hitches. He whispers, "Desdemona."

His whisper pulls my eyes off his neck. In the next instant we kiss. I lose track of the car's engine and the console between us. Our arms wrap around each other as if they have independent lives and their sole objective on this planet is to be in this embrace. The taste and texture of his tongue and lips merge into a powerful force that draws me into him. I lose track of where my body begins and ends. All of me wants all of Hunter. I could easily reach his crotch and caress the bulge that enticed me in high school.

He pulls away first. "How far away do you live?"

"Two miles."

He strokes my cheek, and his fingers track down my neck. He growls. "Let's get there quick."

Fortunately, the directions are simple, and I'm able to guide him. My hands in my lap clutch each other, but I keep them off him, even though my eyes continue their lustful exploration. When he pulls up in front of my duplex, I reach to his face and touch his beard. It is surprisingly soft and thick. My fingers search out the strong jaw that I loved in high school. "I like your beard, but I miss your chin and that dimple you get on one side when you first start to smile."

He pulls me close. "I miss everything about you. I can't believe I waited so long. I should have moved past your mistake years ago. I'm sorry."

I freeze. There it is again. My mistake. "Hunter, what are you talking about?"

He frowns and shakes his head. "Look, you don't have to explain." He pauses and pulls back a little, and his eyes have a deep sadness in them. "Just don't lie to me. It's over and done with. We were kids. What counts is who we are now." He leans in to kiss me again.

It takes every ounce of my power to muster the strength to resist the kiss. But I say, "Wait. Let's go inside. I've got something"—he's out of the car and opening my door almost before my sentence is complete—"to show you."

He holds the door open while I climb out. "How long have you lived here?"

"A little over a year. Moved here when Burt and I broke up."

"You live alone?" His hand is on the small of my bare back.

I unlock the door, and the sweet scent of Ross's flowers greets us. "Yes, come in."

He walks straight to my piano. "You finally got it." He runs his hand across the top of the spinet where Ross's bouquet rests. "I always hoped you'd have your own piano."

I shrug. "Let's talk." I should have written down my questions. Being alone with him scrambles my brain. I take a quick, determined step toward the bedroom to get the journal.

"OK. But you never played my request tonight. Will you play it now?" He waits next to the piano.

I do an about-face. Good idea. Playing grounds me—gets me in touch with my true self. I'll play "Always on My Mind." Then we'll have the talk. I approach the piano and squeeze past Hunter to the front of the bench. His hot breath floods onto my bare shoulder as I brush past him. I drop onto the bench, even though my body urges me upward to continue to bask in his breath. A series of runs leads off the first measure. *Does he notice that this version is much more advanced than my high-school version?* I play softly so my landlady won't be disturbed. As the melody unfolds, he slowly lowers himself to the bench with his legs straddling my body. He wraps his arms around mine and trails his hands up and down each of my arms. He lifts my hair off my back and lays it gently over one shoulder, so that it hangs down the right side of my chest. He touches the left side of my neck and slides his fingers all the way down to my hand that by some miracle still plays the song. His lowers his lips to my neck. His lips and tongue work magic. I hear a moan—too high pitched to be Hunter.

He stops kissing my neck and in a low, husky whisper says, "Tell me if you want me to stop."

He touches the bare skin on my back and slides one hand underneath my dress. His hand, with seductive warmth, slips around to the front and underneath the built-in bra, stroking the skin at the base of my breast. His caress moves toward my peak, and my whole body melts as his fingers tease and pull. His ridge presses against my butt and causes my breath to push out in pants. My deepest core contracts as if grasping for his length even though he's outside my body. His left hand moves from my arm to my thigh. In moments he strokes my folds through the thin fabric of my panties. My eyes are closed and my head is arched back. He pushes aside the fabric and makes direct contact with the spot—now sensitive, awake, wild with energy. I make it to the chorus. A hot tremor curls within my body until I involuntarily squeeze Hunter's fingers that have slipped inside me. I lift my hands off the keyboard and reach behind me for his face as I pant out rapid exhales.

Powerful sensations shatter my concept of time. Somehow I face him. Tear open his shirt. Unzip his pants. Push away every garment until we stand and he's totally naked before me. His gorgeous erection arrests my vision. For long moments my hands freeze, inches away from it. Straight, tan, strong—somehow messaging a magnetism that feels uniquely designed for me. My trembling fingers caress and marvel at the smooth strength of him. I'm not sure how or when, but my dress and panties are off. I push him back to the bench and straddle him—not able to function in any way other than to do everything within my power to get him inside me. As incredible as it felt when his fingers stroked me earlier, nothing, nothing, nothing has ever rocked like the feel of him—hard and ready—flush against my folds that are so ripe to pull him in. I start to sink myself onto him, desperate for him to totally fill me.

"Wait," he says, lifting me off and sliding me onto one of his thighs.

"No," I whimper. *I've waited for this for nine years. I'm not waiting any longer. No matter what happens between us later. I don't care about anything else on the planet. I must have him inside me now.* "No," I say more forcefully.

He reaches to the floor for his pants and pulls his wallet out of a pocket. "Crap," he growls. "No condom."

"I don't care," I say, positioning myself back on his lap. I shake away my mental recording of Dr. Oz's admonitions. *This is a once-in-a-lifetime moment. I'll worry about reality later.*

He gently moves me off his lap. "Maybe I have one out in the car." He lifts his pants and puts one leg in.

Unbelievable frustration rumbles inside me. "Wait." I dash to my bedroom, reach into the drawer of supplies, grab a condom, and hurtle back to him, ripping the foil packet open on my way. He drops his pants, takes the condom, and as he rolls it on, I run my hands from his testicles, up his belly, across his chest. I need to touch him everyplace at once. I straddle him as soon as he's sheathed.

Just before I lower myself onto him, I pause. He holds onto my thighs and looks downward at my hand that is about to guide him in. He raises his eyes to meet mine, and our gazes lock. His beautiful brown eyes, his face that I've loved for most of my life. I want to freeze this moment forever. His lips are parted, and maybe our eyes are communing, and he is trying to freeze the moment as well. Somehow our breathing is synced so that he makes a long exhale at the same moment that I inhale. I can't believe the dream I've carried for so many years is about to come true.

With our eyes locked, I slowly, slowly sink onto him, and as he fills me, a convulsing, melting warmth tremors through my body. His arms wrap around me, I take his face with my hands, and our mouths become one. My lower body bucks on him as if survival depends on pulling him deeper and deeper inside me. And when my consciousness starts to gain enough sense to assimilate that I have just had the orgasm that dreams are made of, a rumbling in Hunter's chest vibrates against me, and he swells and flexes within my core.

He exhales a forceful groan. "Desdemona."

Something deep and alive at the root of me responds to his shudders, and I spasm with more squeezes that leave me weak. "Hunter." I'm too overwhelmed to say much more, but thoughts jet through my mind... *miracle...more beautiful than I could have ever imagined...sublime connection.* I softly say, "Love. Love you."

For long moments we're still. Hunter takes a slow breath and stands, carrying me in my straddle position to the sofa where he drops with me still clinging. He pushes my hair back and looks into my eyes. "Desdemona. I love you." He presses his lips to mine, and instantly my still-quivering interior squeezes him again. He pulls me closer to him and runs his hands up and down my back.

My phone rings. I ignore it.

Hunter pulls out of our kiss. "You better get it. Don't want your friends to be worried."

By the time we disentangle our arms and I grab my purse from the floor next to the sofa, the ring has gone to voice mail. Hunter leans to the side and stretches his arm to reach his boxer shorts still lying on the floor. He folds them like a towel and places them between my legs as he pulls us apart and sets me off his lap. He finds his way to the bathroom.

The caller is my mother again. I drop the phone onto the coffee table to wait for her to leave a message. I relax against the cushiony back of the sofa, pull the throw around me, and watch the doorway into the bathroom. Happiness bubbles through my pores. *So this is what I've been faking all these years.* Hunter, my beautiful Hunter, will come back through that doorway in moments.

He returns, and even though I've already seen him naked, the beauty of him kicks my heartbeat up again. He lifts me as if I were a child and sits on the sofa with me curled on his lap. We're so still that the heaviness of sleep starts to steal over me. I whisper, "I tried to stop loving you. I don't know how to make what you did OK with how I feel about you. My head and my heart can't get in sync."

His body stiffens, and he pushes our faces apart until we're face-to-face and our eyes are locked. That pained expression I saw earlier streaks across his eyes. "Desdemona, please, don't—"

My phone rings again. Hunter reaches for it and hands it to me.

"Mija, we're here," my mother says as soon as I answer.

I jerk upright. "Here? Where?"

"Parking the car. Turn on the porch light for us."

I pop to my feet. "My mother is here."

Hunter grabs his boxers, which fell to the floor when I stood. We both dress on fast-forward. He's clothed and pulls on his shoes, and I run a brush through my hair when the doorbell rings.

"Mija, turn on the light," Mom calls through the door.

I flip on the outside light and reach for the lock but realize when the door flies open that I never locked it. Mom and her friend Alma, like two very short, travel-ready soldiers, stand under the light. They're both five-foot-two and have short, curly black hair. Alma's has more gray mixed in hers, and she's got about twenty pounds on Mom, who stays fit in spite of her love for tortillas. They step in, loaded with their overnight suitcases and several bags bulging with food containers—tamales for sure from the aroma, and maybe empanadas. Mom always brings food and plants.

Eleanor strolls in with them and stealthily creeps over to the condom wrapper I left on the floor near the piano.

Mom's big smile freezes, and her eyes dart from me to Hunter. She wrinkles her nose. "What's that smell?"

I can't help it. My eyes flit to Hunter's crotch. *Could she be smelling his boxers soaked with my stuff?*

Hunter grins. "Hi, Mrs. Lorents and Mrs. Chapa." He approaches and hugs them as if completely unaffected by what we've just done.

I'm rigid and numb, watching a horror movie.

"Oh, Hunter. I'm so glad you're here. I hope you're hungry." Mom thrusts a bag of food at me. "Ah, now I see where the smell is coming from." She points her free hand toward Ross's bouquet on the piano. "I hate those florists who use that cheap, generic perfume on the flowers—makes them all smell the same." She heads for my bedroom with her overnight bag. "Bring your bag in here, Alma."

Alma mutters, "That's not perfume you're smelling." Her accusing eyes shift back and forth between Hunter and me.

Eleanor, with the wrapper trapped under one front paw, calmly bats it with her free paw. I slide over to the bar, relieve myself of Mom's food bag, and smile at Alma, willing her to follow Mom so I can snatch the wrapper before she notices. Suddenly I remember that the goody drawer next to my bed is open from when I grabbed the condom earlier. I barrel past Alma.

Thankfully, Alma ignores the invitation to go into the bedroom. She scurries over to the bar, nudging Hunter along with her, dropping a bulging bag of food containers into his hands. "I love your book, mijo. It is so suspenseful!" She seems to have abandoned the strange-odor topic.

"This smells good," Hunter says, peering into a large rubber container she has opened.

In the bedroom I shove the drawer closed, scope out the room for everything else I don't want Mom and Alma to see, and do a rapid straightening up while Mom is in the bathroom. I skid back into the living room, where Alma reviews in great detail all the evilness in the leading lady from Hunter's new novel. She opens another container and offers the contents to Hunter. He reaches in, grabs and deshucks a tamale, and inhales it in two bites as he grins and nods about her play-by-play from his novel.

I slink toward Eleanor, still next to the piano, to snatch her new toy away. It's gone. She lazily licks her paws, which smell suspiciously like chorizo as I lift her and look underneath the piano. *Where is that wrapper?*

"What's wrong?" Alma asks.

Hunter, chowing down on his third or fourth tamale from the looks of the shuck pile on the counter, waves at me from behind Alma's back. He holds up the condom wrapper before dropping it into his pocket. I force myself to breathe again.

Mom returns and parks herself next to Alma. Both ladies have their hands on their hips as they bear down on me, still crouching from my search for the wrapper. "What's wrong?" Mom echoes.

"Nothing—just checking Eleanor." My voice squeaks and breaks. I'm no good at fibbing, especially to Mom and Alma. "She lost her toy."

They both give me an I-can-tell-you're-up-to-something look but soon switch their attention to chomping Hunter. The two women practically bump into each other opening containers and offering him samples, all of which he takes without hesitation. Alma pulls a large, fresh pineapple from the bottom of one of the bags. "Where's your cutting board?" She opens a drawer and finds a knife.

I hand her my cutting plastic, which she accepts with a resigned shake of her head as she sniffs at the lime-green rubbery surface. "Not wood?"

I linger a few feet away from the bar, still conducting a furtive survey of the surroundings for any other telltale signs of my wanton behavior.

Mom, while she arranges a variety of empanadas on a platter she's pulled from my cabinet, eyeballs me. "So you went to Hunter's book signing today?"

"No!" I shout. My loud voice stills the room. All gazes lock in on me. "I mean, I wanted to—would have—but I had lessons all afternoon right up until time to get ready for Tank. And there was a good crowd tonight—no one special, though. Plenty of people—of course." I bite my lip. Heat crawls up my face. Why must I overtell everything? They continue to stare, so I reiterate. "It was a totally normal crowd—nothing out of the ordinary—no surprises."

Hunter's hand, bringing something wrapped in a tortilla to his mouth, stops in midair. "I went to Desdemona's performance tonight and gave her a ride home."

Alma and Mom, pulling their raised-eyebrow-weird gazes off of me, let Hunter hold their attention again. I love the sound of his voice and his easy laughter while he answers their questions about his book and gives them the feedback they crave about the food. I start to relax. He says something about it being late and he can't eat another bite.

Mom grabs his arm. "Before you leave, would you please help me carry in the plants I brought Desdemona?"

My heart rate gets back to normal. The aroma of the tamales mingled with fresh pineapple rings makes my stomach rumble, so I settle onto a barstool and, realizing I'm famished, grab one of the tamales. I roll it out of its shuck onto a plate and hook a couple of the fresh pineapple rings. *This is a great moment. I've just had the most wonderful sex of my life. The man of my dreams is back in my life. He knows we need to talk about what he and his mother did in high school. We'll get this worked out. We have to. We're perfect together in every way. We have to.* Happiness rolls over me. As I watch Hunter follow my mother out the doorway, I bring the scrumptious, cumin-fragrant tamale to my lips. I pause and close my eyes, relishing the moment, before biting into it.

The front door snaps shut behind Hunter and Mom, and a whooshing sound interrupts my thoughts. My eyes fly open. Alma has swooped in on me like an eagle grabbing a helpless mouse.

With her face inches from mine, her eyes bore into me. "Don't worry, mija. Your mama doesn't know about Burt on *Marriage Exposure*. She only watches the novelas." My mouth, already open to receive the tamale, gapes. My face must be the deepest shade of red. "It's best she not know about you." I drop the tamale back to the plate. Alma plunges her arm into her big, black purse hanging from a shoulder strap and pulls up a small, amber tinted glass bottle. "But I brought you these herbs from my curandera. You mix three pinches of this powder in your first tea or coffee every morning." She puts the bottle into my hand and shakes her finger in my face. "And you must get a Latino. Gringos like Burt will never get you lucky."

Mom and Hunter, already returning, laugh out on the porch.

Alma shoves me toward the bedroom. "Put your herbs away where your mama won't see them—and not in that drawer by your bed." *Alma knows about my drawer.*

I shut the door to my bedroom, gather all my forbidden items, stuff them into a suitcase, and bury it in the back of my closet. Through the bedroom door, the chatter of Mom and Alma, directing Hunter where to place the plants for the best light exposure, gives me time to double-check my bedroom. Mom, finally satisfied with the placement of the plants, appraises the condition of my old plants that have survived from her earlier donations.

By the time I take a deep breath and stroll with fake, nonchalant calmness back into the living room, Hunter again says he needs to leave. Every time I look at him, a warm glow settles over me. It takes all my restraint to keep from touching him.

Alma, a scientist scrutinizing a new specimen, squints at him. "What are you, Hunter?"

Of course, he's totally confused by her question because he doesn't know Mom and Alma well enough to get her meaning, so I help out. "She means what is the country of origin of your ancestors." Alma probably wants to determine whether there's any hope that he may have Latino heritage.

Hunter rattles off a long list—English, Irish, German, Native American.

Alma nods her head solemnly as she considers each one he lists. "You don't think you might have had a Mexican grandmother back there somewhere?"

Hunter laughs. "What's the right answer to that question?"

"The true one." Alma frowns solemnly.

"Well, I'll ask my grandmother." His gaze shifts to me—a mixture of longing, humor, and maybe sadness skates across his face. "Who knows? Maybe I did have a Mexican ancestor."

Alma and Mom sleep in my bed, and I get the sofa. After we all settle in and the lights are off, I listen to Mom's voice mails, which started early in the afternoon. Alma's daughter had volunteered to run the flower shop for a day so the two ladies could come to Austin for Hunter's author talk and my afternoon gig tomorrow. This will teach me not to ignore my mother's messages.

For a few minutes the muffled sound of Alma's and Mom's soft Spanish floats through my closed bedroom door. They finally go to sleep, and I'm alone with my thoughts. *Did the "Always on My Mind" interlude really happen? Did my body really orbit the planet?* My hand drifts down to my girly parts, which are still pulsing as if they can't wait for the next dose of Hunter.

My phone vibrates. *Kari* flashes on the screen in the darkness.

She says, "What happened? Is Hunter still there?"

I whisper a summary to her, leaving out the sex.

"Desdemona, tell me the whole thing. Did you do it? Did the earth move?"

I take a deep breath. "Yes and yes."

Kari lets loose several squeals. "I'm so happy for you. Your long-lost love is back in your life, and your sexual crisis is over—in one sweep. Your world is perfect. It's like a movie—instant love."

"You're right about my world being perfect. But I wouldn't call it instant. Years of high-school angst plus nine years of waiting." As if on cue, a text buzzes in. It's an unknown number, but it has to be Hunter, because it says, "How long are they staying?" I remember that Mom had given him my number at his book signing in Garcia.

Tingles ripple through me. "Kari, I have to go."

She gasps. "He's calling you, right?" She barely pauses for my whispered response. "Oh. Oh. This is so great."

I text Hunter. "Leaving late tomorrow afternoon—going to your author talk and to the mall first."

"Can we get together when they leave?"

"Yes." My face bursts from its huge smile.

He must sense it. "Are you smiling?"

"Yes. You?"

"You know it. I didn't want to leave you tonight."

My thumbs fly across the keys. "I wish you were still here. It was beautiful. I knew I missed you, but now I don't see how I survived all those years away from you. Today I didn't listen to my messages—didn't know they were coming."

"I figured. Can I have your mailing address? Want to send you something."

I text it to him and ask, "What is it?" It must be what he mentioned at Tank when he said he had something of mine, but he didn't bring it with him.

"Let's talk about it and everything—the nine years—tomorrow. Desdemona, I love you."

"I love you, too. My love never went away."

14

We leave Mom's car at the mall and then drive to Café Vuelta, where I drop Mom and Alma at the entrance so I can search for a parking place. Normally the crowds and the traffic would annoy me, but today the very air is infused with an intoxicant that pumps me with a sense of well being. From early morning, when Alma and Mom woke me up frying chorizo in my kitchen, I've been giddy. I smile at odd moments, hum mindlessly, and lose track of conversations. Hunter texts me several times each hour. We figure out that our schedules today overlap a little, so I'll have to leave his event and head to my mall gig before he's finished. But he'll meet me later at the mall. Mom and Alma will go home from the mall after listening to me play for the first hour. I float.

By the time I park and make it back to the rustic café, the place is packed, which is amazing for the middle of a Friday afternoon. Local writers and mystery fans are really into Des Amone. Hunter is already up on the little platform stage in one corner. I gasp. His beard is gone. *Did he shave it for me? Because I said I missed his chin?*

In my peripheral vision, Mom and Alma wave and motion for me to come to their table. Fifty or more people mill around the weirdly mismatched tables and chairs, but Hunter is in a different vibrational plain from everyone else in the room. My eyes can't pull away from him. My body feels light and detached as I move toward the waving ladies. This man who was a handsome boy when we were seventeen, this man whose touch changed my life last night, this man who has delighted my memory all day long, this man in the flesh—the bulk of him, the essence of him, envelops me. It takes labored intention to guide my feet toward Mom and Alma.

Hunter talks to a middle-aged woman who shuffles sheets of paper at the small table where she and Hunter are seated. She must be the president of the local writers' guild. Most of this crowd supposedly consists of local writers. After she interviews Hunter, the writers and fans will dine and chat informally for an hour, and then Hunter will go to a nearby bookstore for a signing. I love watching him in his professional setting. I love the way he listens respectfully to the writers' guild lady. I love the way his naked jaw takes me back to high school but also thrills me with the mature man he is.

Sultry, I mean Zoe, bursts onto the stage with them. Angry track lines crease between her brows. The energy she radiates catches Hunter's attention, and he says something to the writers' guild lady. Then he stands and faces Zoe, who now gestures jerkily with both hands as she whispers in his ear. He listens calmly, unaffected by her obvious rage. She grips his arm and continues her high-octane whispering. I snake my way through the tables and people.

A young woman with a ponytail and a big Ana nametag goes up onto the stage and attaches a small mic to the collar of the writers' guild lady. Then Ana edges slowly toward Hunter as if waiting for a break in Zoe's monologue. Hunter says something to Zoe and turns toward Ana, who attaches a mic to his collar. It seems as if Hunter wants Zoe to leave, but she remains planted on the stage next to his chair. The writers' guild lady hands Hunter a folder, and he opens it as he sits back down.

Zoe, oozing into the space vacated by Ana, bends over Hunter with one hand clamped on his shoulder. She resumes the animated whispering in spite of all the odd glances she gets.

At Mom and Alma's table, their purses are piled on the one empty chair. The two ladies are so absorbed in watching Zoe's antics that they don't notice my arrival. I lift their purses and drop into the chair.

Mom, who's seated next to me, asks, "Who's the redhead?"

"Hunter's agent."

Alma reaches across Mom and takes her purse from me. "What's her problem? I think he should fire her."

A new woman stands in front of the little platform stage and asks for everyone's attention. Most people hush and settle. But Zoe goes on unfazed, and now that everyone else has quieted, bits and pieces of Zoe's staccato words come through. "...were you going to tell me...how long it took for me...how much this is going to cost...what were you thinking... crazy...how much work...and what's with shaving the beard..."

Hunter says, "We can talk later. The program is starting now."

Zoe glances at the audience. Her mouth makes an O, and her eyebrows shoot upward as if she had forgotten the room full of people with her. She pastes on a big fake smile, gives Hunter a friendly pat on the shoulder, and slithers off the stage. I hunker down in my chair, hoping she doesn't see me. The last thing I want is a repeat of her exclamation, "The Desdemona!"

The writers' guild president gives a long welcome to Hunter, and Zoe makes her way to the back of the room. Peeking over my left shoulder, I can see her standing rigidly against the wall. Now that she's off the stage, the fake smile is gone. She pulls a phone from her purse and furiously punches its face.

The guild president asks Hunter to talk about his writing process. His deep, steady voice fills the room. He's fully focused on explaining techniques that work for him. The energy of his words command the room. I force myself to glance around at the audience for a second, and see that they are as mesmerized as I am. The levels and depths of Hunter amaze me. And for inexplicable reasons, his devotion to his craft makes me hornier than ever. I want to devour him.

Mom jiggles my arm. "Isn't it time for us to go to your mall gig?"

I've lost track of everything on the planet except Hunter. I glance at the time on my phone. We should leave, but I whisper, "Soon."

A few minutes later, I'm reluctantly ready to pry myself from my chair and make my dash for the car. The guild president says, "Tell us, Des Amone, about your pen name. It's so unusual. Why do you have a pen name? And how did you select it?"

He casts his eyes down to his hands on the table. Heartbeats pass. He remains still. The room is dead silent. Some subtle shift in Hunter's demeanor signals that the answer he's about to give has special meaning to him. He slowly raises his eyes and makes direct contact with mine. "When I was a kid, I fell in love with a pianist." Mom gasps and clutches my arm. "For years I watched her practice and develop her art." He pauses so long that I begin to wonder if he has finished. "She's a beautiful person, but when she plays, her beauty goes to a level that touches the deepest part of me." My heart is in my throat. "I created the name Des Amone because it reminds me of her. And I wanted to bring the same passion and dedication to my art that she brings to hers."

His words caress my soul. His smile and gaze hook into me. It is the happiest moment of my life.

Mom shoves a tissue into my hand. "Desdemona, everyone is looking at you."

Alma leans across Mom and says, "Go get the car, or you'll be late."

Hunter nods at me as I stand. He knows my time line—knows I'm already late. He mouths, "Later." He turns to the guild president and says, "Next question."

I navigate through the tables toward the door. The guild president says, "That's the most beautiful answer I've ever heard about a pen name. Is this person...your literary namesake...is she somehow connected to the flawed women your heroes are always trying to save?"

I'm about to push the door open, but this question makes my breath catch. *How will he answer?* My heart hurts for him. He won't talk about his mother—how her embezzling sent him to juvie—her long, slow death from cancer. *No.* I answer for him. *Just say no.* His face freezes me. He's still focused on me, and his face is naked. Even though he's silent, his face says *yes* to her question. *His literary namesake equals the flawed women? I am the flawed women?* I look away from his face and push through the door, feeling as if I'm looking at something too stark and raw.

On the street I break into a jog, trying to trim seconds off the time between now and my gig. *He was just thrown by the question. The same as I am by questions about Dad. He won't talk about his mother, just like I never talk about Dad. The flawed women in his stories are all versions of his mother. They are not—*

"Desdemona." A sharp voice strikes me from behind. I know before I turn around. Zoe hoofs down the sidewalk to catch up with me. "Wait. I want to talk to you."

I face her. "What?" I dread a tirade about *Marriage Exposure*. Maybe she's afraid my notoriety will be bad for Hunter—for his concentration and his reputation. My stomach twists. *Maybe it will be bad for Hunter.*

"What are you thinking? Do you want to totally wreck his career? After he spent years working through the crap you put him through? How dare you waltz in, make him change his image, make him cancel the East coast tour?" She talks so fast and waves her hands so frantically, I can't absorb her meaning. "I'm gone a few hours, and you completely derail what has taken years to build. If you want to have a fling with him, fine. I can play the PR to our advantage. But do it without wrecking him again."

"*Marriage Exposure* has nothing to do with him." My voice trembles, maybe because I'm afraid what I'm saying isn't true. "It's old news. It won't have any effect on Hunter." I turn my back on her and resume my jog toward the parking lot. I don't want her to see my eyes tearing up.

She trots right along behind me. "What are you freaking talking about? Don't play dumb. I know what you pulled. His mother told—"

"Zoe!" Hunter's voice roars from behind us.

Zoe and I both spin around. He rushes toward us.

Zoe slaps her head with her palm. "Do not even tell me you walked out of your show to rescue poor Desdemona again. Are you freaking kidding me?" She throws both arms out wide and slices the air in beat with her words. "You walked out."

"Of course I did. I saw you chasing Desdemona out the door." Hunter wraps his arms around me and pulls me to his body. "Are you OK?" I nod, too stunned to say anything. He pulls back, holds me by the upper arms, and speaks softly. "Don't worry about anything Zoe says. She's just overreacting because I canceled some book signings—afraid she's going to lose a few dollars. She'll get over it."

Zoe, with her hands on her hips, sputters, "You...you...you..."

Hunter kisses me on the lips and then whispers in my ear, "Go on to the mall. I'll catch up with you later."

I do as he says, but even though I walk away, his next words to Zoe ring out. "Just because you get twenty percent of my gross doesn't mean you own me. Stay out of my personal life."

"You won't be able to afford a personal life if you don't freaking get your act together. You know what she did to you already—don't be an idiot and throw—"

I slam my car door. On autopilot I drive back to the café. Before I reach the pickup area, I force my face into a calm expression. Mom and Alma climb in quietly, but I can see the question marks in their expressions. I put on my performer's smile, designed to mask stress. "Did you two enjoy the interview?"

Alma, from the back seat, mutters something in Spanish.

Mom says, "We'll talk later when we're out of this traffic." She waits about three blocks. "You and Hunter are in love?"

Her words glimmer through my body. In spite of all the nagging little questions about Zoe and the money in high school, it's awesome to hear someone say out loud that Hunter and I are a couple. I nod. "Yes, we are. We fell in love in high school, but we got separated when his dad died and I moved to Austin. We just now have found each other again." *And we're going to work out the kinks tonight and live happily ever after—we have to.*

Mom brings her hands to her face. "Oh, mija, I'm so happy for you."

Alma pats me on the shoulder from the back seat. "Me, too. Just wish he were Latino."

I shoot her a glare in the rearview mirror. She shrugs and looks away.

Playing at Infinity Mall is always low key. The piano is near the food court and bar area. People are chatty and not too attentive, so I can play anything I want. There are never many requests or tips, but it's a reliable, easy gig—almost like a paid practice time.

Mom and Alma sit nearby at a table in my direct line of vision, enjoying dessert and coffee while I play. Toward the end of my first set, a woman takes the table next to theirs. I notice her immediately—first because she clearly stares at me and second because I know her.

Burt's wife.

She has no food, no shopping bags—she just sits, watching. Dread washes over me—tinged with a little fear. *Is she stable? Will she attack me?* I remember Burt's hurried speech about how she became obsessed with me after they saw me at Zilker Park. Losing her job. Her insecurity.

At my break I rush to Mom and Alma, and amid their exaggerated claps and "bravos," drop into an empty chair.

"Mom, you guys should really leave now. The traffic will get heavy in a few minutes."

Both of them kiss me on my cheeks, patting my hands and murmuring praises for my playing.

I've got to get them out of here—don't want them to witness a scene with Burt's wife. "Really, Mom and Alma—"

"OK, OK," Mom says. "We'll head for home."

And after another five minutes of good-byes, hugs, reminders, and so on, they exit, and I face Jenny, who still stares at me.

"Desdemona, may I sit with you?"

I motion to the empty chairs and nod.

She moves slowly, hesitantly. This is the first time I've studied her up close. She's beautiful, with delicate features. Her hair that seemed brown on TV has a shiny, auburn glow this close. Her small, slightly turned-up nose makes her look almost like a teenager, and her skin, that was red and puffy in her close-up on TV, is creamy porcelain. There's a gentleness and vulnerability about the way she moves. *No wonder Burt loves her.*

She settles into the chair Mom used. "It's kind of you to talk with me." Her voice, which had been wailing and screechy on TV, sounds sweet and sincere. "I won't take much of your time. I realize you must be on a break."

I nod. Unexpectedly, I feel concerned for her—for the effort it must be taking for her to talk to me. I surprise myself by saying softly, "You've been through a lot, haven't you?"

Her eyes, a clear blue that Mom would call *azul de cielo*, meet mine, and I see her painful struggle. "I love Burt, but I'm leaving him."

I'm speechless.

She goes on. "I just wanted you to know—after all we've put you through, you deserve to know. So if you want him back, I won't be in your way."

My mouth drops open in shock. "Wait. No. No."

She grips a small purse in her lap as if she's using it to keep herself anchored, but her sad blue eyes stay locked with mine. "I'm sorry we went on that show—sorry for the way we dragged your name into it." She scoots her chair back and casts her eyes down toward the floor. "Thank you for listening. That's all."

"Jenny, wait." She freezes and slowly raises her eyes back to meet mine. "Burt and I have been apart for over a year. And it was technically over for us long before we split. There's nothing, nothing between us—really never was." Jenny watches me, frozen, as if she's holding her breath. "We were just sort of like in a safety relationship, I think. We never loved each other. And even if we had, I'm in love with someone else." She hasn't moved or made a sound, but perfect teardrops leak—one from each eye.

I shake my head, trying to understand this conversation we have. "Why do you think I want him back? Why do you think he would even want me if I did?"

She takes a deep breath and speaks in a voice so small and low that I have to lean closer to hear her words. "He's never been satisfied with me." I must look puzzled because after a pause, she adds, "Sexually."

I'm about to ask what makes her think that when she whispers, "He fakes his climaxes with me. He pretends. I've tried everything, but I can't satisfy him. And I don't want him to be stuck with me—stuck in a relationship that isn't working for him."

I'm dumbfounded for a moment. "Burt fakes..."

She nods.

Suddenly, like rapid-fire dominos falling in a row, facts line up and drop into place. The rushed, morning-only sex sessions that abruptly ended with his mad dash to the shower to get ready for work. The articles in Dr. Rhymer's file about men's struggles with anorgasmia. The very fact that Burt would think to say on national TV that he couldn't love me because I faked orgasms. He faked. He hated himself for it. And he projected that onto me.

Well, OK, it's true I faked, too. But this explains his awareness of it—his need to blurt it out on TV as a reason he couldn't love me.

"Jenny, he's always faked. It's not about you. It's about something he's struggling with." Her doubtful expression prods me to explain. "Twenty-five percent of all men do this occasionally, and a small percentage do it constantly. Burt's in that small percentage. It's been researched."

A little flash like hope brightens her worried eyes. "What?" But almost as quickly as the flash appears, it disappears. "But I can't help him. I've tried."

"Oh my gosh. I have the solution! A once-in-a-lifetime, serendipitous solution for you and Burt." She pulls back a little as if maybe she thinks I'm crazy. So I lower my voice and reduce my enthusiasm. "Dr. Gloria Rhymer, a national expert on anorgasmia in relationships, is about to begin an unprecedented study, and she has openings right here in Austin. It will involve months of intense therapy, both singly and in couples—for people with anorgasmia."

Jenny's face is blank—her eyes confused—as if she's trying to process my spiel. "Anorgas...?"

"Yes—that's the name for what Burt has. Dr. Rhymer can be his chance to get to the bottom of his issue once and for all and find a solution."

Jenny opens her purse and pulls out her phone. "How do you spell Rhymer?"

I spell it. "I'll also give her a call and tell her to expect you to contact her. You'll love her, and she's an expert on this." I glance at the time on her phone. "My break is over. Good luck, Jenny. And I hope you hang in there with Burt, at least until after giving Dr. Rhymer a try."

Her sweet face breaks into an angelic smile, and her eyes pour out gratitude. "I will, Desdemona. I will."

During the second hour, as I play, my eyes are drawn constantly to the entry area, watching for Hunter. It's still too early, but I fantasize about him coming in. I replay everything he said during the interview, especially the pen-name answer, and I try to block out sultry Zoe's negativity. I'm so thankful that Hunter caught up with us on the sidewalk and shut her down. He rescued me just as he did last night with Burt. Wait. Rescue. What did Zoe say? *Do not even tell me you walked out of your show to rescue poor Desdemona again.*

I don't notice Ross until my second break. He sits at a table close to the piano. Pangs of guilt stab me. I should have phoned him today and given him the update about Hunter and me.

He stands up, embraces me, and kisses the side of my hair. "How'd it go last night? How are you?"

I wait until we sit to answer. "I'm better than I could have ever imagined I would be. Hunter and I love each other—we never stopped." Ross tries to hide his disappointment, but I can see the pain in his eyes. He was probably hoping I'd find that Hunter and I were over. "Our feelings are as strong as they were nine years ago, and in some ways—maybe because we're older—they're deeper." I hate hurting Ross like this. "I want you to know the truth. I don't want you to be dangling, wondering if there's hope for you and me."

He never breaks his eye contact with me. "I appreciate your truthfulness. And I want you to be happy." He starts to reach across for my hand, but he stops and folds his hands in front of himself on the table. "Don't be concerned about me. You and I are best friends, and we always will be." His integrity and goodness touch me. I put my hands on top of his.

He closes his eyes, but his voice stays strong. "Don't feel guilty. You can't control your feelings for someone. I know."

"You're gold." My voice wavers. "The woman who winds up with you will be so lucky. I'm thankful to have you as a friend."

He puts one of his hands on top of mine, so that mine are sandwiched between his. "So Hunter apologized for his mom's stealing and the nine-year blow-off?" His question would sound harsh if his kind blue eyes weren't gently probing mine. I know he asks out of genuine concern for me.

"Well, not exactly." I squirm in my chair. I've been so giddy over our physical connection that I'm still foggy on these reality-check questions. I feel like a blindsided guest on Dr. Phil's show. "But we're going to talk about that. We're going to work it all out."

Ross's brow furrows. "What exactly did he say about it?"

"Well, he said that we could get beyond all that. It was years ago. We're different people now. As long as there's no lying now, we'll be fine."

Ross squeezes my hands, leans forward, and locks eyes with me. "You have to be careful." The intensity in his voice makes me hold my breath. "If he doesn't own up to what he did in the past, he'll hurt you again."

I don't like what he says. I don't want to hear it. But a tiny part of me is scared to death that he's right. "No, you're wrong. Hunter covered for his mother's embezzling and let her kick me out of their lives because of his father's illness and death. That won't happen again. It won't." I pull my hands away from his and stand up. "I have to go back now."

Ross slumps back in his chair.

The joyful giddiness of my first two hours of playing sours. Fear sits in the pit of my stomach. And the little hints of trouble that I've kept submerged for the past twenty-four hours bubble up all at once. *What does Hunter mean when he says he's willing to forget what I did in the past? Does he even know about my Crime Stoppers call?* I didn't exactly share this slant with Ross. Maybe I've been too lustful to share it even with my own consciousness. *And what's with sultry Zoe's grievance about Hunter rescuing me again?* I play flat, simple songs.

Ross comes up onto the platform and bends down to whisper to me. "I'm going home now. I hope everything works out for you. Call me if you need anything. OK?"

I nod. He squeezes my shoulder and leaves.

My eyes constantly drift toward the entrance, hungry to see Hunter stroll in. I hope he'll come to me and explain everything, and we'll go home and make love again, and this time he'll stay with me and hold me all night long.

Minutes drag by. He should be here by now. My breath catches as a familiar form appears amid a crowd in the entrance. But instead of Hunter's taller figure and dark hair, it's Ross's sandy-haired, familiar form. He looks down at his feet as he comes back into the piano area. He avoids eye contact with me. *What's going on?* I stare hard at him, willing him to meet my gaze. But he hurries past and takes a table nearly behind me. I have to crane over my shoulder to see him. He keeps his eyes downward.

Something's wrong. Where's Hunter? Why did Ross come back? I play a simplified version of "Moonlight Sonata" over and over. Probably no one notices because the drifting crowd is noisy. It's almost closing time. I scan the whole area for Hunter in case he slipped in and I missed him. He's nowhere.

Suddenly it hits me. When Ross left earlier, he must have run into Hunter. That's why Ross came back. Something happened.

I stop midmeasure and hustle over to Ross's table. "You saw Hunter?"

"Yeah." Ross's face is the picture of misery. His eyes are downcast.

I drop into a chair next to him. "What happened? What did he say?" Ross finally meets my eyes, but he stays silent. "Tell me."

"It started off fine." He shoves his hand over the top of his hair. "We talked about you—how great you are." He stops again as if he's dreading what he has to say.

"OK." I grip the edge of the table. "Then what?"

"I said you and I are close." He rushes now, getting this over with. "And that I care about you and I don't want to see you get hurt."

Chills crawl over me. Somehow I know the rest is going to be bad, really bad. "Finish, Ross."

"He said he'd never hurt you." Ross clenches his fists together on the table.

"What did you tell him, Ross?"

He sighs and shakes his head. "I said, 'You need to apologize for covering for your mother's stealing and tossing Desdemona out of your life for nine years.'"

OK. Ross probably put it a little gruffly, but I'm sure that Hunter and I can work through this. But where is Hunter? "What did he say? Where is he?" I look around the room, thinking he'll show up.

Pained wrinkles flex around Ross's eyes. "The guy looked like I slugged him. He turned white."

"Was he sick?" I spring to my feet. "What happened?"

"I don't think he was sick. I think he was mad. He said his mother didn't steal any money and..." Ross looks down at his hands for a moment; then he stands and leans closer to me. "You weren't telling the truth about that."

"I'm not telling the truth?" I've looked at that little journal a million times—she must have stolen the money. "If his mother didn't steal it, who did?" This makes no sense. "Did he say he stole it?"

Ross's eyes dart upward at someone behind me. I spin around—it has to be Hunter.

Zoe, towering over me with her hands on her hips, snaps, "Where's Hunter?"

I face her, and Ross stays close to my side. For some reason she totally intimidates me, but I try to keep my voice firm. "I don't know."

"Well, great. Have you two already split again?" Like a shark she senses the blood seeping from my breaking heart. She jerks her phone out of her purse. "He's not answering my texts or calls." She thumbs keys while she broadcasts her concerns at us. "I managed to get the Manhattan signing back on for tomorrow. But he's got to freaking be at the airport in two hours or he won't make it." She reads something on her phone and then drops it into her purse and targets me again. "Look, Desdemona, I'm not trying to interfere in your life, but Hunter needs to be focused right now. It took him years to get over going to juvie for your crime." My knees wobble. *My crime? All I did was call Crime Stoppers. How can she call that a crime?* Ross's arm around my waist keeps me steady. "Now if you're going to waltz in and mess with his mind again, you just need to realize—" She grabs her buzzing phone. "Hunter. Baby. Where are you?" She turns her back to us. "Yeah. Yeah. Manhattan is on... Great. I'll see you at the airport." She marches rapidly toward the exit. "Love you, baby." With her high-heeled pumps click-clacking across the floor, she waves her fingers over her shoulder—telling us good-bye without even turning around.

I slump back into the chair. Ross pulls his chair close to me and sits silently as if ready to catch me—literally and emotionally. And as nice as it would be to crash on my kind, loving friend, I can't let myself do that. Some other person takes over my body and speaks for me. "Well, guess it's time to go home."

Ross says, "Let me drive you. We can leave one of the cars here."

I push my voice out through the numbness. "No. Thank you. I'm good. I'm just going to grab my things and go home."

Confusion swirls in my head. *Could Ross have deliberately sabotaged things with Hunter?* I just want to be away from everyone. "I need to be alone now." Hunter may have called or texted. I want to get out of here and check my phone. "Good night." I scuttle to the employees' locker hallway, grab my things, and race out to my car while my phone powers up.

Hunter's voice mail, as I pull out of the dark parking lot, squeezes my chest. "I think I understand now what you meant when you said your heart couldn't get in sync with your head." There's a long pause, and then his voice, heavy with sadness, says, "I sent you an e-mail." It's not the message itself as much as his tone that tells me it's over for us. Heartbreak, pain, and regret seep through each word.

Unable to wait until I get home to read it, I pull into the parking lot of a convenience store. My hands tremble as I fumble with my phone, and crazy, hopeful ideas torture me: *Maybe I'm reading the signals wrong. Maybe he just needed to go quickly to Manhattan. Maybe the e-mail will explain. He wouldn't just leave me.*

> Dear Desdemona,
> Last night I didn't believe I would be writing this to you. Our time together rocked my world with power I didn't know existed. I'm sorry to end it this way—in an e-mail, sorry that I barged back into your life, sorry that we tasted something great only to lose it.

I grow numb and hollow. This is a breakup e-mail. I scroll down—it's long. How did he find the time to write all this in the past couple of hours? I remind myself he's a writer—he can churn out one or two books a year. This e-mail is nothing to him.

> I've loved you as long as I can remember. But I see now it was the idea of you I loved.
> The first time I saw you in elementary school, with your bright smile, sparkling brown eyes, and shining black braids, you grabbed my little-boy heart and left me tongue-tied. Your laughter during those early years was music to me—I sought you out every day. When you started playing your songs at school parties, I was sucked in, under your spell. The joy with which you played, the way your smile reached out to everyone around. Your whole being seemed a part of your music, and that aura made everyone fall in love with you.
> The year we were ten and your dad deserted you, I wanted to rescue you—make the pain go away. The change in you tore me apart. You worked harder than ever on the piano, but your music turned in on itself. Instead of the songs being your connection with the rest of us, the piano became the barrier between you and the world.

You used music as a shield, blocking out friends and me. I worked for a way to break through for years. After we made our connection in the piano room, you still never talked about your father—never grieved about what he'd done or the way he died.

Seeing you this week made me a little crazy, and I tried to fool myself into thinking we could get beyond the thing with my mother, but I was wrong—the lie, instead of diminishing with time, turned into a boulder. I get this after talking to Ross. Don't be angry at him—the guy is looking out for you, cares about you. He made me see the truth, and it's better to see it now than to string this out longer.

As you probably gathered from Zoe's explosion at Café Vuelta, I canceled my East Coast tour because I wanted to stay here with you. But I'm moving on. Seeing each other right now would make things harder.

Every time I said I love you, I meant it—back in high school and last night.

Hunter

The years of longing I had for Hunter before yesterday were palpable, unending, aches. But this loss of him, after having our one ecstatic night and day, slices me in places I didn't know I could feel pain. I gaze at the message as if looking at a train wreck—horrible to see but impossible to look away from. My phone buzzes. Ross texts, "Have you talked with Hunter?"

I delete his message, drop the phone in my lap, and lean my forehead against the steering wheel. Then, numb, I reread the message, searching foolishly for some *maybe*, some open question, something that leaves hope for us. My phone buzzes again. Kari. "Where are you?"

Ross must have called her. Too weary to explain, I simply forward Hunter's e-mail to her.

15

By the time I reach my duplex, the numbness has worn off, and my body shakes with racking sobs. I don't even bother to stifle my wails or dry my face when I park my car and run to my front door. I don't care who sees or hears. Inside, I read the message again—this time on my computer, thinking somehow it might be different, but the message is as bleak as it was in the car.

Like a possessed person, I grab the tall kitchen garbage can, still half full from Mom and Alma's visit, and make a sweep through my apartment, throwing away everything that is remotely connected to Hunter, Ross, sex, or the hope of having a normal relationship with anyone. Ross's flowers, all the orgasm devices and creams, Hunter's books, all the condoms, and Alma's herbs. I jerk open the drawer where his mother's journal waits. How I want it out of my life, but it isn't mine to throw away. I slam the drawer shut. In my last pass through the kitchen, I grab a handful of paper towels and swipe the slick tears running down my face while I drag the garbage can out the back door, down to the alley to the Dumpster.

I hoist the can up over the side of the stinky Dumpster, and my junk clatters to the metal floor—with the glass flower vase making its own distinct, shattering crash. My heave is so careless that a handful of condoms fall to the ground. Angrily, I snatch them up and pitch the condoms one at a time into the Dumpster. With a maniacal growl, I drag the trash can back toward my kitchen.

The alley gravel crunches under my stomping feet. By now my sobs have subsided into those after-gasps, and I chant with each step, "Done, done, done." *I'm done with men. Done with sex. Done with having hope for a relationship. Done, done, done.*

As I approach my back door, there's movement through the window. I freeze in the darkness. Someone is in my duplex. *Maybe Hunter is back to say it was all a mistake. Maybe my landlady, even though she's hard of hearing, heard my loud crying and banging around.* I can't remember if I locked the front door when I came in.

I edge close to the window, hoping to see or hear whoever is inside. Kari's voice drifts out to me. "I can't find her anywhere. Her car is here, but the duplex is empty."

I open the back door and drag the trash can in.

Relief washes over Kari's face. "Oh, she's here—just was taking out her garbage." Her gaze locks with mine, and tears form in her eyes, as if she's catching my pain. She moves toward me. "I'll call you later." Dropping her phone onto the bar, she wraps her arms around me. "I'm so sorry. So sorry." After a few moments of our crying duet, she asks, "Did you phone him?"

The question takes me aback. "No." *Why didn't I call him? Should I have called him?* I step back, floundering as much physically as I am mentally. *Why is that the first question she asks but the last one that I would have considered?*

Kari nudges me toward the front door. "Let's go to the airport. I'll drive you." I'm like a stump, refusing to move, dumbly processing her idea. "There can't be that many flights to Manhattan. Maybe we can find him." She finally seems to notice that I'm not following her suggestion. "Oh, you're right—he's probably already at his gate even if we figured out his flight. Call him—he probably hasn't boarded or taken off yet." She looks around the room. "Where's your phone?" She heads toward my purse lying on the floor by the front door. "In your purse?" She digs out my phone and brings it to me. "What's your code?"

Still standing next to the garbage can, I call out the numbers and watch as if I'm half-asleep or drugged while she finds Hunter in my directory and calls. She puts the phone to my ear. *What can I say? How can I fix this?* I listen while the rings go to his recorded answer. His voice triggers my tears again.

Kari takes the phone to her own ear. "Hunter. This is Kari. You need to get back here and talk to Desdemona. Now. You two need to discuss this. You can't just send an e-mail without giving her the courtesy of—Crap. I wasn't finished." She redials and continues her lecture.

I drag myself to the sofa and curl up with the lamb's-wool throw, its chocolate-fudge stain reminding me of the horrible beginning of this series of disasters. Only six days ago, Burt announced my secret flaw to the universe, and Mom called about Hunter showing up. I kept myself moving, moving, moving all through the crazy week—made every performance and lesson—kept up a front to the world—thought I could get through anything. But now I'm a wreck.

"Desdemona, I'm going to stay until he calls back." She sits beside me.

"I'm fine. You don't have to stay. The worst is over." I really don't have the energy to talk to her, and talk isn't going to help.

"I'm staying." She heads toward the kitchen. "And the first thing I'm doing is getting us something to eat and drink." A bottle of red wine Alma brought is on the counter. Kari opens it and fills two glasses. She brings one to me. "Drink."

I take the wine from her, so she'll leave me alone, but I don't think I can swallow anything. She busies herself in the kitchen, checking my phone every couple of minutes. Finally, she brings a tray of snacks and coaxes me to eat, drink, and talk.

I awaken on the sofa with the morning sun streaming in as if this is a normal day. Kari's sprawled out on my bed. I get up quickly, shower, and try to make my face look as normal as possible. I know that I'll never be happy or undamaged for the rest of my life, but I've got to put on a front so that the people around me can move on with their lives.

By the time Kari wakes up, I've made coffee and warmed the pumpkin empanadas that Mom left. I nod through Kari's assurances that Hunter will call, we'll get things worked out, love can always find a way. She's wrong. But there's no point in telling her. Let her have her delusions. I want her to go home because I have one more loose end to tie up. Then this week from hell will be history.

As soon as she's gone, I call Dr. Rhymer. "Is it OK if I bring a report over? I found one that I forgot to put back in your folder."

Ten minutes later I pull up in front of her office/home. While I wait for her to answer the doorbell, the memory of my first visit mocks me. How simple my needs were then. I just wanted to figure out how to orgasm. Now I want to figure out how to live without Hunter—how to get through this life listening from afar to a third-rate sound system after I've been in the midst of the most wondrous orchestra in the universe. When she opens her door for me, I rush into her sitting room, almost before she invites me. She already has the white teacups set on the copper-top coffee table. "The water has just boiled. Is tulsi OK again?"

It seems as if my life depends at this moment on having a cup of her tulsi tea. I nod, drop the report onto the table, and sit on one of the brocade sofas.

She pours the water into her little iron teapot. Her way of listening to the water trickle into the pot makes me listen as well. She settles back onto the other sofa. "Desdemona, have you decided to be a part of my study?"

"No. But I gave your name to a friend named Jenny—she's going to call you. She wants to be in it with her husband."

She nods gently. If she's disappointed that I'm still not going to be in her study, she doesn't show it. "I'm glad you came by, and thank you for bringing that report. It will, no doubt, save a printing at some point."

"I have another hypothetical question for you about that person who suffers from anorgasmia except when she's with this one bad guy—the guy involved in embezzlement."

Dr. Rhymer tilts her head expectantly as if she's been looking forward to my hypothetical. She knows the whole hypothetical thing is fake—just like everything about me, but she doesn't object to my game.

I pull out my phone. "So let's say she finally has sex with him, and everything is perfect for the first time in her life. And he says he loves her and that they should just start over—forget what happened in high school—but then he sends her an e-mail that goes something like this." I read her Hunter's e-mail and steal peeks at her expression from time to time, trying to get some clue as to what she thinks. But her face reveals nothing. At the end I drop the phone onto my lap. She stays silent, so I ask, "What do you think is going on with him? What do you think she should do? Hypothetically."

Dr. Rhymer's face is almost impassive as she pours our tea. "May I ask some hypothetical questions?"

I nod, holding my cup between both hands. It's still too hot to drink.

"He mentions that this woman's father deserted her and later died?" I nod, puzzled. "Did she ever have counseling or talk to anyone about her loss?"

"What does that have to do with anything?" The question totally throws me off-balance.

She looks at me with pity. "A woman's relationship with her father can color her relationship with other men."

"Well, sure. Everyone knows that." I want her to get off me—the woman—and focus on Hunter. "But this guy—what's going on with him? Maybe it's the relationship he had with his mother that is totally sabotaging his relationship with me?" There—I drop the hypothetical ruse. "Why does he leave without even talking to me? Why does he do it in an e-mail?"

She points at my phone. "He said in the message that he thought it would be too difficult for you to see each other again. But that said, if you want to talk with him, why don't you?"

I open my mouth to protest that he didn't call back even after Kari lectured him, but I realize she gets at something bigger—the whole fact that I didn't even consider calling him until Kari told me to. That I read his e-mail and dragged my trash can through my duplex to expel anything remotely related to Hunter. That for nine years, I missed him but never tried to contact him.

"Desdemona." Her gentle voice breaks through my thoughts. She leans forward. "Desdemona, did your father tell you good-bye? Did you have closure?"

An involuntary gasp startles my chest. Something brittle inside me cracks open. My voice comes out small, childlike. "No." I never talk about Dad deserting us and later dying. Never.

She reaches forward and takes the trembling teacup from my hands. I watch as she places it farther away. She must think I'll spill it. "I'd like you to take three deep breaths with me. And then you can tell me about your father." Her eyes connect with mine. I clasp my hands together to keep them still. "Breathe in...out...in...out..."

My shoulders begin to shake up and down before she gets to the third breath, and a deep, quaking groan pushes its way up from my chest in choppy beats. She tucks tissues into my hands that cover my face. And I just give it up. Through my noise, her voice soothes, "It's OK. It's OK." Finally, after I've calmed down a little, she touches my hand with a cold bottle of water. "Let's drink some water."

I take a sip. The coldness slides down my throat, and the raggedness of my breathing settles. My voice scrapes out small and somehow old at the same time. "I loved him so much. He had wonderful, kind blue eyes that twinkled when he smiled at me. I loved to ride on his shoulders. His golden blond hair was like fairies had in my storybooks. He taught me to play songs when I was four, and he found a piano teacher for me when I was five. He said I had natural talent like him. But he was just a honky-tonk player. He said I would be classically trained. We were so happy. Mom had her flower shop, and he did lots of different jobs—mostly playing with bands. And one day when I was ten, I came home from school, and the piano was gone. I couldn't believe it was gone. My whole life, Mom and Dad had joked about how hard it had been to move it in—up those narrow stairs. They said the piano would be there forever, even if the rest of us left. I knew as soon as I saw the blank space where the piano had been—I knew he was gone and wouldn't come back."

"Desdemona." I don't realize I stopped talking until she prods me. "Here, have some more water."

I drink. "I begged Mama to tell me where he went, why he left. I begged until she cried and said he needed to leave us to be happy...it wasn't my fault...he would tell me all about it when he could. Every time I asked her about him, she cried. So finally I quit asking and decided to wait for him to come back and tell me." I set the water bottle on the table, take a deep breath, and push out the end of the story. "He never came back. Three years later, he died—we didn't even know until months afterward. The man who told Mama said it could have been an undiagnosed heart condition. Mama contacted his brother, but he never told us for sure what happened."

Dr. Rhymer sort of repeats the story back to me—breaking it apart and talking about how unresolved grief works on kids. She says this talk is a good step for me. Then suddenly we talk about this week—Miguel, Ross, and Hunter. She says I've been in hyperreactive mode ever since the TV program. Two pots of tea and two hours later, she walks me to the door.

I pause before stepping onto her porch. "Thank you for the free advice."

"I didn't give you any advice." She grins and tilts her head. "This was all hypothetical. And remember, I'm the one thankful to you. The *Marriage Exposure* producers would never have contacted me if you didn't live in Austin."

"Well, thank you. I feel drained, but I think I needed to talk about this stuff." I turn to step out.

"Wait, Desdemona. I do have some advice for you. You had sexual relations with three different men in one week. You need to reign yourself in—"

"Oh, believe me. I'm done. Forever." I try to laugh. "Done. I'm shocked at it myself."

Her expression remains serious. "When is the last time you saw your gynecologist?"

Ice shoots through my veins. *What is she getting at?* "Ah, well, it's been a while—haven't been in a relationship for so long. But they used condoms—all three did." *Crap. This sounds awful.*

"Condoms are good." She nods. "I'm glad to hear that, but there's no one-hundred-percent protection from STDs or pregnancy."

Suddenly, I wish I hadn't come here, even though I know she's right. It's crazy how most of my basic common sense has been on vacation for the past week. "Thanks. Good advice." This time I really leave.

On the drive home, nauseous waves of regret wash over me. I slept with three different men in one week. My lifetime number more than doubled in one week. And Miguel is older—has probably slept with hundreds of women. He could have picked up any number of human papillomaviruses or other STDs. And, good grief, Ross has been living with a woman who has a raging history at L and L. And she had a long relationship with tortured Brock. Dr. Oz's voice in my head says, "When you have sex with someone, it's like having sex with everyone they've ever had sex with." How many thousands did I have sex with this week? And Hunter—we never even talked about what he's been doing for the past nine years. I gasp—and I even tried to get him to have sex without a condom. I've been totally crazy for a week, and my chances of having contracted something exponentially expanded. And pregnancy. Pregnancy. *If I am pregnant, I won't even know which man is the father. When was my last period? Was I ovulating this week? Am I nauseous? Are my breasts tender?*

At a long, red traffic light, I Google how soon pregnancy and STD tests can be done, and learn it's too soon for pregnancy and OK for most STDs, except for HIV, which might not show up for six months.

Today is Saturday. There's nothing I can do about lab tests until Monday. *OK. The chances of pregnancy or an STD are miniscule because we used condoms—well, there was that first idiotic attempt I did to sink myself onto Hunter. There was that brief, heavenly nether regions contact.* But still, the chances are next to nothing. *But on the other hand, three different men within five days. Oh dear. That must shoot the statistical possibilities to the moon.* I seriously feel nauseous. *Is this fear or pregnancy I'm feeling?*

A blaring horn alerts me that the light is green. I shoot forward and coach myself all the way home. *Relax. There's absolutely no point in stressing over this. Stress will accomplish nothing.* But the moment I force my focus off the stress, tears of regret over losing Hunter start to flow again.

Mom calls as I pull up at my duplex. "Mija, I'm thinking about you. How are things going with Hunter?" She's still misguided by those golden moments at his book signing. She has no idea how quickly the universe has tilted.

"Mama," I gasp between sobs. "I want to come home."

"What's wrong? Are you sick?" The worried agony in her voice is palpable.

Her alarm makes me calm down. I don't want her to have a heart attack over stress about me. "No. No. I'm not sick. Just sad. He left. He doesn't want to be with me." I take a deep breath. "Is it OK if I come home for the weekend—just for quiet time—you and me?"

"Of course, mija. Come—I'll fix arroz con pollo the way you like it. And flan. All your favorites."

"OK—be there in a few hours. Love you."

"Are you OK to drive, mija? Should I come to you instead?"

"No. I mean, yes, I'm OK. I want to get away from Austin. I'll come there."

I throw a few things into a bag, feed and water Eleanor, lock up, and set out on the three-hour drive to Garcia.

16

By the time I pull up in front of the flower shop, Mom has closed it for the day. I drive around to the back entrance and climb the old wooden stairs to the apartment above. I can smell the arroz con pollo even before I open the door.

Standing in front of the stove, stirring something, Mom's so excited that she drops her spoon and nearly hops to me as soon as I enter.

I force a smile. "Mama." It feels so good to just be home with her even though I could never bring myself to tell her about what has gone on—about my nagging worry that I could have an STD or be pregnant. I won't dump the shame and worry of my past week on her.

"You're home." She squeezes me with each syllable. "I'm so happy, mija. It's so good to see you so soon again." Mom doesn't mention my crying during our phone conversation. She'll want to get us through our meal, catch up on small talk—later, maybe, she'll ask for the details. I realize that's a pattern with us. We dance around the painful stuff—put off talking about it—sometimes forever.

She relaxes her squeezes, and we're both still, holding each other. Her warm arms feel like home. It has been several months since I've come for a visit. The cozy apartment is almost the same as it was when I moved out during my senior year. A small, wooden kitchen table with three chairs stands near the stove. Mom has redone the table since my last visit. The legs now have hand-painted green vines climbing to the top, which is covered with red and yellow roses. Mom loves flowers—either real or painted.

The kitchen and living area are all one room. There's no sofa—just a couple of wicker chairs. My "nook," as Mom calls it, is a twin-size bed in the corner partitioned off with two tall bookshelves. For the first ten years of my life, the piano, a beautiful antique upright, stood in this spot. After Dad left, Mom created my special space. She did it to cheer me up, but every night when I lay in that nook, I wondered where Dad was—why he took the piano and left us. I would have happily continued to sleep on my pull-out bed in the kitchen area if Dad would have stayed with us. The haunting questions spring up as bold as they were when I was ten. *Did he leave because of me? Did he meet another woman—maybe a white woman with beautiful blond hair like his? Or maybe a woman with musical talent like his? Was he bored with Garcia? Mom and her flower shop? Me?*

"Go, mija, wash up. Everything is ready—just the way you like it." She keeps holding onto me even though she has instructed me to go wash up. Finally, she pushes me toward her bedroom, which adjoins the bathroom. Her room is unchanged, a double bed with a night table covered with books, mostly romances. At the foot of her bed, another table holds a small, boxy TV—the same one she's had for years. Memories—her crying in that bed in the nights after Dad left—wash over me. Night after night, when she thought I was asleep, she wept. Just as I now weep for Hunter.

After we eat, she leads me down to the shop to see her new refrigerator, new shelves, new arrangements. The fact that her shop continues to thrive in this small town is a tribute to her work and talent. Several other flower shops have opened over the years, only to go out of business after a year or so of effort.

Back at the rose-covered table, with the dishes washed and put away, she pours her favorite coffee liqueur into the tiny, gold-colored, hand-blown Mexican glasses that she and Dad bought on their honeymoon in Guadalajara. It's one of my favorite childhood stories—how they watched the artisan create each glass, and how Dad carefully packed each glass and bribed the airline attendant to make sure the box was handled gently. Mom and Dad brought the glasses all the way home to enjoy on special occasions—including the day I was born. Dad sneaked Mom's coffee liqueur and two glasses into the hospital. Mom had her drink while Dad held me. They said I wrinkled my nose and smiled at the sweet, dark aroma.

"Mom." My voice takes on a strange huskiness.

She becomes motionless and peers at me—both hands around her glass on the table in front of her. "What is it, Desdemona? Tell me what is wrong."

I take a deep breath. *Everything is wrong—where do I begin?* "What happened to Dad? Why did he leave us?" I brace myself for yet another denial or glossing over with shallow words that I heard throughout my childhood.

She nods slowly. Her gaze drops to her glass. "I often think I should have told you the truth from the beginning. It probably didn't help to try to hide it from you."

I'm frozen, holding my breath. I've never heard words like this from my mother.

She raises her eyes to meet mine, and she reaches for my hands. "Sam was a good man. He loved us as much as he could. He never meant to hurt us." She waits—maybe to see if I'll comment.

I whisper, "What happened? I need to know the truth—all of it."

She stands, reaches into a cabinet for a box of tissues, places the box on the table, and pulls one out. Without thinking, I, too, take a tissue.

"Sam was on heroin when I met him." I gasp, and Mom nods at me solemnly. In all my imaginings about why he left, I never considered drugs. "I loved him from the first time I saw him play at the Mercantile. Something about him was magic for me. His smile. The way he called me his Mexican princess. The way his hands moved over the keyboard. He was a drug to me. But when I found out about the heroin, I broke it off. I knew that she-devil would never let him go, and I loved him too much to watch him be destroyed."

I remain motionless—waiting for the rest.

Mom looks toward the phantom piano—the place where Dad spent most of his time when he was home. "He disappeared for two months after I told him I didn't want to see him anymore. Then one morning, he showed up here at the shop with a Christmas cactus plant—said it was a cutting from his grandmother's plant that had been in his family for a hundred years. He had quit—cold turkey. For me. He had quit. All on his own—no drugs, no help, no rehab."

I glance toward the plant on its stand next to the front door—remembering how Mom nursed it along each year, keeping it in a dark closet for weeks at a time so that it would be covered with red blooms at Christmas. It was our favorite part of Christmas.

She follows my gaze toward the plant. "He gave me his grandmother's cutting, and promised me he was clean—that he had kicked the heroin for me. He kept his promise for twelve years." She shifts her gaze back to me. "When you were nine, I think he started slipping—he was doing more gigs in Austin, and even did a couple in Nashville. I guess being away made it too easy for him to sink back into using. I wasn't sure he was using until he cleaned out our bank account."

Deep sobs come up with her next words. "He lied to me about what he did with our money. I wanted to believe him. I didn't want to think he would ever lie to me." She stops for a moment and steadies her breath. Her voice takes on a hardness. "Everything about him changed—his skin looked different; his eyes took on a wild, distracted look; he lost weight. And one day, while I was out making deliveries, he had the piano hauled away. He said he was tired of it—sick of having it take up so much space. I knew he'd sold it to buy heroin." Her voice squeezes out in a whisper, as though she's horrified with her own words. "I told him to leave and not to come back until he was clean."

She lays her head on her folded arms and cries with as much anguish as if Dad had left only moments ago. I lean over, embracing her back and crying with her. "I'm sorry, Mama. I never knew."

She raises her face, wipes away tears—even though they are still flowing. "If I had let him stay, he'd still be alive." She drinks down her liqueur. "I know it. But I couldn't let him hurt you. I wanted to keep this from you."

"Mom, you did the right thing," I say, but in my heart I wonder. *What if he had stayed with us? What if we had helped him? What if I had begged him to stop the heroin? Would he still be here—still be alive?*

As if she reads my mind, her gaze locks with mine. "I'll wonder until the day I die if I could have saved him. I miss him every moment, mija. I never stopped loving him, and he never stopped loving us—at least the real Sam never stopped loving us. The she-devil took him over and ruined everything."

Numb with this information, I don't know what to say. I hug her and whisper, "Thank you for telling me—I needed to know the truth."

She nods solemnly and pours more coffee liqueur into our glasses. She doesn't comment that my glass is untouched. I pretend to sip but don't swallow the alcohol. There's a chance, a slim chance, that I'm pregnant.

The drive back to Austin Sunday morning gives me time to reflect. Maybe Dad's story and Mom's silent way of dealing with it lured me into a pattern. I've always sensed there was something big and ugly about his leaving, and I've dealt with that dark cloud, as Hunter pointed out in his breakup e-mail, by burying myself in music. My learned response to crisis is to go silent—withdraw. Hence, instead of calling Hunter and demanding a face-to-face, I just pulled into my shell.

I turn my phone on and find several texts and voice mails from Kari and Ross. I'm not ready to talk to either of them—everything is too raw and new. My impulse is to delete Ross from my life—I'm irrationally angry at him for talking to Hunter at the mall, even though Hunter himself stressed that I shouldn't blame Ross.

Finally, while I fill my car with gas, I text them both a bland *Everything's fine, don't worry* message and then drive my emotionally drained body back to my duplex, where I spend most of the night reading every post, blurb, and news release I can find about my infamous splash on *Marriage Exposure*—immersing myself in all the reality that I avoided for the past week. I make myself absorb head-on the full, outlandish trauma of my new normal. No more denial. And somehow, the reality is not quite as bad as the monster I've been imagining.

17

A t 8:07 a.m. Monday morning, my gynecologist's office finally answers the phone, and a scheduler offers me the next available slot—eight weeks away.

"No. I need to come today."

The scheduler, with her bored, slightly irritated voice, says, "You said it was for a routine checkup, and this is the next available appointment."

Uh oh. "Well, it is for a routine checkup, but I'm also having some other issues."

"Are you ill—in pain?"

"No."

"Sorry. The twenty-sixth of next month is the next available appointment."

"But it's an emergency."

"Then you should call nine-one-one or go to the emergency room."

"It's not that kind of emergency." My voice wavers. I can't wait eight weeks to find out if I have an STD. "I have to see her today. I can't wait."

"Would you like to talk to her nurse?"

"Yes."

"OK, let me have a number where you can be reached, and I'll give her the message to call you. She makes her calls between three and five in the afternoon."

Three in the afternoon feels like a century away. Panic wells up in me, and words spill out with a power of their own. "I didn't plan this. It's a long story how it happened. I hadn't been sexually active in over a year until last week. And I'd only ever had sex with two different men in my life." By now I sob. "But then last week something…something horrible happened, and I had sex with three different men, and I can't talk about what happened or the three men. And a psychologist said I should see my gyno immediately." I take a deep gasp and blurt out my worst fear. "I could be pregnant and have an STD."

"One moment, please."

A nurse comes on almost immediately, and I repeat the whole sur-real story, feeling better because she's calm and soothing, as if she hears this every day. But then she asks, "When was your last menstrual cycle?"

My sobbing ratchets up again because I have no idea. I whine, "I'm always irregular—I don't remember."

Between my wails, I hear her say, "We'll work you in at ten this morning."

The visit itself is anticlimactic—the doctor gives me an order for lab work that I can get as soon as I leave the office. But then she hands me a pre-scription for birth-control pills to start after my next period—if I'm not pregnant.

I stiffen as I realize what she's placed in my hand. "I'm never having sex again. I don't need these."

"Take them for six months—then come back. We need to see if we can get your cycle regulated." She was sympathetic earlier in the visit, but now she seems bored and bossy.

I put the prescription in my purse and start toward the door. "Wait." She reaches into a cabinet. "Here's a two-month supply of samples. I mean it. You need to take these until everything is stable."

Her gift shocks me. I don't think doctors ever give samples of the pill. I put them in my purse.

Peering over the top of her reading glasses, she locks a laser stare on me. "Are you going to take them?"

Until she asks me this question, I'm not planning on taking them, but I don't have the guts to say *no.* "Yes."

"Wait until Friday to do the pee-stick. Call me if you get a positive. Otherwise I'll see you in six months—get Myra to schedule you before you leave."

At the lab, during the blood draw, that unmistakable menstrual wetness seeps out at almost the same moment that the lab tech caps his last vial. Until I can get into a restroom and actually see the beautiful red assurance, I'm afraid that I'm imagining my period. *Yes! Thank you, thank you, thank you.* Stress, dread, fear fall away as I bounce out to my car.

The days of waiting for the STD lab results are filled with lessons, minor gigs, and a renewed passion for running. While I run through the streets and trails, I grieve for my father's useless death, my mother's heartbreak, and my shrouded childhood. And I start composing my answer to Hunter's breakup e-mail. I want it to clarify the truth, be kind but truthful about his mother, and serve to close the door on our chapter.

Friday night I meet Kari, Miguel, and Ross for happy hour at the cozy Rascals Inn. Some of my musician friends do this about once a month, and we usually wind up jamming a little, depending on who's there and how crowded it is. This will be Kari's first time.

It's soothing to do something normal. When I walk in, Kari and Miguel and several other people wave me toward their large corner table. Ross is at the piano playing the sentimental duet "Coldplay Paradise" by himself. This is the second duet I taught him—after "Heart and Soul." We've been doing "Coldplay Paradise" together for a couple of years, always trying to out-improvise each other. His skill has developed, and clearly he has practiced this piece. He works in bass runs that deepen the nostalgic tone.

Waving at the table group, I squeeze through the crowd and sit on the piano bench next to Ross. His eyes are closed, but he nods and smiles as if he knows I'm next to him even though he doesn't see me. He gives me a soft shoulder bump. I pick up the treble accompaniment that echoes the tone he evokes. With no prompting, he drops his right arm to give me full access to the keyboard. His base runs throb and support the tripping melody I play.

When we first learned this song, I played the more complex bass, and he took the lighter treble. But now his years of practice show as he plays and improvises the lead segments with as much polish as I could.

It's comforting to be next to the sturdiness and familiarity of him. He finally opens his eyes and turns to me while I improvise, at a higher octave, some of the same runs he just executed. I can't help remembering the night we had sex. He was a friend helping me in a warm, safe way to work through a hurdle that had stymied me. But, as close as I feel to Ross, I will never go that far with him again. After making love with Hunter, sex is in a different plane for me. I can't engage in it lightly. Doing so would feel like stepping on something sacred.

His right hand resumes his melody. "Good to see you, Desdemona."

I drop my left hand and punctuate his measures with some improvising of my own.

The lines around his eyes crinkle with his grin at my new phrases. But his voice keeps its serious tone. "Been worried about you."

"I'm fine. No need to worry."

His jaw flexes, but he remains silent. We both focus on our playing as the song reaches its climax, with all four of our hands engaged.

His part ends before mine. In my peripheral vision, I see him turn to fully face me. "Yeah, there is, and I'm going to fix it. Ten days left before I leave—somehow I'm going to fix it."

I play my last measure and drop my hands onto my lap. "Don't— there's nothing you can do. It's not about you."

He doesn't move, even though we should be leaving the bench for the next person waiting to play. "I am connected. I fucked things up for you when I talked to Hunter, and I'm not leaving the country knowing that you're hurting."

"I'm fine. And the thing with Hunter is done. You can't hang out the rest of my life."

He stands up with me, pushes the bench out, and moves his face close to mine. I can see his faint freckles this close. "I would if you'd let me."

I shake my head and start toward the table. I wish Ross and I could just make music together and keep the talking out of it.

After a couple of obligatory hours, I say my good-byes, and Ross follows me out the door and asks if he can walk me to my car. When I shake my head, he reaches into his wallet. "I just want to show you this chart." Under the marquee light, we stand on the sidewalk, and he unfolds a piece of graph paper that has four large squares—labeled Desdemona, Hunter, cash, and Mom, four small squares labeled Emmitt, Alex, office staff, police—and a bunch of flow chart arrows running among the squares.

I squint at the arrows. "What is this?"

"I put together all the facts you told me, and it doesn't add up." He points to the square with the dollar sign. "So first you discover that Mom has a record of twenty-six thousand three hundred dollars she's taken from the student-activity accounts." I sometimes forget Ross's engineering training and his need to chart everything. "This"—he points to the amount—"is unnoticed until the computer-club seven hundred and twenty goes missing." He points to Emmitt's square. "That's when the police got involved." Ross has a mind like a steel trap—remembers every detail I blabbed. "And the next step would have been their discovery of the twenty-six thousand three hundred." He pauses and peers at me through his glasses. "With me so far?"

I nod, wondering where he's going with this.

"Now we're getting to the disconnect—the part that doesn't add up." He continues with great detail, explaining each flow-arrow illustrating who told what to whom. He remembers more than I do about the string of conversations and events.

There's one huge piece that he doesn't know, though. He'll never know because it hurts too much to repeat. The phone call I made to Hunter's mother the day Mr. Johns died. Her voice, dripping with hatred, cut through me like a blade: *"Don't you ever call here again. Don't you come near my family. You ruined us. You ruined my son."*

Then Hunter took the phone. *"I asked you not to talk to anyone—including my mother."*

That moment cut me so deeply that I've never been able to repeat it to anyone. The grief and hatred that came from his mother made me feel ashamed. It somehow fell into the hole in my heart that my dad's disappearance had created. Ross's replay of the surrounding events scrapes the scab off that old wound.

"See what I mean?" Ross's voice pierces my reverie.

No, I don't. "What?" I say dumbly.

"So what doesn't add up is Hunter's turnaround that night at the mall. Everything was fine until I said, 'You need to apologize for stealing and lying and covering for your mother and tossing Desdemona out of your life for nine years.'"

My eyes bounce from Ross to the chart and back to Ross again. In a small voice, I say, "I think he had just gotten carried away by our old chemistry and tried to forget..." I don't want to say that his mother hated me—that he chose the stealing, lying, and covering for her over me. Back in high school, I made myself move beyond his betrayal because his father had just died and his mother could have been sent to prison for stealing. But now I had hoped enough time had passed that we could move forward. Maybe that's what Hunter hoped as well, but at the mall when Ross put it so bluntly, Hunter backed away, just as he had in high school. At least Hunter sent an e-mail this time.

Ross steps closer. "Forget what?"

I take a step back. "Uh. I don't know. May I keep this?"

"Sure, I saved the file. And let me know if you think of anything else."

"Ross, I want you to drop this. You've got—what? Ten days before you leave for China?"

He nods, but there's a stubborn set to his jaw.

I square my shoulders and take a deep breath. "I do not want to hear about this from you again. Ever. Do you understand me?"

"OK," he says. "You won't."

18

My new normal stabilizes over the next week, and Ross follows my directive—so it seems.

Nothing from Hunter. I track his book tour in New York and the news about the movie, on schedule to be filmed in Austin, which means he'll be back.

Oddly, a letter addressed to him in care of me arrives in the mail. This must be why he asked for my mailing address. The return address is a medical lab here in Austin. Mystified, I put it into the drawer with his mother's journal. Now I have two things to return to him.

At the Thursday night Tank gig, Ross, for the first time, is scheduled to play one song during my set. He hasn't reached the classical-expertise level expected at Tank, but since it's his last week in the states, the manager consented.

From Miguel and Kari's cozy balcony nook, the three of us watch Ross play.

Miguel raises his glass of wine toward me. "You taught him well, Desdemona."

I tap glasses with Miguel and Kari and sip the wine, thinking about my other, secret reason to be toasting—my STD tests came back clear.

"Ross is a hard worker with a lot of natural talent—my best student. I'll miss him."

Kari gives me slight shoulder bump. "Hmmm, maybe you'll miss him so much you'll decide to go visit him?" She makes the statement sound like a question.

"No. He doesn't need me dragging—"

Kari, as if startled, grabs my arm. I follow her gaze down into the main bar area. Hunter sits at the bar. Alone.

Kari says, "Is that...?"

"Hunter," I finish.

Miguel stands up so quickly he almost knocks over his guitar case that is propped beside his chair. "Would you like for me to go and talk with him?" He glances from Kari to me. The ever-thoughtful gentleman, he seems at a loss as to what he should do. "Invite him to join us? Invite him to leave? What would you like?"

Before I can answer, Ross finishes his song, and suddenly the spotlight is on me. My gaze still targets Hunter even though I can't see him because of the glare. The manager's voice booms over the mic. "Thank you, Ross, and thank our own Desdemona Lorents, his teacher. And before Desdemona continues to play, here's a quick preview of our weekend lineup. First..." The spot snaps off me, so I can see again, but now Hunter is gone.

I sit, stunned, still staring at the spot where Hunter had been, reeling from the rush of emotions that I hoped were dead. My very core longs for him. If I could fly, I would be in motion, seeking him out in every nook and corner of Tank.

Kari's voice breaks my trance. "Des—go. It's time for you to play. Ross is done."

Somehow I'm on my feet, moving toward the exit of their balcony. I don't feel my legs as I move down the stairs and out into the open space. It's a miracle I don't stumble, because I move fast, scanning the bar, the nooks, the booths. *Where is he?* I reluctantly approach the stairway leading up to the piano—reluctantly because when I get on that stairway, my view of the rest of Tank will be obstructed.

Hunter. My body responds to him before my brain assimilates his presence at the base of the stairway. Hunter and Ross, talking. Ross gesturing energetically about a sheet of graph paper in his hands—the chart, no doubt. Hunter, with his brow furrowed and his eyes fixed on the page, stares as if the document is a prognosis of a dreaded disease.

"What?" I ask, glancing from Hunter to Ross and back to Hunter. They stare at me silently, and Ross folds his chart. "What is going on?"

Hunter leans close to me as if he's going to kiss me, but he pulls back and shakes his head slightly.

Ross clears his throat, breaking the awkward silence. "Gotta scoot." He backs away a couple of feet but lingers with his gaze locked on me.

My eyes tear. My breathing is rapid and shallow. *How will I make it up the stairs to play? Why can't I just fall into Hunter's arms and make the lying and stealing evaporate? How can I want him so much?*

"I'm upsetting you," he says flatly. "I didn't want to do that. I just wanted to ask if we can talk when you're finished playing."

Finished playing? He thinks I can play. I've always been able to perform—no matter what—but now for the first time in my life, the show can't go on. My years of training and discipline drop away and leave me feeling like melting Jell-O. My default response to stress—babbling—doesn't even kick in.

Hunter steps closer. "I thought you knew I was coming. I thought Ross told you."

Suddenly Kari and Miguel are at my side. Kari puts her arm around me and glares at Hunter. "You should have called back when I left messages. You shouldn't just show up like this."

Ross steps forward again. "This is my fault." He runs his hand through his hair. "I got him here—didn't realize it would be such a jolt."

Miguel says, "I shall go up and play for you, Desdemona?" He makes the statement into a question.

I nod once—sharp and quick. *I'm not going to be the same crushed little girl I was at ten when Dad left. I'm not going to be the person that men leave. I'm going to confront Hunter, stand up for myself, and close this chapter. I'm going to take control.* "Yes,

Miguel," I say too loud. Everyone freezes. "Please get your guitar and finish my set."

"Hunter, I need for you to drive me home. I have two items of yours that I would like to get out of my house."

Kari still has her arm clasped around my shoulders. "Shall I come with you?"

Before I can answer, Ross thrusts his chart forward. "I could come, too—explain the new additions to—I think I know—"

I back away. "No, thank you, Ross and Kari. I'm fine." I almost run toward the exit.

Hunter follows me, but I outpace him and push through the door, not waiting for him to open it for me.

Out on the sidewalk, I bark, "Where are you parked?" I spot his car before he can answer and head toward it, my heels cracking loudly on the cement.

After I settle into his car, I take deep breaths and force myself to be calm. *I'm surprised at how strong I feel now that I'm over the shock of him showing up. I'm not babbling. I'm not desperate. I accept the fact that the physical joy of intimacy with Hunter is not something I'm going to experience again. But I'm my own person, and I can make it alone.*

Hunter remains silent as well. Maybe he senses that there's nothing he needs to say. When he pulls up to my duplex, I don't wait for him to open my door. I shoot out, unlock, and swing my front door open. I gesture toward the sofa. He sits, leaning forward with his elbows on his knees. "Don't move. I'll be right back."

I go into my bedroom and grab his mother's journal and the mysterious letter that came to him in care of me. My heels clack loudly across the hardwood floor. The sound is foreign to my duplex, because I usually kick off my shoes as soon as I enter. And, of course, I normally don't take such hard steps. As I whip back through the kitchen area, I drag a barstool along with me, park it directly in front of Hunter, and plop myself onto it. "I'm glad you came by. I want to finish this once and for all—in person." His eyes glance at the unopened letter I drop onto the coffee table. "Not sure why you had your letter sent here, but there it is. This, however, I took from your mother's desk on the day your father died. I did it to protect you both." I flip open the book to the page of accounts. "I had accidentally discovered this embezzlement record a few weeks before he died."

Hunter's eyes widen as he stares at the open page.

I zip right along, determined not to let him interrupt me. "And on that morning, the substitute secretary was putting your mother's things aside for her. I took this with me so no one else would discover what you were doing. It was bad enough that you took the blame for the seven hundred and twenty she took, but your mother could have gone to prison for the twenty-six thousand three hundred."

Hunter leans back onto the sofa and shakes his head. His lips almost smile, but a sadness takes over, and his eyes rest on me.

I trudge ahead. "I'll never understand why your mother hated me so much, why you banished me from your life. But I accept that it is what it is. I just want you to take these"—I reach for the letter and hand it to him with the journal—"and now we're done. And you don't have to worry—no one other than me has ever seen the journal."

He opens the journal and flips through the drawings and notes his sister made all those years ago. He stops on a page that has a childish sketch of a football next to a helmet with Hunter's number fifty-two on it. Even at five years old, Clara had been caught up in Garcia's excitement over his football scholarship. Across the bottom of the page, her awkward *A and M* stands out in maroon crayon.

The next page is the record of money taken from the accounts. He shakes his head, and his brow furrows. "This explains—" He stops himself when he notices the folded insurance statement in the back. When he unfolds it, the outstanding $11,700 in red holds his gaze.

Feeling as if I'm eavesdropping on a moment that is too private, I slide off the barstool, planning to busy myself in the kitchen.

Hunter stands up and drops the journal and the insurance statement onto the coffee table where his unopened letter lies. "Wait."

I turn and face him. He steps closer, close enough that I can feel his warm breath on my bare shoulders. *How can a man be so gorgeous and yet so wrong? Why does life put someone so desirable in my space when I can never be with him?*

He puts his hands on my shoulders, just as he did the night of the cows. "You're trembling."

I square my shoulders and pull back. "I'm fine, Hunter. This is not a comfortable situation for either of us. But I'm fine." Relief floods through me because this time I really am OK. He's the most gorgeous and desirable man I've ever known, and I'll never forget the magic of our time together, but I can live without him.

He shakes his head as if trying to dislodge something. "If this were a plot in one of my novels, my editor would say it's too unrealistic to be published."

This is not what I expected him to say. "What do you mean?"

"Desdemona, I didn't know about my mother taking this money or about the unpaid medical bills." He angles his head toward the journal and the insurance statement. "But now that you've told me, it explains a lot—like after Dad died, and Mom got his life insurance money, she donated twenty-six thousand three hundred dollars to the Garcia High School activity fund. I couldn't understand why she would give that much money away when she still had Clara to raise. But this explains it. She was putting back what she stole." He steps closer, raising his arms as if to embrace me.

I move back and hold my hands up to block him. "Wait. You didn't know about her stealing?" I feel as if I'm watching this play out through glass that has just been etched with millions of scratches. Things that were clear are now distorted. "But that day in the practice room, you guessed that I was concerned about the money, and you said you'd fix it no matter what."

He drops his hands to his sides. "I thought you were upset about not having money to buy a piano. You used to talk about that a lot—about how you wanted to get your own. And then you put that cash on my mother's desk and—"

"How did you know that I—"

He seems to anticipate my question because he gets his wallet out and pulls out a folded slip of paper that appears old and worn. "Look at this."

I open the slip and squint at key phrases that jump out in faded blue print. *Garcia First National Bank...Desdemona Lorents...Savings Account Withdrawal...$720.* "Where did you get this?" But even before my words are out, I realize I must have left it with the cash that I planted on Mrs. Johns's desk. "This is what you were talking about at the Tank when you said you had something of mine."

He nods. "I saw you leave something on my mother's desk, and I found the cash with your withdrawal slip. I figured you must have taken the computer-club money, deposited it, and then decided to return it. So I took the slip out, and when the cops showed up, I said I had taken the money."

Now I'm the one shaking my head. "Why did you say you took it?"

"I didn't want you to go to juvie. It would have been too tough on you. But I knew I could take it."

"But I didn't steal any money. This"—I hold up the withdrawal slip—"was from my savings. I put the cash on your mother's desk so that she could replace the computer-club money and the police would stop investigating. I was afraid she'd go to prison if they found about the thousands." Hunter wraps his arms around me and pulls me close. With my head against his chest, I hear the thudding of his heart as we embrace. "You gave up your A and M scholarship so I wouldn't go to juvie?"

He makes a little huffing laugh. "And you gave up your piano savings so my mom wouldn't go to prison." He squeezes me tighter. "We're like Della and Jim in that O. Henry story. Remember?"

"Yeah. Jim gave up his gold watch to buy Della silver combs for her long hair, but she sold her hair to buy a chain for Jim's watch." But our story is more complex—Hunter's mother is in the middle. "So that night at the mall, when Ross said you needed to stop lying and covering for your mother, you thought I had been blaming your mother for something I did? That's why you left."

"I'm sorry, Desdemona. I didn't realize until Ross came to one of my book signings with his chart and—"

I pull back so I can see his face. "What? Ross went to New York?"

He grins. "Yeah. Bought a book, stood in line, handed me a chart, and gave me an overview of all the loose ends that didn't make sense."

I laugh at the image and snuggle back into our embrace. "I love Ross." But then before I get too relaxed, one more big unanswered question jerks me to alertness. "Wait." I back away from him. "Why did your mom hate me so much? Why did she say that I'd ruined you when I called the day your father died?"

"Oh yeah." A shadow of pain crosses his eyes. "There's that." He picks up the little journal again. "When I got nailed, and then the next day Dad died, Mom was pretty fragile. She blamed herself for my arrest because she thought I'd stolen the seven hundred and twenty to help her out. So I told her I had stolen it because I wanted to buy you a piano. It was the only plausible excuse I could think of." He looks down at the journal. "I hated lying. It was a bad time for us."

I overflow with love for him, and I don't have the heart to remind him that his mom stole the $720 and with a twisted, maybe grief-stricken, rationale, let her own son take the punishment and me take the blame. But maybe in her worry about her husband, she somehow got confused—after all, she never entered it into her journal. My body, moving with a will of its own, slams into him. I reach for his head, stand on tiptoes, and press my lips to his. He's not the thief, and the only lie he told was to spare someone's feelings. An energy surges through me and sings with lightness as the nine-plus-year burden evaporates. He lifts me higher, and I wrap my legs around his body. I want to be as close to him as possible with nothing between us. I want him inside me. Now.

A deep groan from his chest resonates against mine. I can no longer tell where his mouth and tongue end and mine begin. Our lips separate for a moment. "Desdemona, I love you."

"I love you, Hunter. I love you. Love you. Love you. I want you inside me."

Our lips and tongues entwine, and he walks toward my bedroom with my legs still wrapped around him. He grins as he breaks our kiss. "OK if we use the bed this time?"

I press my lips against his while he lowers me onto the bed. With one arm around his shoulders, I reach with my free hand to tug my dress up. He helps me slide it up to my chest, and our lips break apart for a moment while we pull it off over my head. Kissing again, I unbutton his shirt while he undoes his pants, and he slides them and my panties down at the same time. Finally, we are together with nothing between us.

I scoot toward the center of the bed and pull him toward me.

Hunter lies next to me and pulls me close, but then he pauses. "Desdemona, where are your condoms?"

I point toward the drawer of my night table. With one arm around me, he reaches into the drawer. I stroke the smooth skin of his hardness—unbelievably grateful that the man I love, with his heaven-on-earth package, is in my bed this very moment—and wrap my legs around him, desperate to have him inside me.

Hunter pulls out of our kiss and turns his head toward the drawer. "No condoms in here."

I suddenly remember my tirade the night he left the mall without talking to me. "Oh yeah. They're all gone."

He pulls back a little with his eyebrows raised. "All of them?" He must be remembering the huge supply he witnessed me purchase a couple of weeks ago.

"I decided to never have sex again, so I threw them away."

He sits up. "You decided what?"

"But I changed my mind. Now. Today. Because of us."

He tilts his head with a lopsided grin, as if he's waiting for the punch line.

I sit up too, eager to explain so we can get back to making love. "The night you left the mall, I was so upset that I decided to never have sex again. I threw out everything related to sex, including the condoms." I climb onto his lap and straddle him. "But I'm on the pill now, and I had an STD screening." His erection is snuggled between our bellies. I finger the smooth head that is already slick with his essence. "We don't need condoms." I know Dr. Oz would say you shouldn't have unprotected sex unless you're monogamous, but I am monogamous. For me, it's going to be Hunter or no one for the rest of my life. Our lips come together, and I raise up so he can slip in.

Hunter's body stiffens, and he pushes me away. "Stop. We have to stop."

I make an involuntary moan of protest. "No. We have to make love."

His strong arms lift me off his lap and back onto the center of the bed. "Wait."

Before I can say anything, he slides off the bed and goes into the living room. Watching his gorgeous back and butt move away from me, I scoot to the edge and hop off to follow him, but he returns quickly with the mysterious sealed letter from the coffee table.

A chill slithers through my stomach and raises the hairs on the back of my neck. This must be serious. He wouldn't stop moments before having sex to go get a letter unless it contains something lethal. *Maybe he doesn't really want to have sex with me.* Feelings of insecurity jitter through me, but I check out his evidence, still solid—huge and solid—and know that he's as physically ready as I am. I hold my breath while he sits beside me on the edge of the bed.

He looks down at the letter. "I haven't told you about my past."

"I don't care. Nothing that happened before this moment matters." *That letter is from a lab. Maybe he has some fatal disease or some awful STD.* I wrap my arms around his chest even though he's still facing forward with both his hands holding the letter. "I love you. I want to be with you no matter what."

He faces me and strokes my cheek. "I love you, too. I always have. But I need to be as straight with you as you were with me. Remember that first night at Tank? You blurted out your whole sexual history of four the first moment you had the opportunity—spring-break Victor, Burt, Miguel, and Ross. I love that about you. How the truth is always right there with you."

"OK, OK." I squeeze him impatiently. "Give me your number and their names. I guess Sultry, Sexy Red is on the list." I try to keep the hate out of my voice.

He grins. "Zoe's gay."

"I love Zoe!"

His smile fades. "But there were a lot of short-term relationships—a lot."

What does this have to do with the letter he's still holding? "Hunter, what matters is us now."

"I agree. But I never had an STD test done." He looks down at the letter. "I never saw the need to do one because I always used condoms."

"Are you ill? Do you have something now?"

"I don't know. I don't think so. But after the Tank, when we came here and made love, I didn't want to use a condom. I wanted nothing between you and me. So the next day when I called and asked for your mailing address, it was because I was having testing done and sent here." He holds up the letter. "That's what this is—my STD screening."

I snatch it from his hand and rip it open. "Negative, negative, negative, negative. You're negative for everything! Listen." I drop the letter to the floor and grip both his shoulders. "I'm only going to say this once." I peer into his eyes, feeling our connection, hoping I say this right, hoping I'm not wrong in presuming he's as committed as I am. "I want you, only you, forever." My voice is husky. "I want naked sex with you." He starts to speak, but I put a finger on his lips to shush him. "If you don't feel the same way, you have one second to get your bod away from me and to the drugstore—"

He interrupts my sentence with a long, slow, probing kiss that leaves me breathless when he pulls away. "You're never getting rid of me again." His eyes burrow into mine. His one-sided smile takes over. "Never."

I grab his face. "Fuck me now, Hunter Johns. Now."

He laughs. "Let me see." He reaches toward the floor for the letter.

I lower my face to his gorgeous erection and lick the glistening tip and then suck while I gently cup his base with one hand and stroke the strong shaft with the other. He gives up on reaching for the letter because both of his hands are in my hair, and the deep groan from his chest sounds purely involuntary.

I love being in full possession of his most intimate part, and I love the pure passion that I can sense rippling through his body. I love him with every fiber of my being. I love this moment. I lower my mouth, taking him in as deeply as I can, loving that this wonderful man is mine—at least for this perfect moment, he's mine. Nothing else in the world matters.

His breathing becomes rapid—each exhale accompanied by a rumbling growl. I let him out of my mouth but hold onto him with both hands while I raise my face to his. His mouth is slightly open, his expression helpless and waiting. I flick his lips with my tongue, and speaking so close that I feel his lips, I pronounce the words. "Want to read the letter now?"

He pushes me back onto the bed and looks down at me with pure hunger in his eyes. With our gazes locked, he strokes my clit, and I pull his cock toward me—pushing his fingers away and stroking myself with his tip. This exquisite prelude connection—his tip, my clit—creates a harmony beyond description. And slowly, slowly he slides in, and instantly my body, as if it has waited my whole life for this moment, convulses in wave after wave—squeezing my beautiful Hunter. And when I think that nothing on the planet could be more fulfilling, he swells within me, triggering another round of my squeezes. I love hearing his helpless growl as he releases into me.

He collapses on top of me with his heart pounding. "I don't want to squash you," he whispers. We roll onto our sides. "But I want to stay inside you."

His words and his kiss trigger more spasms in my core.

Entwined, we find a comfortable position, and the next thing I know, hours must have passed, because I open my eyes to Hunter's sleeping face. His arm is still under my neck, but we've drifted apart a little, no longer connected. My heart fills with love for him as I watch his body asleep, relaxed, and completely open to me. He rolls to his side and wraps his free arm around me, pulling me closer and mumbling my name. As if our lips are synchronized on some kind of magnetic string, we come together in a kiss, and then I doze off again.

When I awaken the next time, Hunter slides out of the bed. I love watching his strong back and shoulders tapering down to his muscular butt as he glides away in the darkness. I slip out of bed and follow him into the kitchen. He grins at me as he opens the fridge. "What have we got to eat?"

"Eggs, tortillas, salsa. Want a taco?"

"That works." He pulls the eggs out, and I turn away from him to grab a pan. He comes up behind me and wraps his arms around me. He sets the eggs on the counter in front of me and runs his hands up and down the front of my still-naked body, brushing my nipples. I gasp a little and, for some insane reason, reach into a cabinet for the bowl to break the eggs in—even though there is no way I can do anything at this moment other than fuck this man.

Breathlessly, I say, "If you want to eat, you might want to slow down a little. I'm not sure I can concentrate with—" His firmness rises against my butt, and my core immediately responds like a hungry tigress wanting to devour him. He slides one hand down to my crotch, pressing a finger inside. "Oh, Hunter." I turn to face him. Our lips meet, and he lifts me onto the counter. I spread my legs wide with my pelvis tilted and pull him toward me. He slides in, as if coming home. And, with the most leisurely rhythm I could imagine, he slowly plunges again and again—moving himself from side to side—finding pressure points that come alive. Even if he weren't deep inside, our skin against skin would transport me. For the first time in my life, I try to delay my orgasm—try to stretch out this exquisite cliff that my quivering core is teetering on. As if Hunter reads my intention, he moves slow, so slow with each deep plunge uniting us more completely.

For a moment, with one deep plunge, he pulls away from my lips. "I love you, Desdemona. I never want to be apart from you again."

My voice, which I wouldn't have thought could make a sound, comes out husky and low. "I love you, Hunter. I'll never let you go."

He continues to gaze into my eyes as he changes the rhythm of his plunging, somehow tilting his pelvis so that he finds a new pressure point on my clit that totally shatters my resistance to orgasm. I hear a breathy, high-pitched scream and realize it's me. For some reason this makes me laugh. Hunter slowly continues his tilted plunge that triggers ricochets of spasms that leave me weak, helpless, limp.

He watches me with a grin. "I love it that I can feel your orgasms. I love those crazy flexes."

I collapse against him, wondering if I'll ever be able to move again.

He lifts me off the counter and carries me like a child toward the piano. "Know what we need?"

I shake my head and murmur, "No."

"'Always on My Mind.'"

"Hmm?"

"It was one of my high-school fantasies to fuck you while you played that song." I laugh in spite of my exhaustion, but he goes on. "You always looked so sexy at the piano—always gave me a hard-on."

The image of us fucking on the bench while I play seems crazy.

He pulls out of me, leaving me hungrily empty, and he sits on the bench and rotates me so my back faces him. "Come on, will you indulge a high-school boy's fantasy?" He strokes my clit and thrusts into me.

Each time he enters me, even though I may be spent, something sparks. Something deep and wild inside me comes alive. I feel my core ready to grab him again. I exhale, "You're not a high-school boy."

He nuzzles my neck. "But we got interrupted in high school." He caresses a nipple with one hand and my clit with the other. "This is what kept me in torture every day and night." I gasp as he presses deeper into me. "Play the song for me just once this way."

Thankful that I know this song so well, I play the melody. Hunter's mouth explores my neck while his hands continue their stroking and his hardness sends reverberations throughout my body. Before the chorus, that familiar, delicious swell and flex tells me he's there—at the point of no return.

With a low gasping groan, his head drops onto my shoulder. "God, Desdemona, I love you—totally, completely. I love you."

We say "love yous" over and over, but each one carries a magic connectedness. I reach back for his head. "I love you, Hunter. Totally, completely."

He takes a couple of deep breaths, and his body regains its strength. He lifts me up and stands. "Sorry I didn't make it to the end. Can I have a do-over later?"

I throw my head back and laugh from the deepest part of myself—wholeheartedly, freely—like a child in delight. "A million do-overs. As many as you want, forever and ever."

He carries me back to the kitchen and drops me onto the counter. "Can we eat now?" He pulls paper towels off the roll and starts blotting my very soaked inner thighs.

"Maybe a shower first?" I slide down and pull him with me into the bathroom.

I love our domesticity—fucking, cooking, showering—orgasm after orgasm. I'm living the dream.

He follows me obediently. "Even as hungry as I am, a shower with you can keep me distracted."

I adjust the water temperature and nudge him in. "I'm going to wash every square inch of your body."

He grins, already running his hands all over me. "I guess that works both ways."

I squirt shower jell onto our hands, and the fun begins. I love running my hands over his skin, but as distracting as this mutual bathing is, a question keeps nagging me. "Hunter, can I ask you something?"

"Anything." He tenses for a moment. He must sense my seriousness.

I feel nervous about probing his writing, so I talk fast. "In all your books, there's always a flawed woman. And the hero is always tormented by her—never finds peace because he's trying fix her flaw and trying to release himself from his love for her. And some psychologists might say that your main character is actually you—struggling with your own demons."

He throws back his head and laughs.

"I don't think it's funny."

His hands, newly slicked with more shower jell, rub circles on my butt and slip down my thighs. He's very distracting, but I press on. "I used to think your flawed women were versions of your mother, but now

I see that they're versions of me. So will you be able to continue to write bestsellers, now that you know I'm not the flawed woman you thought I was—not that I'm perfect, but, well, you know..."

"Well..." His roaming hands caress my breasts, carefully massaging the nipples. "I guess my career as a novelist is doomed."

I gasp, maybe from his touch—maybe from his assertion.

"Ah, Desdemona." He grins down at me.

"Yes."

"Are you going to just wash my dick and skip everything else?"

"Oh." I realize that almost the whole time we've been in the shower, all I've done is massage his man parts. "Well, it's hard to let go of this gorgeous, perfect package."

19

Too early the next morning, my phone wakes me. "Mija?" Sunshine streams in above the curtains. Hunter lies on his back next to me. I stroke his bare chest with my free hand.

"Hi, Mom." Hunter turns on his side to face me. He wraps one arm around me, and with one leg, he pulls my body close to him. His erection, pushed against my thigh, triggers a melting sensation deep in my core. I love looking at his chest in the morning light. His skin, under his clothes, is lighter than mine, and his chest is covered with soft, dark-brown hair. His naked maleness in my bed in the morning feels like an impossible dream come true.

Mom chatters. "I know you are broken up with Hunter, but I just read on the Internet that he's coming back to Austin because they are filming the movie of his book there." Hunter nuzzles my neck, and his lips and tongue awaken sensations I didn't know my neck could feel. "I didn't want you to be caught off guard in case you see him." He caresses my breast.

"Thanks, Mom." His tongue on my nipple forces an audible inhale from me. "He's actually in Austin already." Another gasp.

"Oh no." My gasps must have heightened her concern. "Did you see him? Maybe you should come home for a long visit." Now his hand slides down to my mound, and my pelvis, of its own accord, tilts into his palm. "Mija, are you there? Desdemona?"

"Yes, Mom. I can't talk right now, and I didn't think this would happen, but we worked out our misunderstanding. We're back together."

"You and Hunter are back together?"

"Yes, and I have to go—I have a date with him this morning."

"For breakfast?"

"Yes."

Hunter covers my chest and stomach with his mouth and free hand while the other hand stays on my mound. He slowly slides fingers in.

Mom says, "Well, I'm glad things are better, but be careful. Be sure he means it this time. I don't want you to be disappointed again. Is he coming to your house?"

"Yes."

"What are you cooking?"

"Yes."

Hunter's mouth and hands are everywhere. Last night I thought I was having the happiest experience of my life, but now having Hunter in my bed in the morning, working my body the way he is—this experience is too exquisite to be real life. His tongue and lips knead my lower belly. *How can this much joy exist? How can waking up with this gorgeous man be possible in this life?* His tongue circles my clit while his fingers push deeper toward my core.

"What did you say?" She doesn't wait for me to answer. "Just don't do waffles. Your waffle iron doesn't work right—always burns the edges and leaves the center gooey."

"Yes."

"Sounds like you're in a hurry, so I'll let you go. Bye, dear. I love you."

"Love you, Mom." I drop the phone and pull his shoulders upward.

He raises his head and stares into my eyes. "Good morning, Desdemona." His grinning face comes closer to mine. "Are you in a hurry?"

I'm about to reach for his gorgeous cock to guide it home when it slides in on its own as if my magnetic core has suctioned it. His grin fades, and his lips lower to meet mine. And we are one. His rhythm, uniquely his yet sublimely in tune with mine, takes me slowly, slowly to the peak and holds me there.

"What did your mother say?"

"Don't make waffles," I pant as he pushes me over the edge.

He watches me closely as wave after wave shakes my core. I force myself to keep my eyes open this time—I want to commune with him visually during this intimate happening. His eyes dilate, and within me, he swells even more. Then freezes. With our gaze connected, I feel him flex, and his climax begins thrusting into my spasms. Connection. Unity. Completion.

Our bodies become one and play out a primitive, synced rhythm. Slowly we roll onto our sides, facing each other. I place my hands on his face and gently stroke his lips. He sucks my fingers into his mouth and pulls me closer to him so we are flush together.

My phone rings again, and Hunter hands it to me.

"Good morning, Desdemona. It's Gloria Rhymer."

I jerk into an upright sitting position and pull the sheet up to my neck. "Yes, Dr. Rhymer. Good morning."

Hunter watches me, his head tilted with curiosity. I haven't told him about her yet. There just hasn't been time.

"I wanted to let you know that my contract with *Marriage Exposure* is finally set up. So I'd like to ask you once more if you'd consent to be in the study."

"No!" I shout. "I mean, no, thank you." I lower my voice. "I haven't changed my mind."

"OK, I didn't think you had, but I did want to let you know that the door is still open." I turn my face away from Hunter. Embarrassment seeps out my pores—he must be able to see it. "Also, there's a new story about you and Burt in a couple of the national tabloids this morning— this time with pictures of you. *Marriage Exposure* is probably going to be doubling their pressure to get you. I suspect that a producer, Jake Rawls, from the show will reach out to you."

"Well, thank you for letting me know. I have to go. Good-bye." I cover my face with my hands. "Will the *Marriage Exposure* ever go away?"

"What's wrong?"

"There's tabloid articles about it with my picture."

"Why?"

I uncover my face. "You know—about that time that Burt and his wife were on TV."

Hunter frowns. "You said something about that at Tank. What does that have to do with you?"

"It's what Burt said about me on the show." He studies me as he slowly sits up beside me. "Burt and his wife were on the show, and his wife, who'd struggled with some self-esteem issues, was insecure because she thought that Burt still loved me, which he did not. But she, for some reason because of the Zilker Park concert, which I didn't even know they had attended—"

Hunter puts his fingers on my lips. "Take a breath and slow down. We have plenty of time, and nothing you're going to say—nothing that happened before matters to us now."

I nod and take a breath and grasp both of his hands with my own. "So on the show, she blurted, 'You still love Desdemona.' And Burt said no, he could never love Desdemona because she fakes orgasms."

"She fakes? *She* meaning you?" I nod, and Hunter's eyes widen. "Why would he say that?"

"Well, he said it because I did it." Silence hangs between us as Hunter waits for more, so I add, "Fake orgasms. That's what I did."

Hunter shakes his head and furrows his brow. "You faked orgasms?" I nod. "Why?"

I take a deep breath. "I have secondary anorgasmia." He gasps and reaches for me. I quickly pat his arms and assure him, "It's not as bad as primary anorgasmia."

"Desdemona." He clasps my shoulders. "What is secondary anorgasmia?"

"It's the condition of not being able to have an orgasm, and it's secondary if you've ever had one, but primary if you've never had one." My explanation doesn't relieve his alarm. "And I had three, almost four, with a vibrator, so that's why I have secondary anorgasmia and not primary."

"So you aren't sick." The worry lines slide away, and he gets that half-smile that means he's amused. "This secondary anorgasmia isn't a disease?"

"Oh no. Well, maybe it is for some people." I grasp his hands that are still on my shoulders. "But no. There's nothing wrong with me—at least not anymore. Now, with you, I'm totally"—I kiss him—"totally"—I kiss him again—"totally orgasmic."

He pulls me close. I lay my head against his chest and listen to his heart thudding.

With his arms wrapped around me, he rests his chin on my head. "And who's Dr. Rhymer?"

"A psychologist who studies anorgasmia, and *Marriage Exposure* wants her to do a study of people who have it and put together a show. They offered me ten thousand dollars to come on the show and talk about why I fake it."

He pulls back and grins at me. "You're kidding, right?"

"No. And Dr. Rhymer called to offer one more chance to be in her study and to tell me that Jake Rawls will probably be calling me again to persuade me." I can tell by his puzzled frown that he's wondering who this is. "He's a producer for the show. Burt gave him my number, and Jake's already called me once, but I said no—never would I go on the show."

Hunter's jaw clenches. "I don't want you to have to talk to him again."

"I can handle it."

"I know you can, but I have an idea that will keep this show off your back."

"What?"

"You can sign a contract with me—give me an exclusive on your story. Then everyone else will have to leave you alone. We can make them go through Sultry...ah, Zoe." He must see the alarm on my face because he cups the side of my face with his hand. "You don't have to worry—I would never really write a story about you. I'll just sit on it, and eventually interest will die down. In the meantime, no one bugs you. They bug Zoe. OK?"

Relief surges through me. "OK."

"Where's my phone?" He finds it on the bedside table. "I'll call her now."

He puts his phone on speaker and Zoe answers immediately. "Where are you? The hotel said you never checked in."

He relaxes back against the headboard with one arm around my shoulders. "I'm staying at Desdemona's. Write this down. Ready?"

I can picture her fuming, but her voice doesn't give it away. "Uh, yeah. I'm ready."

"*Marriage Exposure* producer Jake Rawls."

"OK, and what about him?" Rapid clicking—she must be at a computer looking him up.

Hunter grins at me. "Get a new contract drawn up for me. I'm doing a book about Desdemona Lorents. She's given me an exclusive on her story."

"Hunter, have you lost your mind?" Now she sounds like the Zoe I know. Over-the-top exasperated.

Hunter goes on, unruffled by her reaction. "Contact Jake Rawls, and let him know I have an exclusive on Desdemona's story. He offered her ten thousand dollars for one show, so he's chomping to get her signed on."

"What? Why?" Zoe sputters.

"Just get the contract done—move fast or we could lose this one. Bye—"

I grip Hunter's arm. "Wait."

He looks at me with raised eyebrows.

Zoe is still clicking away. "Yes?"

The memory of her reaction when she heard my name the first time rips through me. "Zoe, don't you already know about this—about my being mentioned on the show?"

"Nope—never watch it."

"Then why did you say, 'the Desdemona' that morning outside the drugstore?"

"I'd heard about you from Hunter's mom—how he went to juvie for stealing money for you—how he threw away his A and M—" She gasps, "Holy shit. This is in the tabloids. 'Man Dumps Lover for Faking It.' Oh, and 'Beautiful Pianist Can't Perform.' This is freaking gold—and perfect timing. You get this drafted—I'll pitch to the studio while they're filming. This will be an insane new twist on your flawed heroine—"

"Zoe. Stop. Your job is to get the contracts done, and notify Rawls to back off. I'll take care of everything else."

Hunter cuts off the phone and pulls me close. "You know that I would never write anything about you unless you wanted me to, right?"

I cuddle up to his chest and close my eyes. "I trust you completely." We're perfectly still, and I feel safer, more complete than I've ever been in my life. Nothing could make my world better. I could stay in this room forever and be giddily happy.

His chest starts shaking. I sit up, alarmed that something's wrong. He laughs—trying to muffle it, but his laughter won't be squelched.

I grin, trying to get in on the joke. "What is it?"

"You're the most orgasmic woman I've ever known." He pauses to laugh some more. "In fact, I never knew a woman could be so orgasmic." Deep rumbling laughs break up his sentence. "And you've got this infamous title—reputation, in the tabloids—on *Marriage Exposure*."

It does seem funny when he says it that way, but his take on this as a joke worries me. "Does it affect your feelings for me?"

His smile instantly turns serious, and his gaze locks with mine. "It does, Desdemona. It does affect my feelings for you."

Fear coils in my chest. The idea of our perfection being marred by my past looms up and triggers an ache, worse, far worse than the loneliness I felt for Hunter in the past. The possibility of losing him now, after everything we've gone through, paralyzes me. I can't breathe. I don't want to hear that this joke tarnishes his love for me.

Something deep and serious shades his eyes. He inhales and exhales slowly as he shifts in the bed so that he's squarely facing me. "Desdemona." He pauses and looks down for a moment as if casting for his next words. He raises his eyes and speaks with a low, husky voice. "Before Rhymer called this morning, I thought I loved you. I thought there was no woman on the planet as right for me as you are. I didn't think I could possibly love anyone as much as I loved you. Do you understand?"

I make myself nod, but I can't make myself speak. What he's about to say may break my heart.

He casts his eyes downward again and shakes his head. Finally, he looks up at me. Something new is in his expression. I thought I knew every nuance of Hunter, but now I see a shift that scares the hell out of me. "Desdemona, I was wrong."

My disappointment crashes with my anger. I feel tears welling up in my eyes. But I continue to face him. I can handle whatever he has to say. I'm not the wounded little girl anymore, and I'm not going to be defined by what he says or does. I'm my own person, and I'll make it just fine, if I have to, without Hunter.

He moves closer, his eyes searching my face, as if he's looking for some message written there, or he's exploring a face he's never seen before. "Knowing about your past, and knowing how responsive your body is to me, made the love I had for you expand into something I've never imagined. I love you even more—in every way—than I did before that phone call."

Gasping sounds fill the room. I don't realize at first the sounds come from me. I throw my arms around him. He pulls me close, and I wrap my legs around him. Even though we're not having sex, I've never felt closer or more connected to him before this moment.

"Desdemona," he whispers in my ear. "Is it too soon for me to ask you to marry me?"

Now I'm full-on weeping and nodding, unable to speak.

"Are you OK?" He sits up, alarmed. "Are you nodding yes it's too soon?"

I shake my head. "No," I croak. We've been together really only a day and night, but in a way it's been nine years and four months. "I mean, I don't know if it's too soon."

He comes close to my face. "If it weren't too soon, what would you say?"

I take a breath and manage to say, "Yes. Yes. Yes."

"Good." He kisses my nose and grins. "I'll do it right. Ask your mom's permission, get the ring, plan a surprise for you. Then propose."

"Is this really happening?" A wondrous, warm calm settles over me. "Is everything really turning out perfect for us?"

He nods, and his expression turns serious again. His eyes lock with mine. "It may be too soon for a proposal." He takes a deep breath, pulls me closer, and whispers, his voice husky with emotion, "But we're so lucky it's not too late."

Epilogue
Garcia High School Ten-Year Reunion

"M om," I call as Hunter and I climb the steps to her apartment. "We're here."

The door flies open. "Oh, mis hijos." She manages to grab us both at the same time, kissing first my cheek, then Hunter's as he bends low enough for her to reach him. "I'm so happy you are here early, so we can visit before you go to the party. Here, mijo, I have all your favorites." She nudges Hunter toward the kitchen counter, where an array of snacks waits. His capacity for food is an endless source of pleasure for her. He pauses to frown at his buzzing phone.

I head toward the food as well. "Zoe again?" I ask, but at the same moment, a stack of wedding RSVPs and sketches on Mom's painted-roses table grabs my attention. "Oh, Mom. These are beautiful." Her sketch of the flower-covered archway being built for our garden wedding is music to my eyes. "And look, an RSVP from China." I rip it open, and a picture of Ross with his sweet girlfriend, Meili, falls out. With beaming smiles, they stand next to a small rippling waterfall. Ross has his face leaning on her shining, long black hair. They both have their arms wrapped around each other. "They're coming!"

Hunter pockets his phone. "I'm glad."

While he fills his plate, Mom stands beside me with one arm wrapped around my waist. She points out all the features she plans to incorporate into the decorations at the wedding reception.

"Mom, it's amazing. I can't believe what you're doing." I almost wish we could skip the reunion and just stay here, working on wedding plans. Neither Hunter nor I actually graduated from Garcia High School. After Hunter's father died, I dropped out, got my GED, moved to Austin, and attended junior college. Hunter graduated from high school in juvie. Then his mother relocated the family to El Paso to live near her parents; however, the class reunion committee has been relentless in their insistence that we attend the reunion.

Hunter stands behind us, holding his plate and looking over our heads at the pictures. "Um. Nice. Thanks, Mom—for the food and the plans."

She clears the papers away to make room for our plates, and while we eat our predinner, dinner, she regales us with all the latest developments in the reception plans.

An hour or so later, she takes off her apron. "Now I'll go to Alma's so you two can get ready." Mom has planned a sleepover so Hunter and I can stay in her apartment.

Dressed, I stand in front of the narrow mirror in Mom's bedroom. I meant to check out my pale-green sundress, but as usual my eyes drift to the sparkling, princess-cut, double-carat on my left hand. Every time I see it, a thrill rushes through me.

Hunter steps up behind me, so handsome in jeans that hug his butt and a loose, gray, natural-fabric shirt that sets off his broad shoulders. "You look beautiful." He kisses my shoulder and nuzzles my neck. "That color makes your skin look even sexier than usual." His voice drops low and husky. "I want to eat you." I turn to face him, and he slips both hands up under my dress and squeezes my butt. "I'm going to have to fuck you while we're at school. Being back there is going to drive me crazy with horniness that I suffered all those years in high school."

"Mm." He makes me remember my own unresolved horniness in high school.

His cell buzzes again. He glances at it and shoves it back into his pocket.

"Is Zoe still trying to convince you to write a story about me?"

He wraps his arms around me again. "Yeah, but don't worry. My contract gives me the option to decide what I write. She's just sniffing the potential dollar."

"But why now again? I thought she'd forgotten this idea months ago." Every time I feel the scandal has died, some new version of it trickles into my life again.

He squeezes me. "She's got something going with the producer—some idea about a romantic comedy with a lead character like you. She'll get over it, or we'll get a new agent."

Even though I've visited Garcia countless times over the past ten years, neither of us has been back to the high-school campus. When we walk past the spot where Hunter was taken away in cuffs, dark memories of those last days sink onto me—heavy, black clouds, the struggles of his mother, the morning his father died.

I lean closer to Hunter. "Was this a mistake? So many sad memories."

He squeezes my hand. "We'll be OK."

A squeal from behind us cuts into our conversation. "Oh my gosh, Hunter and Desdemona. I can't believe you're really here." Georgina, the class president, who hasn't changed a bit since high school, rushes up to us, pantomiming silent claps.

Her excitement attracts at least half a dozen other smiling faces—I recognize the whole cheerleader squad—faces I haven't thought about in years. When we entered, they had been milling around in the main hallway ahead of us. Now they surround us with excited chatter, hugs, shoulder bumps. More people collect around us as we walk toward the gym. Someone brings us name tags. Someone else hands us booklets that contain a brief bio of all 148 members of the class. They have Hunter and me listed, even though we didn't graduate with the class. Bald jokes. Prom stories. Baby pictures.

My somber mood is replaced by something unexpected—a bright, nostalgic connection with all these people we grew up with.

It seems that every person there has several of Hunter's books to be autographed. And they've parked the old spinet practice piano right in the middle of the gym floor, so I bang out an oldies jam session while Hunter signs book after book. Some class members sing. A few dance. Everyone shares memories.

I chat with the noisy crowd around the piano, laugh at the stories, play their requests, but my eyes keep drifting back to Hunter. He's a miracle—so handsome, good, talented, and mine. That we made it through all the loss and the nine-year separation is more than a miracle.

No one requests "Always on My Mind," but the emotions that are colliding within me guide my fingers to our song. Hunter cuts his eyes past the crowd around him and focuses on me. His lips part, and he takes a step toward me. Somehow just his subtle expression of hunger leaves me melting and quivering. Drinking him in and flushing from head to toe, I finish one stanza and switch abruptly to the school fight song. He grins and shakes his head, but then frowns down at his phone—more texts from Zoe, no doubt.

Finally, Georgina asks for everyone's attention. "Thank you! Thank you! This is the best reunion ever! Every single member of our class is here except for two people. Let's have a moment of silence for Jesse, who's overseas serving our country. Let's pray for his safety and for his presence at our fifteenth reunion."

We all stand quietly—sending Jesse our thoughts. Georgina breaks the silence. "Thank you. Now it's time to leave these hallowed halls and take the party to Lassie Park!" Hoots and cheers break out. "The catered barbeque and kegs will be delivered in twenty minutes. Be there or be square!"

People start gathering their belongings and families to head out. I make my way to Hunter and tiptoe to whisper in his ear, "Who's the other person that's missing? Did someone die?"

Hunter grabs my hand and pulls me out of the gym and down the long, now-dark main hallway. "No one died. Someone told me Emmitt Straus is in prison." Before I can express my surprise, Hunter grins at me. "Embezzlement. He owned a company and set up a scheme to report funds missing—turns out he was stealing the very funds he was reporting." He continues to lead me down the hall.

"Emmitt!" The annoying anger I'd felt toward him many times throughout school rears up into a boiling rage. "He must have stolen the seven hundred and twenty he reported missing." At this moment we turn into the main wing, past the office where Hunter's mother used to work. "So that's why your mom didn't enter the seven hundred and twenty in the journal." Her desk in the dimly lit office still looks the same. "She didn't steal it." An odd relief settles on me like a warm blanket. I have always been perplexed at why she would try to blame me and why she would let Hunter take the blame for her own theft. Now I see that she really believed Hunter stole it for me. With one last glance at her old desk, I whisper, "It was Emmitt. We were both wrong."

Hunter, still focused on leading me deeper into the empty school, nods without breaking his pace. "Yeah. Funny thing. That's what Ross said when he followed me to New York with his chart."

"Where are we going?" I hustle to keep up with him as we round a corner into a dark hallway lined with lockers.

"I told you...I want..." His voice, suddenly thick and low, trails off. He pushes me against the lockers and kisses me long and deep. His mouth closing in and his tongue sweeping mine trigger a flow of reaction deep in my body. He releases my mouth and slowly runs kisses down my neck and across the front of my chest. He pushes one strap of my sundress down and lifts out my breast, totally practiced in all the intricacies of working around my undergarments. His mouth locks onto my nipple. I hear myself gasp as he slips one hand up under my dress, hooks my panties, and slides them down. I step free of the panties and he shoves them into his pocket.

He releases my breast, and whispers, "God, I wanted to do this in high school."

Before I can respond, he drops to his knees and his tongue finds the spot between my legs as if attaching to a magnet. My pelvis, with no conscious message from me, pushes into his face, and my thighs spread farther apart. My heart pounds, and my breathing puffs out in pants as he caresses with his incredible sense of the right pressure and suction.

Voices and footsteps approach, but in that moment I honestly don't care who comes or what they see. I'm lost with Hunter. My body desperately wants him inside me—nothing will budge me. Nothing.

Hunter, though, has more control than I do. He stands up, grabs my hand, and pulls me further down the darkened hallway. In a husky whisper, he says, "I'm going to fuck you in my favorite place in this building." He opens the door to the old piano room. The long-forgotten scent of sawdust greets me as we slip into the room. Another text buzzes in his phone. His frown shows from the lighted face of his phone. "Look at these. She's gone nuts."

I take his phone and scan the dozen or so texts. Phrases jump out. "Hot market topic—faking phenomenon—chasing the big O—producers primed for romantic comedy—big bucks—diversify your writing portfolio."

Hunter props a chair against the door—just as he did when we were seniors. My eyes adjust to the darkness—there's only a few chairs and one bookshelf in the room. The piano is still back in the gym.

All the old longings from high school well up within me. "I wanted you to make love to me in this room. I wanted it every day after that first day you touched me," I pant. I set his phone on the bookshelf next to us and reach for his zipper. "I love you so much." I slide his pants down and caress his magnificent shaft.

Every time I touch his manhood, something deep inside me sings, "Enter."

He backs me against the wall between the door and the bookshelf and drops to his knees in front of me again. Involuntary sighs push out of me, as his tongue swirls just the right spot. He knows me so well, but each time—though familiar—is new and surprising. The physical sensations coupled with our love create a symphony that grows more beautiful with practice. He leads me to the edge—he knows that my favorite orgasms are with him inside, and he's learned just the right moment to enter.

Footsteps and voices approach in the empty hallway. A male voice says, "I think that's the room where the piano goes."

The knob rattles. Hunter stands up and shifts to his right far enough to quietly wedge his foot against the base of the door—I guess to ensure that the angled chair holds. I slide along the wall until I'm directly in front of him, and I lift my skirt. Silently, Hunter thrusts into me.

A voice on the other side of the door says, "Yeah, this must be it— music room. Let's hope there's a dolly in here." The doorknob rattles. "Must be locked."

Hunter's mouth melds with mine, his arms lift me up, and he slides in and out, filling my body as well as my soul.

A different voice from further down the hall calls. "Just leave it. Eddie said the custodians will put it back."

The footsteps and voices retreat.

Wave after wave curls through me, punctuated by his own thrusting climax. I can feel his heart pounding and his exhales forcing out with each thrust, but he whispers anyway, "I love you." His voice low and husky—almost in a growl. "I love you."

We cling together, relishing the closeness, delaying the moment of separation. By now it seems as if we've uttered the *I love you* sentence a million times. Those words have become a living thing that demands its moment over and over. Like a beautiful song—hearing it once is never enough. And each time you hear it again, even though it's the same notes and beats, something new and beautiful happens. "I love you, Hunter."

He kisses me—long, gentle—as our heart rates slow down.

His phone buzzes again. We break our kiss and look at the screen lit up on the bookshelf next to us. Zoe's text flashes. "Got 2 titles...which do you like?"

Hunter scoffs one short laugh, shakes his head, and kisses me again.

Maybe because I'm feeling extra happy in this moment, or maybe because Zoe is finally wearing me down, my giggle bubbles up, breaking into our kiss. Close to his lips, I whisper, "You know, I think I like her titles. Let's see again."

We both look at the screen, still lit on Zoe's text: "Desdemona Finds the Big O in Love" or "Faking Lucky"?

www.ingramcontent.com/pod-product-compliance
Lightning Source LLC
Chambersburg PA
CBHW060926120626
46557CB00003B/884